THE RED KING

WILDE JUSTICE, BOOK 1

JENN STARK

ISBN-13: 978-1-943768-44-8

Cover design and formatting by Spark Creative Partners

This book is a work of fiction. References to real people, events, establishments, organizations, or locations are intended only to provide a sense of authenticity, and are used fictitiously. All other characters, and all incidents and dialogue, are drawn from the author's imagination and are not to be construed as real.

Books by Jenn Stark

Wilde Justice Series

The Red King
The Lost Queen

Immortal Vegas Series

Getting Wilde
Wilde Card
Born To Be Wilde
Wicked And Wilde
Aces Wilde
Forever Wilde
Wilde Child
Call of the Wilde
Running Wilde
Wilde Fire

One Wilde Night (prequel novella)

JENN STARK

Demon Enforcers series

Demon Unbound
Demon Forsaken
Demon Bewitched

For Nikki
I knew you were amazing the moment I met you.

KING of CUPS.

CHAPTER ONE

With its endless mountain vistas, crisp, clean air, and granola grunge vibe, Boulder, Colorado was considered the happiest place in America. Not for this guy, though.

"You can't touch me! I'm protected!"

Ricky Berrit shouted this declaration over his shoulder as he darted away from me, which didn't speak volumes for his faith in his own inalienable rights. The dude could move, though. I gritted my teeth and bolted after him.

My lungs burned. Mad dashes up snow-covered mountain paths were yet another aspect of my job as Sara Wilde, Justice of the Arcana Council that hadn't been fully explained to me. Granted, there'd not been a lot of time for orientation. After agreeing to search out, apprehend, and deliver unto Judgment any magic-wielding criminals who crossed my path, I'd been given a couple of fancy bracelets, a quick primer on protocol, and a folder of starter jobs. Ricky was the second of my two newbie assignments, and he was already jumping on my last nerve.

But he also bore the mark of Justice across his temple, a telltale silver slash of energy that pegged him as a psychically gifted offender in desperate need of my particular services. Whether or not he wanted them.

Ricky twisted around to face me at the end of the trail, trapped between a rock and a hard place. Over the edge of the cliff was a bunch of rocks; I was blocking his way back down the trail. I wasn't liking his odds in either direction.

"I have rights!" Ricky protested again, his eyes jacking everywhere but me. "I want my lawyer. A cop!"

I shrugged, doing my best not to gasp as I sucked in the bitterly cold and unreasonably thin air. "Funny thing about that, Ricky. They save the cops and lawyers for people who break ordinary laws. You didn't."

His eyes widened slightly. I wondered how much he knew about the product he was shuttling back and forth across the Rocky Mountain west. According to his file, Ricky had mostly made his name shilling low-level weed up until a few years ago. He certainly looked the part of low-key pot dealer, with his hipster beard, fast-drying pants, and cheerful fleece over a heavy-duty flannel shirt. Unfortunately, then the good voters of Colorado had gone and made pot legal.

Not to be deterred, Ricky had quickly come up with something new and illicit to push. It was his bad luck he'd stumbled into technoceuticals, the half-pharmacological, half-arcane drugs of choice favored by folks looking for the kind of high that came with enhanced psychic powers. The arcane part of the drugs could be inorganic—crystals, metals, nanobot energy conductors, you name it—or it could be organic. Sadly, technoceuticals with organic components were where the big money was.

And the biggest money of all was currently in a new drug called Black Elixir, which I happened to know was what Ricky was packing on this beautiful Colorado morning. I'd encountered the drug's dark signature in a few hapless victims of Ricky's on my way to finding him but unfortunately, once Black Elixir got into someone's bloodstream, it dissipated fast. To get a real fix on it, I needed the source material. Ricky had it.

"Do you have any clue what you're selling these days, Ricky? Or what effects it has?" I pushed. "Those buyers back at the trailhead looked like they were coming back for their third or fourth hit. You want to know why I think that? Because no one survives the fifth one."

"That's a lie." Still, Ricky's expression changed at my words, his eyes going craftier. "What happens after the fifth hit is *transcendence*. Nothing more, nothing less."

"Uh-huh." I knew Ricky wasn't manufacturing the drugs he pushed. He didn't have the brains for that. Most likely, he was a low-level psychic, several miles downstream from the source of the poison he was witlessly dumping into the nervous systems of his equally witless customers. That didn't mean he wasn't accountable, though. "You ever see anyone hit transcendence and come back to tell the tale?"

"*Lots* of people…" Something shifted again in Ricky's energy, a grifter seeing an easy mark, and I got my first glimpse of the drug dealer lurking beneath all the organic deodorant. Excellent.

"Wait a minute," he continued, as if struck by a new, startling thought. "You're curious, aren't you? Want to try Black Elixir out for yourself?"

"And if I did?"

"I can be generous."

Good man, Ricky. He was making this easier all the time. "First tell me what you think it is, exactly."

"It's *magic*," he said, stepping toward me, away from certain death over the side of the cliff. If he knew where I planned to deliver him, he probably would've taken his chances on the mountain. But some sort of fever had taken hold of Ricky, and his eyes were alight. "The best stuff anyone's ever seen. And it's not what you think. It's not heroin or something cut into heroin. That shit's for children. This is the real deal. The kind of juice that the shamans used back in the day."

"Shamans." I kept my hands loose. "Medicine men."

"*Magic* men, I'm telling you," he said, sounding awestruck. "Women too. Lix is the real deal."

"Lix?" I wrinkled my brow. "What the hell is Lix?"

His grin went lopsided. "Short for Black Elixir. I made it up myself."

"Really."

"You can tell your friends all about it, then you can tell them where to get it. Or, you want to work it a different way, you can be my contact, and they can only deal with you. You do that, I'll hook you up royal."

I paused, startled. "Are you seriously running a pyramid scheme on me right now?"

"Ground floor," he said, taking another step closer. "Premium product, reliable delivery, best word-of-mouth advertising you've ever seen."

"You can't see word of—never mind."

"I know what you're thinking."

"I seriously doubt that."

He bobbed his head, flush with sudden confidence. "Oh, I know. Rocky Mountain High guy doesn't know shit from the real stuff, couldn't get his hands on anything major if he tried. But *you* found me, didn't you? You knew where to look. Who told you?"

"Someone gave me your card." I didn't bother explaining that the card in question was a Tarot card—

the Fool, as it happened. I used the cards to find anything that needed finding, and right now, the top three on the deck tucked into my pocket were the ones that'd brought me to this impasse with Ricky. The Fool, the Eight of Swords, and the Seven of Swords. Not the clearest spread, but it'd gotten me to the Seven Forks Trailhead at eight a.m. sharp, early enough to catch the worm.

Once upon a time, I'd used Tarot cards to find arcane artifacts; the more ancient and arcane, the better. These days, I used them to find those gifted humans—known as Connecteds—who'd done very bad things, so that I could bring them to Judgment. It was a calling that'd already started looking like a twenty-four seven commitment. Lucky for me, Hotel Judgment was always open.

Since I'd upgraded from tracking down objets d'art to actual humans, however, my targets were a lot more prone to chatter. Which worked out, because I needed to keep Ricky talking long enough for me to get within cuffing range.

Fortunately, that didn't seem to be a problem.

"The Black Elixir will give you visions, man, visions of the person you could be if you believe. If you transcend. But it doesn't wait to give you its gifts at the end. First time I took it, it showed me my future."

"Prison?"

"*Gold,*" he corrected me, with a fervency that made my skin crawl. "Everywhere around me. All of it mine for the taking. My second hit, it gave me the plan. Showed me the people I needed to meet, what I needed to say to them. And boom, they showed up. Like magic."

I'd gone still by this time. "You could predict the future?" I asked carefully. I'd heard as much about

Black Elixir, but every drug on the arcane black market promised that kind of thing. I got the feeling Ricky wasn't quoting brochure copy.

"Give the lady a prize." Ricky laughed delightedly, tapped his pocket. "I got some of the stuff right here, if you've got the cash. You can see for yourself. If you're lucky, it'll take you all the way to the Red King."

My brows shot up. "The Red King? Is that your supplier?"

Ricky's chortle rattled along the rocks. "Oh, man, you don't know anything do you? While I know everything!"

Irritation riffled through me. "Uh-huh. If you're so all-knowing, how come you didn't see me coming?"

A gun cocked behind me.

"Because Ricky learned his lesson early about sampling the product," said a new voice. High, thin, scornful. "Anything he sees under the influence of Black Elixir, he tells me."

Crap.

Ricky's face split into a broad grin. "You had your chance to cut in on the deal, babe. Mine was a legit offer. Leonardo, he's not so good with the deals."

Babe? Ignoring that, I turned slowly, my gaze sweeping over a wide swath of Colorado skyline before it fell on the newest arrival on the trail. *Double Crap.* This was the problem with Tarot cards. They usually made the most sense after the dust settled.

For tracking Ricky, I'd drawn the Fool, the Seven of Swords, and the Eight of Swords. The Fool pulled double duty serving as both Ricky and the whole concept of walking off a cliff, which was why I'd followed the idiot up this edge-of-the-abyss dirt track. The Seven of Swords seemed a shoo-in for the Seven Forks Trailhead. It was also, however, a card about strategy and being double-crossed. I'd discounted that interpretation because I'd only been given Ricky's name, and I'd been sure he hadn't known I was coming, so there was no double to be crossed.

I shrugged mentally. My mistake.

The Eight of Swords, finally, could have been eight a.m., and maybe still was, but the card's predominant reading was all about feeling unreasonably restricted...or that you were facing an obstacle that wasn't truly an obstacle, more a mere pain in the ass. So, all things being equal, I wasn't particularly surprised to see someone else here.

I *was* surprised that it was a kid.

"Um," I began helpfully.

"Looks like you were right, Ricky." The boy—Leonardo, apparently—held his gun low and away from his body, but his stance meant business. He knew how to fire the weapon he held, or he thought he did. Leo looked barely fifteen years old and was maybe a hundred and twenty pounds soaking wet. But he also had a slash of spectral silver above his right ear, and his eyes were twitching with the fervor of a hard-core high. I didn't need to use any psychic powers to see that he was juiced on something. But was it truly Black Elixir? All the intel I had was that upper-level Black dealers didn't sample the stuff. Not the smart ones, anyway.

"What're you staring at?" Leonardo demanded.

"I guess I'm staring at Ricky's boss." I settled my weight on my heels. "You guys out here for a convention or something? Maybe a doubleheader with Mary Kay?"

"The Black Elixir advised you'd be coming. Said you'd be strong." The boy sneered. He was well made, with dark skin and big dark eyes, black hair catching the breeze. Everything he was wearing and carrying looked straight out of Eddie Bauer, except the gun part. I was pretty sure Eddie Bauer didn't sell guns. Then again, I'd read you could 3-D-print the damned things in plastic these days, so any idiot could get their hands on one. "You don't look all that strong."

"I get that a lot." I wasn't wearing hiking clothes so much as catch-you-and-throat-punch-you clothes—sleek, black, and minimalist. "Who else you have back down the trail, Leo?"

"The Black Elixir said we should come with weapons, backup." He rolled his eyes. "But I know these trails, and I know Ricky. He's lived here his whole life. No one understands the trail system better. I wasn't worried."

I heard the clatter of stones and gritted my teeth. *Freaking great.* If Ricky had truly been climbing up and down these trails his whole life, chances were good he knew a way down. This job was beginning to seriously suck.

I refocused on the kid. "Sounds like you might have gotten pretty close to your fifth hit if the drug said all that."

Leonardo grinned. "Holding steady at three. Three keeps you tight, keeps you close. Three gives you what you need without taking anything away."

"Congratulations. You're a model of restraint." Irritation sawed away at my good humor. "Did Three say anything else while it was turning your brain to soup?"

"It said I should kill you before I listened to your lies."

Without any more fanfare, the boy raised the gun and shot.

There are few things more alarming than being shot at by a kid, especially one who knows how to shoot and who doesn't flap his gun around for show. But Leo managed to take it one step further. The movement of the boy's arm and the tightening of his finger on the trigger was accomplished in one motion, as if he was either some sort of superhero or a high-level Connected juiced to the gills. Which was it?

I indulged in that question during the split second it took for Leonardo's arm to lift, then got busy. I was *not* going down to a kid, no matter how Connected he was.

I thrust out my hands, and a web of power burst into life, a ball of magic as blue as the Colorado sky and a hell of a lot more useful. But before I could direct it to do more than eat Leo's bullet, I was pounded into a snowbank by a hundred and eighty pounds of flannel and neoprene.

"Oof!" The sudden burst of cold startled me almost as much as Ricky's impressive ninja moves. The dealer flipped me over in the snow and jerked my arms back, pinning them behind me. A tumble of cards fell out of my pocket, Eight of Swords right on top, the quintessential picture of a woman bound.

But I was the one supposed to do the binding, dammit.

"Stay down," Leonardo growled. "Ricky, get away from her, or I'm going to shoot you too."

"What the hell, man, you don't have to be an ass—" A single shot cracked, and Ricky yelped, then skittered away from me. I was alone, defenseless, and sunk in a snowdrift. I'm sure I looked pathetic.

"This isn't going to end well," I offered, but Leonardo wasn't having any of it.

"Shut up! I don't care about your lies."

He leveled the gun at me again, but this time, I was ready. I crossed my hands so my fingers snagged my cute little cuff bracelets, ripped both of them free, and flung them at the Wonder Twins before Leo could get the shot off.

The cuffs hurtled through the air. Not as flashy as a golden lasso, maybe, but a girl had to use what she had. And what I had was a designer set of Justice-themed jewelry that'd come with the job title.

Ricky reacted first, his wrists locking together as he flopped around in the soft powder like a demented snow angel. "What in the—"

"Can it!" I growled, hauling myself out of the snow and staggering forward a few steps to get my bearings.

I headed his way, and his eyes widened. "Seriously, who are you? *What* are you?"

"Not the ATF." With more force than I expected, I cracked Ricky on the side of the head, enough to knock him out. Then I grabbed him by the shoulder of his jacket and dragged him over to Leo, who'd apparently been cold-cocked by my bracelet before it'd snapped around his wrists.

Excellent. I'd essentially bagged two bad guys for the price of one and hadn't had to listen to their explanations as to why I'd gotten it all wrong about them. That was for other ears.

Ears I now had to go bend.

I sighed, but there was nothing for it. These bozos weren't going to perp-walk themselves to Judgment. Unfortunately, this next part was yet something *else* that hadn't been fully disclosed regarding my new job title: covert transportation of my quarry was a requirement. Painfully covert transportation.

I collected my cards and stuffed them back in my jacket, then pulled Leonardo and Ricky together in a jumble of limbs. Securing each of their upper arms with a hand, I squared my shoulders. Then I drew a long, steadying breath. This…was gonna hurt.

I burst into flames.

Chapter Two

Sweet *Christmas*, that hurts." Still smoking, I stood up and turned around in the concrete entry bay of the abandoned warehouse that Judgment of the Arcana Council was using as her intake HQ.

Ramrod straight and well muscled in full leathers, her thick, dark hair braided into heavy ropes, Gamon had come to her role of Judgment by way of ex-Mossad international terrorist, but there was no question she was the right woman for this job. She paused a second longer, smirking at me, then her eyes cut to the two figures beside me.

"Who's the kid?"

"Ricky's boss," I said, also transferring my attention to the boy on the floor. "I didn't plan for him to be there, but he was both marked and one notch higher on the supply chain, so I figured, fair game." I nudged the bodies with my foot. "Aren't they supposed to wake up?"

"You catch a man on fire, it's going to take him a minute to recover," Gamon said drily.

I made a face. To effect corporeal travel, I had to make myself lighter than air. So far, I didn't know how to do that unless combustion was involved. "I don't see why I can't simply put them in the car and drive them."

"You could barely drag them three feet in the snow. You really think you could've hauled them down to a car?"

"Were you there? No, you weren't," I said sourly, flinching as the cuffs snapped off Ricky and Leonardo and reappeared around my wrists again, once more delicate bracelets. The bonds of Justice lasted only as far as Judgment's door, I'd already learned. I wasn't yet sure how I felt about that. "I could have totally gotten them to a car."

"Secure them." Gamon directed this comment to two dark-robed attendants who arrived with oversized rolling carts. The two men—I assumed they were men—picked up both Leonardo and Ricky and laid the boys on the carts, strapping them down ruthlessly.

I flinched despite myself. "Ricky didn't seem completely irredeemable, for the record. He was just another dude selling the newest version of weed under the open sky. And the other, Leonardo..."

"He shot at you," Gamon put in reasonably.

"He did shoot at me, but who knows what his life has been like up to now? I mean, seriously, what is he, fifteen? And yes, I see the mark on him. But he's totally a kid."

By now, Gamon was full-out staring at me. "You really do suck at this," she said, not bothering to hide the tone of derision in her voice.

"Look, all I'm saying is that—"

"No, *you* look." Gamon turned from me and gestured to a wall full of TV screens. I hadn't noticed them before.

"What're those for? You catching up on *The Bachelor* in your free time?"

"I had them put in after the last time you pulled this. Which was the last time you brought someone to me."

I winced. "She seemed like a nice enough old lady."

"Who also had the mark of Justice upon her. That should've given you a clue." Gamon flicked her hand, and a dozen screens lit up with hundreds of faces. "These are all the people who Ricky has damaged—or killed—by cutting his harmless pot with technoceuticals even before he had the Black Elixir in hand, all of it under the direction of Leonardo."

I stared. Some were obvious long-term users, some were…not. "Those are kids."

"Those are kids," Gamon agreed. "Pot is legal now in Colorado, but that doesn't mean it's easily accessible for those who need it most. Those whose parents are desperate, whether they're Connected or otherwise. Those who—"

"Enough," I muttered, my stomach roiling. With a flick of my own hand, the screens went blank again. "I get the point."

Gamon was glaring at me now, her eyes flinty. "I don't want to have to go through this explanation every single time, but I will for as long as you need me to. You see someone marked, their time for Justice has come. And that's what you are. So you bring them in."

"And you judge them."

Gamon gave me a thin smile. "I let them know the error of their ways and their path to redemption. Some take it, some don't."

"The old lady from the Strip?"

She shrugged. "Took her chances on a different higher power. But at least she wasn't selling street kids into the Connected sex trade anymore."

"Well…good." I'd sensed the woman was bad news when I'd first seen her, despite the appearance she displayed to anyone without my quirk of vision. She'd appeared to be a dozing old drunk enjoying an early morning snooze in the gardens at Caesars Palace, but there'd been no denying the silver slash along her right temple—a scarlet letter for Connected modern times. She couldn't see it, no one around her could see it, but ever since I'd ascended to the role of Justice a few weeks ago…I could see it.

This brought up yet another key fact I'd learned about my role as Justice, though it made a certain sort of sense. I wasn't called upon to track down *every* soul who'd trespassed against a fellow human, only those who were psychic, otherwise known as Connected, and who'd also passed a threshold of villainy I hadn't yet entirely figured out. I had a bad feeling there would end up being a hell of a lot more bad guys than I'd ever expected.

The information of the old woman in her file hadn't been clear on her crimes, but I'd seen the mark across her temple and had acted. I'd grabbed her, and a second later, we'd arrived at Gamon's front door. The old woman was passed out. My ears were on fire.

Screw this lighter-than-air stuff. I needed a teleporting Uber, stat.

"We need to know more about this Black Elixir," I said as Leonardo stirred on the gurney. "And there was a guy Ricky mentioned, someone called the Red King. I want to know who that is, too." In Tarot, the Red King meant the King of Cups, a good-natured patron of the arts, heavy on the emo and mindfulness, light on the soulless analytics. But I hadn't heard of any dark practitioner called the Red King, and from Gamon's flat, unconcerned expression, she hadn't either. So either the guy was pretty new to the scene, or Ricky was out of his head with the drugs he'd already taken. Or both.

"Fair enough," Gamon said. "Since Ricky is taking his time rousing, we'll start with the formal judgment of Leonardo deSalvo." She followed my gaze and signaled to another attendant, a hooded human whose face was impossible to read beneath the shadows of his or her heavy cowl. I didn't know where Gamon got her minions, and I didn't particularly want to ask. Either way, the attendant moved forward with surprising grace, snapping off Leonardo's restraints before the boy fully realized he'd been bound. As a result, when he came to, he bolted upright and swung his legs over the cart, his eyes darting around the room.

He wasn't an idiot. He was surrounded on all sides by hoods, walls, and now-dead screens, with Ricky on the cart beside him and Gamon and me blocking the only exit. His shoulders dropped almost immediately, and despite the obvious evidence of his supreme fail as a human being, I grimaced at the forlorn expression on his face.

"You're so pathetic," Gamon muttered beside me. She fixed the boy with a glare. "Who's your dealer? And who's the Red King?"

Leo's gaze immediately hardened, teetering between mutinous and desperate. "Who're you?"

Gamon didn't hesitate. It was one of her defining characteristics, so in its way, it answered the boy's question without words. Her hand went up, palm out, and with absolutely no physical contact, the boy was punched off the cart and hurled backward against the far wall. The minions in the area neatly sidestepped the movement and also appeared unmoved as the boy's angry shout turned into a terrified scream. Not surprising, given that his feet were now a pool of blood and goop below his shins, the putrefaction rolling up his legs like a red tide.

"I don't know any Red King! My dealer's name is Coronado, and he's in LA. LA!" the boy cried, his words coming more urgently as his kneecaps dissolved.

Gamon was, among many other things, a master of manipulating fear. She needed to work on her finesse, though.

"Gamon," I warned as the boy started to hyperventilate.

"Wuss," she muttered back, but with another wave of her hand, the boy's legs were back where they were supposed to be. He collapsed against the wall, breathing heavily. He wasn't a high-level Connected, I realized, no matter how quick on the draw he'd been. Probably a couple of steps up from your basic intuitive, which made him ideal at picking out his foot soldiers and marks to support his drug trade.

The screens around him flickered to life again—more of them, this time. Not only Ricky's clients, but dozens, hundreds more. Leonardo had been busy, mostly targeting kids. Why these kids? Was there something special about them, or were they truly random marks? I had so many questions, but this was Gamon's rodeo. Ricky and Leo were supposed to be my warm-up act, nothing more. Then again—the mention of the Red King clawed at me, digging at my cerebral cortex. Why did it sound so familiar? Was it simply the Tarot reference?

"What's Black Elixir?" Gamon demanded, refocusing my attention.

"It's *magic*." The boy looked up at the name of the drug, his eyes saucer wide as he uttered the words exactly like Ricky had not two hours earlier. "You can do anything, see anything, be anything with it. When you mix it with another base, you got no pain for days—

days, not hours. And you can maintain that dose, without issue, forever."

"Okay," I cut in. "Then what's all this with the fifth hit?"

Leo's smile turned craftier, less full of wonder. It made him look far older than the fifteen years I suspected he'd lived on this earth. "If you increase your dose, even a little, that's a new hit. But with each new hit, you get more. A lot more. You get visions. You don't just lose your pain, you lose some of whatever it is that's hurting you—cancers diminish, broken bones go back together, your memory returns, whatever. That's hit number two. And even then, you can return to the lower dose, and you're good, you maintain. But…"

"But there's always the allure of hit number three," I supplied.

Leonardo had returned his gaze to his knees, as if reassuring himself they were still there. "You brought them back," he murmured, stretching his fingers down to brush his thighs.

"Not for long," Gamon said noncommittally. She lifted her hand, and the boy must have sensed the movement.

"No," he blurted, his head jerking up again, words tumbling out of him. "Hit number three and you can predict the future, your personal future, anyway. You can't know if your sister or your cousin will be killed, but you know what's going to happen to *you* within the next day or two, no more. You can almost make out the people around you when it happens, so you can predict when the thing you got in your vision will happen exactly, you see?"

"It always works?"

"Always," he said with a certainty that bordered on reverence.

I pursed my lips. What the hell was this drug?

The magical drug trade of the Connected community had been going full tilt for half a century now, each new concoction worse than the last. But to make the best technoceuticals, the kind that worked on Connecteds and non-Connecteds alike, you needed strong genetic material as a base. Which meant humans. Connected humans. And all too often, Connected kids.

It'd been a decade—more than a decade—since I'd first stumbled over that reality. Sometimes, I liked to think I'd evened the odds a little bit in my work to protect the most vulnerable of the Connected community. Most times, I knew better. I'd been a fringe player, a mercenary. At least until a few weeks ago, when I'd exploded the war on magic and then leveled up to Justice, with a whole lot more than merely the children of the world to look after.

I stared at the still-shimmering, faintly visible silver slash across Leonardo's right ear. "So how'd you not know I was going to haul your skinny ass to Judgment?"

It wasn't an insignificant question. Leonardo hadn't been surprised to see me. He'd clearly started following me the moment I'd gone after Ricky. If he'd known I was going to take him in, though, why hadn't he run instead? Had the elixir shown him something of his future that I didn't fully understand? Did he know more about what was going to happen than I did?

It was Gamon who answered. "He never took the third hit," she said stonily. Leonardo had turned his attention back to his legs, which had started another rotting rotation. "He made Ricky take it."

"He wanted to take it," Leonardo insisted quickly, his face jerking up again.

"I'm thinking as juiced as he is, Leonardo here has never actually sampled Black Elixir. Have you?" Gamon continued inexorably, her flat glare pinned on the kid. "You've seen the effects too many times. You've seen how the allure of the next hit becomes too much to bear. Even though someone doesn't need it, even though their pain is managed perfectly well to the point where they can pursue other forms of healing to take care of whatever it is that ails them. It isn't enough. They can't stop. The visions, the dreams, they always keep thinking that the next hit will make it all worth it. And that they can always stop in time. How many people have you seen take the fifth hit?"

Leonardo's expression had turned mulish, but Gamon didn't let him think about his answer too long. His hands started to quiver too, fingers liquefying as he yelped and jerked against the wall. "I don't know—I don't *know*. Fifteen, twenty, maybe. Enough. I've seen enough of them." His fingers reformed, and he shook them hard, as if reassuring himself they were still there. "Ricky was up to three doses, and he..." Leo shrugged, his gaze darting over to his comatose friend. "He may have had four. He's been acting weird."

I glanced to Ricky as well. How much of the Black Elixir *had* he taken?

It didn't matter. He was in Judgment's capable hands now and out of mine. He'd wake up again, even if he didn't want to.

Gamon leaned forward, still focused on Leonardo. "And you weren't about to start acting weird, so you never even took the first hit. That's pretty disciplined, Leonardo. I'm proud of you."

Gamon's voice was laced with malevolent disdain, but not all of her disgust was targeted at the boy, I knew. Gamon's past was longer than most and darker than most. She'd murdered men, women, and even children in her quest for a vengeance I still didn't fully understand. She'd trodden the worst paths of the arcane black market to build her strength and destroy her enemies. Some of those enemies had been people I'd known, respected. There was a core of darkness inside Gamon so deep and wide that I wasn't sure she could ever fully step into the light. Her ascendance to the role of Judgment had been as much to control her Connected abilities as to put them to greater service, not unlike me. And one day she—both of us—would be judged as well.

But not today.

"Take him," Gamon snapped out the order to the assembled minions. "I'm not done with him yet."

"Wha—what?" Leonardo looked at Gamon in confusion as her attendants moved closer to him. "What're you going to do me?"

"We'll have to see about that. You've got a lot of dead kids to account for, and I don't think you're going to like your rehabilitation plan." Gamon's lips twisted as understanding finally lit Leonardo's eyes. Understanding...and terror. "Maybe you should've taken your own hit after all."

Chapter Three

Two hours later, across Vegas and back on the Strip, I stood in the hallway of the penthouse floor of the Palazzo casino hotel, eyeing the single door at the end of the long hallway. My office as Justice of the Arcana Council was the legit penthouse level of the building, part of the original luxury Vegas hotel. The Palazzo was one of the jewels anchoring the northern end of the Strip, along with the Venetian, Treasure Island, and the Wynn casino. I'd been a fan of the Palazzo since my earliest days in Vegas, when I'd reluctantly visited the city as an artifacts hunter for hire. That'd been over five years ago and felt more like five hundred.

Now I was someone different, something new. Frankly, after today, I wasn't so sure I'd made the right employment choice.

I was even less sure when I strode the length of the hall, pausing only briefly at the door. There was a small brass plate to the right of it, etched with the number eleven, the number for the Justice card in the Tarot's Major Arcana. I hadn't decided yet what else the placard should say, mainly because I hadn't stepped foot inside my own office yet.

Clearly, it was time.

The door unlocked as I approached—another perk of my position. I turned the knob and pushed the door half open, then shoved it the rest of the way, wincing as something loud crashed to the floor behind it. I edged into the room and peered around. There were boxes. Lots of boxes. All of them open and brimming with paper.

"Um…what is this?"

"Yo! Dollface." The shout came from another room, through one of two doors that exited what should have been the reception lounge of the brand-spanking-new Hall of Justice, a name that usually made me grin, except right now when said hall looked like an episode of *Hoarders*. "Give me a sec, I'm stuck in 1973."

"You're…" I blinked as Nikki Dawes emerged from the door to the left of the lobby, which should have led to the library of my new office. "You don't look like you're stuck in '73. More like World War II."

"Well, duty calls, so I'm workin' it."

Nikki grinned, flexing her impressive biceps. At six foot four not counting her heels, which today were heavy, thick-soled work boots, Nikki would be remarkable when she wasn't even trying. But she'd never be known for not trying. She currently was rocking a Rosie the Riveter ensemble that had her springy dark brown curls tied up in a bright red-and-white polka-dotted hair scarf, her heavily mascaraed eyes flashing brightly as her glossy red lips parted in a generous smile. Her denim jumper's sleeves were rolled high, but in a sartorial move that I suspected would've left Rosie aghast, the jumper itself terminated in a set of cuffed short shorts, exposing approximately eighteen miles of leg atop Nikki's red socks and black boots.

"What is all this stuff?" I asked, gesturing to the cardboard box modern art sculpture surrounding me.

"Case files." Nikki reached back inside the door and pulled out another long, slender box—no, not a box, I realized instantly. A very large scroll case. "And a whole bunch of these bowling pins."

I stared as she leaned the case against the wall. "Those are our case files? No one in this office ever heard of a computer?"

"Apparently, when you don't fill a position for nearly two hundred years, things pile up. New jobs would come in, but they'd…" She shrugged, jerking her thumb over her shoulder, "be sent here. For filing. All this stuff out here in the lobby was simply to give me room in the library to get the lay of the land."

"I don't suppose you've figured out how many backlogged cases we have?"

"Yes, sir, I have." Nikki saluted. "First I had to remove all the jobs that had expired, due to, well, people expiring. I figured that would cut down the load considerably."

"Makes sense."

"You'd think so, but you would be wrong. As it turns out, the sins of the fathers had a nasty way of working themselves down Connected family trees. And as it further turns out, even if the perpetrators are long dead, in some cases there are still those crying out for justice, whose souls cannot rest until it is served."

I wrinkled my brow. "I don't think we need to worry about some outrage that occurred in the 1300s, no matter how many people are still frosty about it."

"Well, look around you." Nikki waved. "There's a whole lot of sorrow on ice in this fridge, and even if you backlog these bad boys, some of them will eventually need to be dealt with. That's the job."

"That is the job." Once again, I was reminded that I clearly hadn't considered the fine print of said job when I'd agreed to become Justice a few short weeks ago. And my recruiter hadn't exactly been forthcoming either. Something I planned to discuss with him. Later. "So, what are we looking at exactly? You've been through all of it?"

"I've been through a lot of it. Best I can figure, you should be done with your backlog of cases by right around…" Nikki cast her gaze skyward, pantomiming mental calculations. "The year 2417. Give or take a decade."

"*What?*"

Her grin widened. "Good thing you're immortal. I plan on retiring before you even get through the bowling pin room."

"But there's no way that's—" I stopped and shook my head. "Never mind. There's something else I want you to follow up on, a dark practitioner drug dealer apparently known as the Red King."

"The Red King?" Nikki's brows went up. "One of the Houses? There is no King of Cups that I know of, and that house was Gamon's old stomping grounds."

"She didn't recognize the name either." I blew out a breath. "I don't know. It could be nothing."

"I'm on it," Nikki said, pulling out her phone. "Ma-Singh said if I ever needed intel, to give him a ring. He'll be thrilled to help."

I smiled and nodded as I thought of the general of the House of Swords, my gruff, protective partner in arms up until a very short while ago. "Good. If anyone knows, he'd be the one—"

"Incoming!" The squeak to my right was completely unexpected, emanating as it did through the open door of the other room leading off the lobby, which was my office. My *private* office, a fact which didn't seem to have impressed the diminutive creature who rushed through the door and leapt up on the first box she encountered. At first I thought she was a little girl, then I realized she was a full-grown woman, barely four foot eight, as weathered as old bark, her white hair wound around her head in a kind of fluffy bun. She launched a long, slender glass canister at me with remarkable gusto. It flipped toward me end over end, and I jerked back as it hurtled through the air.

"What in the—"

"Catch it!" The shrill command was issued with so much force, I reacted instinctively, reaching out for the tube—and missing it entirely. There was a reason I hadn't played sports as a kid.

The heavy glass canister smashed into my chest, toppling me backward over a large open box. I managed to get my hands around the thing before it slid off me, then winced at its extreme heat, and I fumbled the canister like a hot potato as its clasp flipped open to reveal its contents. A sheaf of papers lay nestled inside.

"Freaked me out the first time too," Nikki offered from the sidelines. "It's apparently how new cases show up. Pneumatic tube system, right behind your desk." She grinned and pointed at the case. "That must be a hot one."

I blinked from the canister to her. "Please tell me you're joking."

"The system's never been upgraded," interrupted the woman on the box. "How could it be, I ask you, with no Justice to oversee it? We've been keeping up as best we can, but it's not for the likes of me to change a system I didn't put in place, and that's the truth."

I glanced up to see the woman looking down at me severely, and for the first time, I noticed her dress. It was something out of a time capsule itself, a dark gray Victorian-era gown with a skirt that showed white ruffles sticking out of the bottom, an old-time crinoline. The bodice of the dress was buttoned all the way up to a high neck, also edged in white lace, the whole thing as crisply pressed as if it had been delivered that very morning from the costume shop.

"And you are…?"

The woman straightened. "Mrs. French. Not Frenchie, French Kiss, the French Lieutenant's woman *or* French Fry," she added severely, cutting a glance at Nikki. Who winked, thoroughly delighted with herself. "I am the caretaker of the library of Justice. This disarray you see has nothing to do with me."

"That's for sure," Nikki allowed. "Mrs. Frenemy here had the shelves as neat as a pin when I opened the door to the library, but there was no way I could fit into the narrow walkways she'd allowed between the shelves. So I improvised."

"With cardboard *boxes*." Mrs. French could do aghast better than anyone I'd ever heard. "The case files strewn about as if these weren't the outcries of the wronged and the afflicted."

"Yep. So anyway, here we are," Nikki said. "Until 2417."

"But how…" I poked at the contents of the pneumatic tube, the papers now cool enough to touch. They were still barely more than parchment, and the information on them had been hand-lettered with an ink pen. I slid the documents out, squinting at the first page. Then I stiffened. "This is written in Hindi."

"Hindi?" Mrs. French hopped off her box and bustled over, a movement I'd never seen performed by someone actually wearing a bustle. It suddenly made a great deal more sense. She set a pair of tiny glasses to the bridge of her nose and squinted at the paper. "Nepali, actually. They're very close. You can read it, I assume?"

"Well enough." I shrugged. One of the perks of my evolving status was my ability to translate. Most of the time it was a boon; sometimes I mourned the bliss of ignorance. "It's a complaint against spirits roaming the countryside, whispering tales of enlightenment to lure children from their beds and the elderly from their fires. Apparently, there've been some villagers going missing."

"Dark days, dark days indeed," Mrs. French tutted. "Now that this has cooled off right proper, I'll be about filing it." She took the papers from my unresisting fingers and cast a baleful eye around the room. "And about cleaning up this mess."

"I…" I couldn't finish the sentence. All I could think about was dark spirits roaming the streets of Nepal. Spirits that could be anything from true demons to the dark practitioners of the Connected community, constantly on the hunt for the newest source material for their dark potions. I'd thought becoming Justice would make me feel more capable of addressing this issue, not less.

"Take a breath, dollface." Nikki had made her way to my side. "You gotta go at this slow, get used to it."

"That's quite right." Mrs. French turned with a rustle of skirts, eyeing me more closely. "The last Justice broke down several times with hysteria before she accepted her first case. And more than a few times after that, I'm sorry to say."

"She did?" I asked, frowning. "Why?"

"Such a mess we have here," Mrs. French said briskly, picking up one of the smaller boxes and carrying it to the side of the room. "But she soldiered on, lasted longer than any of them before her too. She was a good and sturdy sort, that one. I'm sure you'll do her proud, her and all those who came before."

"Hold on there, French Dip." Nikki lifted a hand. "You didn't mention anything to me about the other Justices that came before the last one. Or about any breakdowns."

"Well, it's not as if we had a lot of time for idle chitchat." Mrs. French sniffed. "And I don't recall you asking about any of the ones before. Goodness knows we had a lot to do to make room for your, ah, substantial presence in the library."

"Was that a body slam? Because that's some sizeist crap right there—"

"Enough," I interrupted. I didn't know what had gotten the two of them off on the wrong foot, but I wasn't about to start sorting out stilettos right now. I focused on Mrs. French. "You've been tending the library for the past two hundred years, then, since the last Justice served?"

"Since 1855, dear. I was her intern, bless her soul, and kept on. It's been a satisfying life."

"You're…two hundred years old."

"Oh, go on. I'm not as old as that." Mrs. French flapped her hands at me. "And I've done my job right good and well. Justice Abigail and I got on famously, and I suspect you and I will be no different, and Mistress Dawes, of course." She ignored Nikki's snort. "As difficult as her parting was, it did my heart good to know that Justice Abigail never lived to see the death of dear Prince Albert or the failing of the queen. They were all fast friends, you see."

I'd never really given much thought to the previous Justice. Looking at the lobby, I realized yet again how much I'd not considered about this new role.

"Eighteen fifty-five," I repeated. "But there are documents and files from well before then."

"You got that right," Nikki put in. "That scroll I showed you was definitely not from Victorian England."

Mrs. French tsked. "Same as you, Justice Abigail couldn't handle every cold case on the shelves when she came into her station. She did what she could, but her attention was much more heavily fixed on the issues of the present moment than on righting past wrongs. And, too, there was the issue with formal versus ad hoc cases. Still and all, she made quite a name for herself during her tenure, as I'm sure you will too."

I tried to follow everything Mrs. French said, but something was niggling at me, pricking my senses. "How long did Justice Abigail serve, exactly?"

"Oh, well then." For the first time, Mrs. French seemed a bit nonplussed. "Where *are* my manners and protocol? You deserve a rightful introduction all around." She patted her skirts abruptly, then stuck her hand in the folds and drew out a small whistle, which she blew into, three shrill, staccato blasts. I shot my gaze to Nikki, who looked as mystified as I felt.

We didn't have long to wait. A patter of feet sounded from deep inside the library, and Nikki barely had time to get out of the way before several figures emerged from the dimly lit room—a group of boys who looked like nothing more than cleaned-up Victorian chimney sweeps, down to their snap-brim caps, which to a one they snatched off and held in their small hands, looking up at me with large, soulful eyes as they canted their heads down respectfully.

"There, there we all are, the six of you. Well, look smart, then. It's our new Justice here to see you, and you can be proud of all you've done."

I stared as a scattering of mums, ma'ams, and m'ladys rippled through the group. "But…those are children."

"That they are, Justice," Mrs. French said, seeming to consider my title the proper form of address for me. "All of them scamps, mark my words, but they work hard at being respectful and doing their jobs."

"But—how—?"

"How is it they're all still living, never aging a day?" Mrs. French beamed at the boys, who were openly staring at Nikki as if they'd never seen anything like her. Which, I supposed, they probably hadn't. Nikki, for her part, merely looked more and more dismayed. "Well, now, that's a story in itself, but suffice to say they were some of the afflicted that Justice Abigail encountered even before she entered her service, and though she handled their tormentor as quickly as she could, the damage to the boys had already been done. She couldn't very well leave them running about, never growing up. So she offered them lodging and work in the library, where there are plenty of doorways to the outside world. They weren't fools, our boys, even back at the beginning," she said. "They'd lived a good ten years under the heel of their captors before Abigail learned of their plight. They knew a good bargain when they saw one."

"You're here…by choice?" I managed.

"We are, mum," one of the boys said, a skinny kid with light blond hair. "It's not so bad. We can go anywhere and come right back, so long as we're careful. We tend the library, file the papers. And we can all read, of course."

"Every language!" another one piped up, his gray eyes wide as he nodded several times.

"That they can, and they're quite circumspect when they go out into the world. They've only put their foot in it one or two times." Mrs. French continued. "That poor Mr. Barrie, he never did recover from seeing them, but one can only do so much."

"Ah—right. Hey, have we got any cases that center on someone called the Red King? Maybe technoceuticals, or…" I looked around the shambles of the room. "It'd be recent."

"We haven't, I can tell you without looking," Mrs. French said crisply.

"Good thing, since there's no way you could have found it if it was here," Nikki cracked.

"Now, that's exactly the kind of attitude that isn't helpful, Mistress Dawes, I'll thank you to understand. It—"

Mrs. French looked like she was about to hold forth in a surprisingly epic rant, but a sudden rumble that seemed to shake the very foundations of the Palazzo Hotel had the diminutive woman gasping and turning around. She raced back into my office. Unable to stop myself, I wove around the boxes, then stuck my head for the first time inside what was supposed to be my private sanctuary.

The place was perfectly spotless, a masterpiece of Victorian architecture, gilded and curved and carved. What drew my attention, however, was a series of glass tubes that stretched from the ceiling to about waist high, with openings at the bottom. A velvet-lined trough extended along the bottom of the tubes. For overflow, I assumed.

"Oh dear, oh dear, oh dear," Mrs. French murmured, her gaze on the visibly trembling ceiling, as if that was the origin of all our difficulties. "I was afraid of this."

"What is it?" I asked. Nikki crowded in behind me, surveying the room, and took several steps forward as the noise increased.

Mrs. French wrung her hands. "It's been two hundred years, nearly, since the last Justice served. Now you're here, though no one should have known quite yet. Word travels fast, of course, it always has. It was bound to cause some commotion, couldn't be helped. But I'd hoped…well, I'd rather thought—"

"Watch out!" Nikki lurched forward and swept Mrs. French out of the way as a half-dozen of the pneumatic tubes began clanging and rattling. Fat cylinders pounded down their lengths and burst into the room, completely bypassing the padded trough. Nikki caught the first, then the second, but another four more blasted down the tubes and were violently ejected into thin air, clanging against the opposite wall as I ducked.

Then…silence.

I stood shakily, my eyes on the rolling canisters. At the door to the lobby, six faces poked in, all of them pale as chalk.

"We might need to adjust our intake procedures, Justice," Mrs. French said faintly. "It would seem you've been announced."

Chapter Four

It was another several hours before I staggered to my suite at the Palazzo—a totally ordinary suite, not like my office on the penthouse floor of the casino hotel, where the library of Justice Hall started in the Palazzo proper but then extended up dozens of floors beyond it, soaring far up into the sky. I could have created a palace in the heavens for my personal residence as well, like the other members of the Arcana Council, but I hadn't wanted that in the end. I never wanted to forget where I'd come from, no matter who I'd become.

I didn't want my old life back, truly. I did want my old room back, though.

Waving the card at the door, I heard an entire series of locks disengage. So far as I knew, I was the only one who lived on this floor anymore—at least, I'd never seen anyone else. But you couldn't be too careful.

And as it turned out, the suite wasn't empty.

My heart did a weird sort of sideways samba as the door swung shut behind me and I took in the other occupant of the beautifully appointed living area, who was currently sipping from a glass of wine. If this was what coming home meant, I'd have to do it more often.

Taller than most ordinary humans, ridiculously attractive, and brimming over with power, Armaeus Bertrand had, in many ways, gotten me exactly where I was today, pneumatic tubes and all. Five years ago, I'd been a mercenary artifact hunter, arguably one of the best of the business since I was Connected and had a particular knack for using Tarot cards to find the items most coveted by my clients. The combination of psychic ability and crack search skills put me one step ahead of my competitors and kept me in high demand. At least until the Arcana Council had gotten wind of my abilities. The fact that the Council was made up of demigods who embodied the Major Arcana of the Tarot, my particular flavor of crazy, hadn't been lost on me, and they'd paid me well for my artifact-finding services.

As to their organizational hierarchy, I rolled with that, too. They weren't the only super special society who liked to call their leaders funny names. The Elks had their Grand Exalted Ruler, the Templars had their National Bishop, the Freemasons had their Grand Master, and the Arcana Council had their Magician. So far, so good. It also hadn't hurt that the Magician of the Arcana Council was a particularly delectable hunk of man meat.

"Your mental barriers are down. You must know I can read your thoughts."

"Just checking." I tossed my jacket onto the counter, then walked deeper into the room. It smelled of cinnamon and possibilities. I couldn't deny the pull the Magician had on me, but wasn't letting go of the fact that I had an axe to grind with him. "You held out on me."

He, of course, knew immediately what I was talking about. One of the benefits of being the Magician. Way better than a Grand Exalted Ruler, in my book. "You didn't ask."

"How was I supposed to know what questions to ask about a job that hadn't been filled in almost two centuries? I picked the role of Justice because it called to me, but it's not like I had any idea what I was getting into. You did."

He turned, slanting me a look I chose not to interpret. "You were born to be Justice," he said, his words an exotic mix of rolling syllables I'd come to love, even when the owner of the voice irritated me. Armaeus Bertrand was French by birth and Egyptian by lineage, his father a twelfth-century soldier in the Crusades and his mother a high priestess to Thoth, god of language and spiritual father of the Tarot, by many accounts. Armaeus, quite legitimately, *had* been born to be the Magician.

My lineage was a little more problematic. My father was a member of the Arcana Council, which had a strict nonfraternization rule when it came to other celestial beings. My mother was most likely the reason for the rule.

"No," I replied gamely. "I was born because you guys couldn't keep a collar on the Hermit, and he didn't have the sense any of the gods could've given him to stay away from my mother. There was nothing in there about me becoming Justice as a result of that extremely screwed-up union, any more than there was anything ever written about Gamon becoming Judgment."

"She's adjusting to her new role quite well," Armaeus observed.

"She's looking forward to years of joy. And speaking of years…"

"Twenty-four seventeen. Nikki told me." He nodded, eyeing me over the rim of his wineglass. "You won't lack for distractions as Justice. In fact, distractions will serve you well."

Right. I was beginning to notice a disturbing trend of nonanswers when it came to my questions regarding my new position. "And how long did the last Justice serve, exactly? Mrs. French was remarkably vague on the topic."

"Was she?"

A trend that apparently was going to continue. "Yes, she was."

I watched the Magician as he took another long sip of his wine. Armaeus was many things, but straightforward was not one of them. However, he wasn't the only one who'd learned how to play Reindeer Games. Since I'd ascended to the Council, I'd leveled up as well. It didn't take special powers for me to realize he was avoiding the subject.

"Tell me about her, or I'm going to go to the Devil. He'll tell me."

"He would, yes." Armaeus strolled over and sat on one of the deep wingback chairs, and only then did I notice the redecoration.

"These weren't here before," I said, frowning at the deeply plush furniture.

"I took the liberty."

I started for the sitting area, then detoured for the refrigerator. I opened it, taking a moment to register its contents. It'd never been so full of food. "It looks like you took a lot of liberties."

"Since you insist on living somewhere that relies on the laws of physics, it was—quite literally—the least I could do."

"I'll keep that in mind." I grabbed a plastic container of some vaguely dip-like substance that looked like it had been made with a pound of cheese and snagged a box of crackers from the counter. I blinked at the shiny metal surface. "What was wrong with the granite?"

"Mm." Armaeus watched me as I moved across the floor toward him, his dark eyes hooded and more mysterious than usual. I could barely make out the faint lining of gold around the pupils as I sat and braced myself. The deeper the Magician was into his magic, the blacker his eyes. Given the depths of dark his pupils were currently rocking, I expected him to poof into an alternate reality at any minute.

"Okay. Hit me," I said, adding a liberal scoop of cheese to my cracker. Cheese made everything better.

He lifted a hand, stalling my progress. "Before you lose all capacity for speech by eating that in one bite, perhaps you could clarify your question. What specifically do you want to know about the previous Justice?"

I paused. It was a fair question. And I wanted to enjoy my food, which meant I needed a long-winded response. "How about you give me the full run-down on Justice Abigail. Where she came from, what she did, why she stepped down from the Council, and where she is now."

Armaeus watched as I shoved the cracker into my mouth, his lips twitching with amusement as the concoction hit my taste buds. It…was ambrosia. On steroids. I also couldn't remember the last time I'd eaten, which certainly helped.

"Mmflggh," I groaned. I slapped my hand over my mouth to ensure none of the miracle escaped.

"I'll convey your compliments to the chef," he said drily as I reached for the wine.

"Abigail," I finally managed.

"Abigail," he agreed. "Justice Abigail Strand ascended to her role at the age of twenty-seven, not much younger than yourself. Prior to her work on the Council, she'd been employed as governess to the children of a very reclusive psychiatrist, whom she revered far longer than she should have. One day, she discovered that the doctor's particular brand of psychiatry was far less circumspect than she had at first imagined."

I tried to ask a question but couldn't form words around the cheese, and Armaeus elaborated. "Her employer was Connected, of course, and an experimenter of high reputation, as well as quite pious in his outward appearance. He brought Miss Strand on as a governess to several wayward street urchins, and as the months passed, she began to notice something…peculiar about the boys."

"Oh." I knew this part, and Armaeus nodded.

"Sadly, before she could satisfy her curiosity, her situation took a drastic turn. The boys, who had come to care for her by this time, revealed that she had also become the subject of her employer's experimentation. He'd secretly begun augmenting Abigail's abilities without her realizing it through tinctures she consumed in her evening tea. She was aghast, then distraught, then outraged."

"Which was when you showed up."

"Merely to intervene to ensure that the abilities of her employer did not grow too far, too fast. Balance was essential in the mid-1800s. The world was reeling from political and scientific revolutions, and in times of great chaos, magic can proliferate unchecked. Unfortunately, I arrived on the scene too late."

"Too late?" That surprised me. "What do you mean?"

"Abigail Strand had already confronted her employer, surprising him in the midst of an experiment that was both depraved and breathtaking in its savagery. She wrested the machine from him, freed the young woman who was being subjected to his torture, then turned the machine on him."

"She did?" I stared at him. "I mean, go her, but how was she able to do all that, exactly? I thought she barely understood her own abilities."

"She didn't. Her employer did, but he believed he could direct her. Miss Strand was a victim of sleepwalking. When she slipped into her trance state, she would—and did—perform atrocities of appreciable ferocity. She'd entered such a condition before I arrived, and by the time I reached her, Randolph was dead. However, because I was present, Miss Strand came to her senses most abruptly, fully cognizant of what she had done. While she had no particular love of Randolph, her horror at how he'd been using her knew no bounds. She demanded to know of the crimes she had committed and, once we determined what they were, how she could make amends."

I narrowed my eyes. "And you were exactly the guy to give her a suggestion."

Armaeus spread his hands. "There was no question that her abilities had grown beyond those an ordinary mortal could handle. She'd been augmented within an inch of her life, and she had no training to control it. Raising her to the Council allowed her that control, and becoming Justice afforded her some solace for the lives she had unknowingly taken. She was, at heart, a good person."

"Okay, fine." I stared at the empty box of crackers "Some man came in here and stole all my food."

"It's so difficult keeping out the riffraff," Armaeus sighed.

"So, how long did she serve? I don't believe you mentioned it."

Armaeus sat forward, his gaze suddenly intent. "That's not truly what's bothering you," he said mildly. "Do you want to talk about it?"

I glared back at him. "Pretty sure I don't."

"Miss Wilde."

"Don't you Miss Wilde me. You didn't tell me about the backlog of cases in ye olde Hall of Justice. You also didn't tell me I'd be chaperoning the Lost Boys."

"Mrs. French keeps them well in line."

"That's not the point. What else haven't you told me? Because I'm starting to think it's quite a lot." I straightened. "And speaking of, who's the Red King?"

If I thought I was going to surprise Armaeus, I failed. His expression didn't change. "Where did you hear that title?"

"Oh, I don't know, just the second of the two jobs that showed up with my cool bracelets and decoder ring."

His elegantly arched brows lifted. "You didn't get a—"

"Focus. You know the title, who is it?"

"I know the title." Armaeus inclined his head. "But much like the role of Justice, it's not one that anyone's claimed in centuries. It was an accolade that originally implied a powerful sorcerer, the greatest among his peers."

"Originally," I repeated. "And now?"

He shrugged. "Now it's no longer in use, unless you're about to correct me."

"I...I don't know." I sat back in my chair. "A guy used it today, one of the drug dealers, but he was half out of his mind on Black Elixir."

"The new drug of choice for the dark practitioners." Armaeus considered that. "Tied to the Red King? That's…interesting."

"I asked Nikki to look into it, but she's gotten nothing yet, and it's been over twelve hours. The guy's a ghost. If he exists at all."

"It was definitely a title of some renown in the Middle Ages, but…" Armaeus got that faraway look he assumed when his mind started running through his internal Encyclopedia Arcania. His voice was ever so slightly dazed when he continued. "Gamon advised that she recovered enough of the unspent drug to analyze. We're doing that now."

"She did? You are?" I straightened. "Did she get anything else out of Ricky?"

"He's the older of the two." The Magician blinked, refocusing on me. "He has not awakened yet. From her preliminary assessment, he's deteriorating quickly."

That…didn't sound good. "Aww, man."

"He was a drug dealer, Miss Wilde."

"Yeah, well. I know," I grumbled. "But I didn't take this job to sweep up bodies. The point was to give people a path to rehabilitation. Kind of hard to do that if they're dead."

"Your tasks will not always end happily," Armaeus reminded me, not unkindly.

"Well, once again, that was something I didn't think through all that clearly. You knew better than I did what was entailed. You could have *warned* me."

"And why ever would I have done that? We've needed a Justice to sit on the Council since Abigail—left."

I didn't miss the slight hesitation at the end of that sentence, but Armaeus recovered quickly.

"I admit I didn't know how you would handle the criminals you encountered," he continued. "But you solved that in short order with the recruitment of Gamon."

"Which also saved me from making her my first collar."

He nodded in agreement. "The fact remains, the world is more in need of your skills as Justice than ever before. Magic isn't merely proliferating, it's exploding. The genie is out of the bottle, and it's not going to return on its own."

He seemed strangely…ambivalent about that. Which was odd, since for as long as I'd known him, Armaeus had been the most vocal opponent of the world becoming more magical.

"I hope you don't think I'm going to put it back in."

"I don't," he said, his words suddenly far softer. I blinked up at him, startled to see Armaeus regarding me with an affection that should have put me on edge.

It didn't, but it should have.

"I'm relying on you to help bring the world to a different place than I could ever have imagined on my own, Miss Wilde." He watched me with his hooded, black-gold eyes. "A different light is shining on this earth, and I can't capture it, I can't mold it. I can't walk with one foot in the stars and one on solid ground. You can."

That…sounded suspect. "Since when?"

"Since you became Justice of the Arcana Council…" His mouth twitched into a smile. "With enough cases to last you until the year 2417."

My phone buzzed, and I fished it out of my pocket. I froze when I glanced at the screen, then bolted out of my chair. "Mrs. French!"

"What?" Armaeus demanded, also rising as I turned to race back up the short stairs toward the door, leaning over to snag my jacket and stuff my arms into it.

"The office—there's someone—an attack—"

I'd made it to the door, glaring at the eighty-seven padlocks, all of them installed for my protection. "Oh, for the love of—"

Instantly turning incorporeal without even a hint of fireworks, Armaeus blew into me with a rush of smoke, wrapping me close, and we were gone.

CHAPTER FIVE

We poofed back into existence on the penthouse floor, but there was nothing to be seen. The hallway was quiet.

"Let's go," I snapped as Armaeus held out a hand to stop me. "And how do you *do* that? Because lighting myself on fire *sucks*."

"Who texted you?" He began walking toward the door after another moment, his gaze hard on it. As we approached, the faintest amount of industry could be heard at the other side of the door.

I scanned the hallway. It was an ordinary hallway. An ordinary, nonpsychic hallway, accessible to anyone who could punch the right button on the elevator panel. Maybe my office location hadn't been such a good idea after all. "Mrs. French."

"Are you sure?" he glanced at me. "She didn't strike me as very technologically savvy."

"I—" I grunted in exasperation as I pulled out my phone. "Unknown number. But who else would—I mean there's somebody in there. I can hear them." I frowned. "Why aren't *we* in there, for that matter? Why didn't we show up inside?"

"Your wards, Miss Wilde," Armaeus murmured.

"Oh. Right." Like the locks on my suite door, those had seemed like such a good idea at the time. I'd wanted the office secure for ordinary access, a safe haven for anyone who should come to see me. So, I'd barred forced magical access of any kind. Including, perhaps most especially, anyone on the Council besides me. Yet something else that I needed to rethink. Maybe. "Well, that's kind of obnoxious."

"Shh." Armaeus raised a hand as we drew within five feet of the door. The disturbance was more pronounced now, but there was nothing to indicate that the door had been forced. "There are five, maybe six intruders inside."

"But…" Something wasn't adding up. "How is that even possible? The door is even more heavily warded than the walls and ceiling. There's no access."

"It must have been—"

"The *canisters*. Son of a bitch."

Springing past Armaeus, I burst through my own door with a fireball of magic strong enough to send the barrier flying into the center of the room, then I raced in behind it. The chaos of earlier in the day had been replaced by an apparently different type of disruption. Two of the junior librarians were out cold on the floor, lying in their own blood, though not a lot of it, thank heavens. The remaining four were barely visible, mere blurs of waist-high movement around a knot of men who were attacking the door to the library with something that looked like a battering ram.

A battering ram that was working.

The last of the intruders turned and looked at me, but rather than expressing the fear and panic he should have, he grinned and jostled the man beside him, who also turned, his eyes alight with eagerness. That…didn't seem right.

And what else didn't seem right? These guys weren't human, I'd bet my life on it. They were too…smooth, too perfect. I couldn't quite explain it, but something was definitely off.

Armaeus murmured behind me, "I fear there are certain elements I should have already disclosed to you about Abigail's life—and her death."

"We'll take it up with HR." A panicked wail sounded from the other room. "Get Mrs. French."

"If you're sure—"

"Go!"

The thug-bots abandoned their battering ram and rushed at me with the air of the possessed, so frenzied, so excited that once again I knew there was a trick in here, knew it in my bones. But I didn't have time to work through the intricacies of the bad-guy plan. I hurled a bolt of blue fire at the three thug-bots coming at me, and with a speed I hadn't expected, they dodged to the side. I braced myself, fully expecting them to come charging after me, while one small part of my brain remained occupied by the screaming boys. No one did outrage like a ten-year-old boy.

But then things got weird.

Well, weirder.

The thug-bots *didn't* come after me. My fire bolt blew past them, straight into the library door, which seemed to absorb all its weight for a long, fraught moment before bursting off its hinges. At that point, the thug-bots viciously kicked and ripped at the boys, flinging them aside, and dove for the library.

What the hell?

"They can't!" howled the young boy on the floor beside me, hugging his knee to his chest as blood oozed out between his fingers. "You have to stop them from finding—"

He passed out, which wasn't his most helpful move, but I didn't need any more giant blinking neon signs to get his point.

"Miss Wilde." Armaeus interrupted my mental chatter. I didn't need him either.

"Busy!"

I raced for the door and burst into the library as well, pausing a second to get my bearings. As Nikki had said, the place was a warren of narrow alleyways between enormous stacks of books, scrolls, boxes, and cases, and a fair amount of rolling ladders and scaffolding as well. I could hear the steps of the thug-bots ahead of me, but the acoustics of the place were alarming—footsteps seemed to be coming and going at once, growing louder and fading into obscurity all at the same time.

To my surprise, Armaeus kept talking. *"For nearly two hundred years, there's been no Justice of the Arcana Council, but two things have now changed with that situation. One, you're here."*

"I picked up on that," I muttered aloud, edging my way down a long hallway as I lifted my hands, readying to create another bolt of magic. Ordinarily, that wouldn't be the brightest of moves. Nobody likes a fire in a library, especially a library dedicated to lost and tormented souls. But my fire didn't ignite anything I didn't want it to. It was, first and foremost, a burst of electricity. Electricity didn't have to proceed to fire.

Then again, I didn't know this place, these books and cases. I should've brought something less magical as a weapon. Like a gun.

"The second is that many cases thought lost to the mists of time with the departure of the last Justice have reappeared with you. Those cases have returned to this library."

And you knew that would happen. I switched to my inside voice as the library quieted, the steps leading away and toward me now hushing to silence.

"It was but one likelihood among many, but it was one of the more viable likelihoods. Magic and the power that drives it does not spontaneously generate in a vacuum, and neither does it disappear without a force exerting itself upon it. That magic was merely waiting for its portal. You provided the portal. You made it appear. You can make it disappear."

Can we get to the part on where the bad guys are? It was tough to imbue exasperation into mere thoughts, but I did my level best.

Armaeus hesitated. *"The only Council member allowed in the library is Justice herself. That's not due to your wards but Abigail Strand's. Only Justice can see what truly is. Which means that only you could find the intruders. If only you had a particular skill at that."*

"Oh, for the love of..."

I shook out my hands and shoved them into my jacket. Sure enough, the cards were there, and I roughly drew two of them. I already knew that the thug-bots were hitting some sort of case file in the library, so this particular game of Clue was going to be short-lived. I simply needed to figure out—

I flipped over the card, and despite myself, I smiled. The Hermit. Seeker of Truth and Knowledge—and a guy who virtually always, no matter the deck, no matter the time period, no matter the artist—was depicted as holding aloft a bright light to see by.

If these bad guys were tied to someone's long-past crime in some way, they probably knew where to find his case file. But even they would need light to see by.

I placed my hand flat on the nearest wall, shooting a pulse of energy into every surface. The room went dark.

To their credit, the thug-bots didn't reveal their surprise with so much as an exhalation of disgust. They didn't need to. There was a light in the room, all right, but it wasn't coming from anyone's iPhone.

I took off at a run, snagging the first ladder I could to climb up to the next level of the scaffolding-like floors of the room. I realized the intruders I was chasing had somehow circled back beneath me, which meant they were now, technically, chasing me. As I raced through the library, I realized something else. The room *moved*. The variation was subtle at first, but as I leapt from one ladder to the next, where I ended wasn't necessarily the same spot I'd fixed on when I started. The effect was dizzying, and by the third level, I had stopped paying much attention to anything but the mark at the top of the—

The crack was distant, but there was no denying the accompanying burst of pain in my shoulder. "Hey!"

I whipped around, hanging off the ladder with one hand as I craned my neck to see what'd happened. Sure enough, a bloom of blood had emerged along the sleeve where I'd been hit. And yea, though I was an immortal member of the Arcana Council, with a particular skill at healing myself, that didn't mean gunshots didn't *hurt*. Besides, since when had golems become gunslingers? I glared down into the gloom, but I couldn't see anyone else. However, I also couldn't climb up ladders with a lame arm. Which meant—

"Screw this," I muttered. I burst upward…

Nothing happened.

"Yo." I sagged against the ladder, gripping my arm. With a concentrated blast of psychic energy—far more concentrated than I really should be expected to produce so many hours after my last caffeination—I felt the muscles of my arm knit back together, blood pouring in behind to reenergize the area and speed the healing process. With gritted teeth, I began climbing again. My healing efforts were working, but they were taking their own sweet time about it.

"What's going on?" I muttered aloud to the Magician. "What's wrong with me?"

"I'm not sure," Armaeus said in that way of his that always made me feel like a particularly interesting bug he was studying. *"It could be Abigail's legacy wards on the library."*

I grunted, hauling myself onto another platform. "Wards against a future Justice too? That seems pretty stupid." I paused for a second, staring blindly at the cases lining the shelf at eye level. Gradually, they came into focus. Apparently, we were in the "D" section, because this entire shelf looked dedicated to dark practitioners, dating back to the Middle Ages.

Good to know they rated their own section.

Armaeus continued as I used a box of some forgotten Renaissance Master of Disaster to pull myself upright.

"We know very little about Abigail's final days as Justice. We do know that with each official case, her mind fractured a bit more and, well, she wasn't exactly stable to begin with – "

"Her mind *what*?" I didn't bother keeping quiet, because somehow during my impromptu healing session, I'd lost my advance position in the labyrinth. Either that or the people below me had found a shortcut. How was it I didn't know shortcuts in my own library? This place had a serious Chutes and Ladders problem.

Either way, I arrived at the glowing box only milliseconds before the bad guys did. The prize they were after shone brightly behind another scroll tube, and I shoved the obstructing case away to grab the box. It was a very small box, but ornately carved, and its glow intensified as I held it in my hands. I noticed something else too: a date, in a faint silver script. Of course, the date was in Roman numerals, and I'd always sucked at reading those. But still, this little box was *old*.

To my surprise, the men around me had gone stock-still as soon as I'd grabbed the prize. They stared at me, their eyes remarkably…empty-looking.

"Who sent you?" I growled, not forgetting the boys in the lobby. "Because there's going to be hell to pay if you hurt one of my team."

"You don't have the right to keep the contract active," one of the thug-bots said. To my disappointment, the voice that emanated from its mouth sounded vaguely intelligent, almost rational. I really preferred my golems to be stupid. The voice also sounded Middle Eastern, which narrowed things down not at all. "It's been dormant for five hundred years."

"Well, it looks like it's moved up in the queue. In fact, I have a feeling it's going to be next in line." I hefted the box, shook it. "What'd he do?"

"He has *returned*." This from the golem standing behind the first one, a thin, reedy figure with hollow cheeks and shaking hands. In fact, none of these guys were looking nearly as robust as they had when they'd first entered the library. I narrowed my eyes, trying to pick out the rest of the intruders. There'd been four, right? Six?

Oblivious to my attempt at recon, Trembling Man kept going. "Mak'rep has returned from beyond the grave to reclaim his place among his people. He has sent us to make him whole."

"Uh-huh. And Mak'rep would be?"

"Time is short," rasped the head guy. "You cannot pass judgment on a crime you did not witness and do not know.'

"Fortunately, Judgment's not my department. And she's happy to take a pass at anyone. So why don't we take a peek at what Mak'rep did that was so—"

"Stop!"

Opening the little box was clearly not on this group's itinerary, because my move to do so goaded them into action. They exploded into movement around me, emphasis on the explosion. I whipped around, and several of my Tarot cards fell out of my pocket to the floor. At the first burst of activity, the lead guy's head fell off his shoulders. A pool of light spilled out of him, illuminating his fellows. They now looked like little more than wraiths. They lunged toward me with howls so garbled that they defied translation, and I curled my body around the box, bracing myself for impact.

It never came.

I peeked up, and the men had been incinerated to ash in a circle around me. Scowling, I spoke aloud to Armaeus, who I assumed was still tuning in. "They shot me. I bled. I didn't have any sort of protection then. Why do I now?"

"It is curious..." Armaeus's voice was faint, preoccupied, and I rolled my eyes, then looked down at the box.

"Who's Mak'rep?"

"There are several gods attributed to that name, and god-kings besides, mostly dating from the Akkadian period."

"Right..." I said, turning the box over in my hand. "But this date isn't Akkadian, it's Roman." I frowned, trying to see how to open the latch. "I don't know what the deal is with this guy, but he's pissing me off."

"No—please, stop—"

It was the sound of pounding feet in an ungainly gallop that interrupted me this time, and the wide-eyed face of one of the scamp librarians who'd apparently not been hurt poked into view. "You cannot open that, Justice Wilde. You'll go mad!"

I blinked, my thoughts immediately flying to Armaeus's comments regarding Abigail's fragile mental state, but I wasn't going to let fear get ahold of me my first day on the job. "Dude, no. I'm going to be okay."

Without another moment's hesitation, I opened the box, ignoring the boy's terrified gasp and retreating footsteps. As had happened with the canisters before it, a sheaf of tightly wrapped pages fluffed up, with a burst of some sort of powdery substance. Hopefully not anthrax. Did they have anthrax in ancient Rome?

I slid the pages over and scanned the contents. "Mak'rep wasn't a god. At least this one wasn't," I reported. "He was a sorcerer who lived in Rome during the reign of some dude named Tullus Hostilius…great name, by the way." I pursed my lips, continuing to read. "Yeah, he deserves to be here."

"Do I?"

I jerked my head up, realizing that my young librarian had vanished back down whatever corridor he'd sprung from. In his place, all the golem ashes had reassembled into…a much bigger guy. A guy who spoke English, though he was rocking some serious prophet robes.

"Um…Mak'rep?" I shook the box again and sized up the man standing in front of me. "Wow, golem animation. That was awesome magic. Looks like you really are a sorcerer, and a bad guy too. So guess what, you win. You're going to Judgment." Mak'rep's silver slash didn't stop at his temple. His whole head was lit up like a disco ball.

"I didn't expect to be found," the sorcerer said, his words a bare whisper in the silent library. He lifted his hands and waved them. Nothing happened. "The previous Justice had allowed far too many cases to pile up."

"Yeah, well. I'm not her." After Mak'rep made another complicated gesture with his fingers and frowned, I glanced down at the cards I'd dropped. They were now lying faceup on the floor. Lovers, Devil, Justice, High Priestess.

Interesting.

Each of the cards was a perversion of the others—similar, yet decidedly different. What was truth? Or what did I merely want to believe? What was a real threat, and what was merely smoke? What was actual, and what was a mere shadow of itself?

Opposite me, Mak'rep muttered something I assumed was an ancient Roman curse. "I have no magic," he said, clearly irritated. "But you can't take me anywhere either. You're not as strong as I am."

That brought my head up, and I considered Mak'rep anew. He...wasn't completely wrong, I decided. I could feel the power rolling off him in waves, even if he couldn't wield it quite yet, and though I'd never heard of the guy, there was no denying from his paperwork that he'd packed a serious punch back when he'd been Mak'rep the Magnificent or whatever. Time to go before he figured out a way around the library's wards.

"Be that as it may, your little minions were right to keep me from trying to open your box. This place is hell on sorcery, and you're a very bad man."

I stepped forward and grabbed the sorcerer by his toga. To Mak'rep's obvious shock, he was too weak to twist away. Tightening my jaw, I prepared to destabilize us both enough for one quick, smokin' hot trip to Judgment.

"You can't do this," the sorcerer insisted. "You're not Justice Strand."

"And *you* are super observant. I like that in a case file."

As fire exploded around us, Mak'rep was still coherent enough to manage a startled scream.

Good man.

Chapter Six

Mrs. French and the boys weren't in the lobby or my office by the time I made my way out of the library, and by then, thankfully, most of the blood had been cleaned up. I still spared an extra second to glare at the place where the boys had fallen, though. The golems had come through on my watch, in those blasted pneumatic tubes. There was no other explanation. Which meant the harm that had befallen the boys had been my fault.

My gut churned at the thought of that. Some things never changed.

A familiar voice jerked me up and out of my spiraling self-disgust.

"Why is it I only hear of you returning to town *after* you've caused a disturbance?" Detective Brody Rooks of the LVMPD stood in the center of the room, his usual hangdog look achieving entirely new kennels of somber. He was tall and strong without being bulky, with the kind of toughness that had been earned the hard way from his years as a beat cop in Memphis, Tennessee. That was where we'd first met. I'd been a scrawny teen with some skill at reading cards and serious stage mother issues. He'd been a rookie, and he'd drawn the short stick and had to work with me and my mom as members of the community wanting to help with local child disappearances.

Brody and I had made a good team back then. Now too. Usually.

The good detective had also developed a healthy understanding of my recklessness over the years, but I'd done nothing to deserve this particular scowl.

"It wasn't my fault," I said flatly. "I took a new job, and the terms of that job were not clearly laid out to anyone, least of all me." I glared at the Magician, who'd taken up his post out of the fray, leaning against the far wall. His eyes gleamed with curiosity, which was never good. "Did you know I had a *sorcerer* in my library?"

"Not until you uttered his name. It was a fascinating gambit," Armaeus said, his gaze unfocused enough that I knew he was still rehashing the events in his mind, exploring all their myriad angles. "Your essence is trapped in a case that can only be opened by Justice. If you're Mak'rep, do you tempt a brand-new Justice into opening the case and run the risk of annihilation, or do you bide your time, running the risk that she will only get stronger?"

I shook my head…then had to stop myself from continuing to shake it. Something…felt a little sloshy in my skull. That was weird.

"How did he send his minions in for him anyway?" I asked. "I thought sorcerers were barred."

"Not barred from entering, merely barred from forcible entry. Only Council members other than you, as well as gods or demons, are truly barred. Humans can enter, even the Connected." He raised a brow. "Otherwise, your young assistants wouldn't be able to do their work."

"Right." I nodded gingerly. "So they got in by approved means, somehow." My brains had seemed to settle a bit, but I felt the curious need to hold my arms out to my sides, as if I might trip over my own feet. It wasn't that I was dizzy, exactly, but...

Brody sighed loudly. "Will someone please explain to me what is going on?"

I focused on him. "Bad guy in the library attacked me. I attacked back."

"And said bad guy is now..."

"With Gamon. I didn't stay to chat."

Brody looked a little green. He'd known Gamon about as long as I had. "Gamon. Who's, um, Judgment. And probably acting in ways that are decidedly extralegal. In my jurisdiction."

"If it helps at all, it's technically above your jurisdiction," I offered, pointing skyward. Unlike me, Gamon had had no problem creating an aerie for her own personal use. To those who could see it, it looked like a giant Mount Doom made out of meatloaf, hovering above what was now named the SLS Las Vegas, a place I'd always know as the Sahara no matter what they called it.

"It doesn't help, no." Brody grimaced. "Why do you smell like smoke?"

I ignored that and glanced back at the doorway to the library, which was now an empty hole. "Um, I need a couple of new doors. And a new security system. And...I don't know. Magic-sniffing dogs, maybe."

Before Brody could respond to that, a sharp rap sounded on the doorframe to the outer corridor, and Nikki strode in. "Yo, Loverboy," she said to Brody. "Glad you finally made it."

"Do you know what's going on here?" Brody complained, sounding very close to a whine.

"I know the good parts." Nikki flopped onto a couch I hadn't noticed before. Then again, the only two times I'd been in this room, it'd been stacked with either boxes or bodies. "Word's out that Sara here has taken on the role of Justice. No one here seemed to think that was going to be a big deal, but the rest of the world begs to differ."

"And..." Brody made the hurry-up gesture with his hands.

"And now she's a target, it would seem. Both by people who want her help and by those who want amnesty on their library fines. Which is the case with Mak'rep the not quite so powerful. Am I right?" She looked at me. "Mrs. French called, said she thought he was the perp, based on what the boys told her. Though she didn't use the word perp. She used..." Nikki furrowed her brow. "Miscreant."

I sank into my own chair. Armaeus remained propping up a wall, though with a wave of his hand, he replaced at least the front door. Apparently, the library door was beyond his dice roll for the moment. Brody simply stared from me to the broken library door. "You got attacked by someone named Mak'rep?"

"It's been a really long day."

"So here's the lowdown, love chop," Nikki said. "Sit, sit. This is going to take a minute."

Brody sat. Heavily. "I have to report *something*," he grumped. "There was a disturbance. The hotel was concerned. The guests directly beneath this floor were concerned."

We all looked at the floor. "I hadn't thought about that," I said.

"Should we rent that floor too? I've been looking for someplace to store my winter clothes." Nikki tapped her chin. "And we can install the bodyguards you clearly need."

My lips turned down. "I don't need bodyguards. I need magic-sniffing dogs."

"You need more than that." Brody pulled out his notepad and flipped it open. "Guests reported explosions, screams, children crying, and gunfire. They flooded the front desk with calls, and for obvious reasons, it was everything the staff could do to hold off a panic. A report was filed, and that means paperwork, and paperwork means a trail." His scowl got deeper. "You do *not* want a trail, Sara. Not until you figure out exactly what this Justice thing is all about. The moment the local police think you're some sort of vigilante—or God forbid Interpol does—you can kiss your freedom goodbye."

"I agree with Detective Delish," Nikki put in. "But to bring you full circle, boy-o, Sara here got hit with a number of new jobs earlier today. As per protocol, they were lined up on her desk for her to review, with nobody realizing that they were part of a spell. The lights go out, the pages become thugs, the library aides come in to investigate."

"Library aides."

"Never mind that part. The aides alert Mrs. French, the head librarian, she sounds the alarm, chaos ensues. Sara shows up, blasts a hole through the door, giving the thugs entrance to the library, and then they perform another change-up act, becoming Mak'rep in the flesh when she opens his magic box."

"They were golems. It was one of Mak'rep's more advanced skills," Armaeus put in. "They led you to the box, and you opened it. He believed his power would overwhelm yours. It didn't."

"Right," Nikki said, sending Armaeus a sharp look. "And why didn't it, again?"

We all switched our attention to Armaeus, but I was already watching him, so I saw the reaction the others didn't. A reaction which honestly didn't make me feel all that good.

"You don't know," I said, a hollow pit opening in my stomach. "His power *should've* trumped mine."

"Mak'rep was an exceptionally powerful and ancient sorcerer. By all rights, yes, he should have given you at least some minimal trouble. He didn't."

"He tried." I thought of the sorcerer waving his hands around, then back to my own issues when I first entered the library. "I figured the library hit him with the same dampening effect it hit me with."

Armaeus nodded. "Yes..." he said, though that didn't seem to make him any happier. "The role of Justice ended abruptly with Justice Abigail Strand. She made several unorthodox changes to the library without advising me. When she died—"

"Wait, what?" Nikki cut in. "She died? That's how she left the role of Justice?"

The Magician slanted her a look. "If she was among the living, don't you think she would still be occupying the role?"

"Not necessarily. She could have retired. People do that. They retire. Play shuffleboard. Drink mai tais. She sure as hell would have earned it, given the Library of Neverending Stories in there." Nikki folded her arms tightly against her chest. "You didn't tell us she died."

"How'd she die?" I interjected.

"Poison," Armaeus said briskly, and we all gaped at that. "Meant to look like a suicide, but almost certainly not."

I felt a little dizzier. What had the boy said inside the library, one of Mrs. French's diminutive staffers? That I'd go crazy if I opened that box?

Was that really a thing?

Brody's startled voice drew me back. "You let her get killed on your watch?" he accused Armaeus.

"She was on a case, alone. She lost her focus."

"So then she lost her life," Nikki said bluntly. "Who did it?"

"Most likely someone whose crimes also remain interred in the library, but who knew the dangers the library itself presented." Armaeus cocked his head, then shook it. "Not Mak'rep."

"So are these bad guys looking to knock off the next Justice too?"

"Unlikely. We established several mock Justices over the next twenty years, and the bait was never taken. Whatever Abigail knew died with her. So did any interest in killing her specifically. Tonight's actions are unfortunate but unrelated."

The Magician spoke with enough confidence that I should've been satisfied, but I wasn't. My head was beginning to pound. "How likely is it that we'll *continue* to get interested parties who are, ah, interested in partying in the library, then?" I asked. "One of those golems shot me. With a gun. That's some serious animation ability."

"They didn't bring the gun with them."

The voice came from my office, and I turned to see Mrs. French, her fussy gray Victorian dress and starched white collar in stark contrast to the body-length black apron she had lashed around her body.

"Wait, what—" Brody began, but Mrs. French ignored him. Her gaze was steady on me, her chin up, and she was practically quivering with repressed emotion.

"Justice Abigail kept guns in the library. A lot of guns. Many I've found and removed, what with the children about. But every time I'm back there, I find another pistol or derringer or rifle or something. The boys know to look for them now too, but no sooner do we confiscate one than another seems to appear."

Brody spluttered again, but I didn't have time for his sensibilities either.

"Brody, this is Mrs. French, custodian of the library. Mrs. French, Detective Brody Rooks of the Las Vegas Metropolitan Police Department. So how many guns are we talking exactly, Mrs. French? And how is it the golems knew about them?"

"Pleased to meet you, Detective." Mrs. French bobbed a very proper curtsey, and Brody opened his mouth, then shut it again, staring at her. "Justice Abigail told me once, she'd planted five hundred. I've only found two hundred and thirty. Two hundred and thirty-one, I should say, with tonight's discarded piece." She patted her apron.

"Five hundred…" I echoed.

Brody clapped his hands to his head as if trying to keep his brains from falling out, then spun toward me. "You have more than two hundred loaded weapons in that room, and you have no idea where they are? And this—whatever it was who shot you, did? How the hell is that possible?"

Mrs. French fielded that one, her hands now clasped tightly in front of her. "Begging your pardon, sir, Justice Abigail made no secret of her arsenal while she was alive. And she kept unusual company. It's possible some of the locations of the weapons were more widely known. I have tried to find them, I surely have. But because of the wards—both yours and Justice Abigail's—there's no way we can use magical means to discern them. And without magic..."

"We'll deal with that later," I said, rubbing my head. I really didn't feel well. "Armaeus, back to the issue of who else is going to play Raid the Library. Because if we've got weapons in there...that's not good."

"Dogs," Brody said abruptly. "We can get dogs in there, right? They're not magic."

"They're not." Despite myself, I smiled at Brody's outburst. It was a good idea. And it would certainly keep the boys' minds off what had happened here tonight, at least somewhat. "Dogs," I echoed, liking the sound of it.

"On it." Nikki pulled out her phone.

Armaeus shifted in the doorway, reclaiming my attention. "After we publicize Mak'rep's attempt and failure, especially the part about the library being far more than people think, I suspect we will have no more than a few who attempt to remove their cases from your inventory. But some, certainly. It would be alarming to know that your long-buried crime is suddenly back, as they say, in circulation. The worry would prove difficult for some to bear."

"Right." It made sense. "I'm going to need to expedite those cases somehow."

"Twenty-four seventeen," Nikki intoned miserably.

"What's that?" Brody asked. "The number of cases you have back there?"

"Not exactly," I said, my eyes still on the Magician. "There's got to be a way to weed out the more sensitive ones. Everything in there is ladders and scaffolding and gears and pulleys. It's insane."

"C'mon, you don't like the pneumatic tube system?" Nikki asked.

"There is an advantage to the system the way it is," Armaeus said. "If you can't digitize it…it remains tangible. Finite. Impossible to duplicate, or to hide evidence of a breach." He waved at the very obvious evidence around us of tonight's breach.

"That's fine for out here, but have you *seen* that place?" Nikki jerked a thumb toward the blown-open door. Brody followed her gesture, then stood, wandering that way. "You wouldn't have a hard time hiding evidence of a war, let alone one little scrap of paper going sideways."

"Everything's marked," I said suddenly. "That's what you mean. Like Mak'rep's box. There was a date on it in silver. But only one. Its intake date."

The Magician smiled. "Of course. You check something out of the library, there's a record. The system is inviolate."

"And the library catalog is…"

"Oh my God. Are you serious?"

I glanced over to see Brody standing at the ruins of the door to the library.

"There has to be at least twenty levels in there that I can see, floor-to-ceiling with books," he said. "Forget the weapons, there's no way you're going to be able to sort all those cases out to determine which are the most problematic. And even if you did, something that you might consider to be completely inconsequential may in fact be the number one priority for someone on the other side. There's absolutely no way of telling."

"It's not quite that unsophisticated," Armaeus returned mildly. "Justice Abigail knew the most challenging tasks before her, but it was always her choice as to whether or not she would address them straight out. Toward the end, she completely ignored the backlog of cases for Justice in favor of handling assignments that came to her more directly."

"Why?" I asked.

"Much like the guns, I suspect. It gave her a sense of control." He looked at me, his gaze probing, intent. *"And then there's the small problem of potential insanity that the cases that came in through official channels seemed to exacerbate. A condition of which Justice Abigail was very much afraid,"* he said, his words audible in my mind alone.

I kept my expression neutral, but Abigail's paranoia was making more sense all the time. *You've got to be joking. That was real?*

"That was real. Your friends…"

Don't need to know.

Armaeus nodded sharply. "For now," he said aloud, "it's enough to know that a balance between ad hoc cases and those which come through more traditionally is probably your safest course. That and managing your time effectively."

"If you say I need to focus on what's important instead of what's urgent, I'm going to cut you," I grumbled. My headache and sloshy brain was getting worse. "This is feeling more and more like a corporate job all the time."

The Magician spread his hands, but his eyes glittered with amusement. "It's far more straightforward than that. You simply have to ask what's next."

"Maybe try that again in English?" A knock at the door cut me off mid-scowl.

Brody turned away from the library entrance. "You expecting anyone else tonight?"

"I wasn't expecting the first people," I said, standing. We all stared at the main door, no one making a move to open it. After a brief pause, the knock came again. It was light, professional, courteous. And as it echoed softly in the room, I realized my headache was going away.

I slanted a glance at Armaeus. Who'd disappeared.

"I didn't ask what's next," I complained, staring at the empty space. "Did anyone hear me say it? Because I didn't say it. I just want to point that out."

"At least he fixed the library door before he went." Brody reached out, then grunted as he laid his hand on the vertical surface. His hand floated about an inch beneath the plane of the door, piercing the very effective illusion. Then again, the Magician was all about effective illusions.

"The game has changed, Miss Wilde," came the voice in my mind. *"There's still too much I don't understand. That said, you are right. You didn't say the words. However, that doesn't change the fact that there is a man at your door with a need that only you can satisfy.*

My first thought was a gigolo, but of course it couldn't be that easy.

"Fine," I said, drawing both Brody's and Nikki's surprised glances. I stalked across the room and opened the door.

Definitely not a gigolo.

Standing in front of me was a man I recognized instantly, for all that I'd met him only once. It'd been a few short months earlier, beyond the sumptuous front entrance of one of the world's finest and grandest old hotels. I'd had a meeting scheduled, and this man, the hotel manager, had graciously shown me to my reserved rooms.

And he'd then proceeded to point out the staff gunmen he'd secreted in elegantly carved alcoves around the room, should I have any need to blast my associates to kingdom come. Definitely the best hotel service I'd ever received.

"Mr. Stone. Welcome." I stood back and allowed him to enter.

As it had that day in the Hotel Metropole Geneva, Luca Stone's elegance struck me first—he moved with a grace and complete mastery of space that should have tipped me off immediately that he was no ordinary hotel manager. He was maybe sixty years old, with neatly cropped gray hair and a wiry, slight build. One elegant silk patch was affixed over one eye. When I'd seen him last, he was wearing a tuxedo, but his suit tonight was equally effortless and bespoke. Despite the elegant attire, there was no questioning the strength in his slender form. The man looked like he could break someone into little pieces, then brush off his fingers, shoot his cuffs, and return to a garden party.

"Madame Wilde," Stone said. "I do apologize for the lateness of the hour, but I was encouraged to come here immediately, on the off chance you were available." He glanced around the room. "I see now this was good advice."

I stiffened. "Good advice from whom?"

"Your former compatriot, General Ma-Singh."

"Ma-Singh?" I reached out mentally for Armaeus, but the Magician had left the building. Handy of him.

"Indeed. I was en route to the House of Swords to shore up some routine contracts when he telephoned. When I heard what he had to say, well. I knew I could assist." He looked past me toward Nikki and executed a bow. "Mademoiselle Dawes. It is my absolute pleasure to see you again. I'm so glad to see you in such good health."

The dots stopped jumping around my brain and connected with an audible click. "The Red King," I said, and Nikki straightened too. “You have information on the Red King.”

“Ah, Sara?” Brody prompted.

“Right—right, sorry. Luca Stone, this is Detective Brody Rooks, Las Vegas Metro Police Department. Brody, Mr. Stone is an acquaintance of mine from Geneva. He took great care of me when I didn’t realize I needed it.”

Brody made an appropriately welcoming noise as Stone’s gaze shifted to him, and Stone betrayed nothing in his expression but the faintest lift of his brows. “It seems I’ve caught you at an inconvenient time.”

“I’m getting the impression that’s going to happen a lot going forward,” I said. “But I appreciate you coming here so quickly.”

He smiled expansively, then gave me an elaborate bow. “As it happens, you’ll be doing me the favor. Rumors of the Red King have been plaguing one of my closest associates, who has asked me for assistance.”

“Really. And who is the Red King, exactly?”

“That, I’m afraid, no one knows as yet,” Luca Stone said. “But if you wish to unmask him quickly, you must go to Carnevale.”

Chapter Seven

Unable to contain herself a moment longer, Mrs. French went into full fluster, ordering everyone to sit before attacking the sidebar and muttering dire imprecations about tea.

We arranged ourselves on the couches and chair, but I didn't miss the jump in the shadows at the far end of the room. Neither did Brody. His eyes narrowed as he fixed on the spot where I suspected one of the Lost Boys had darted behind a collection of boxes. Rather than explain who else was roaming around the library, however, I turned my attention to Stone.

"Carnival. You mean in Rio? That's where this Red King is?"

"The Rio de Janeiro carnival is truly an experience worth savoring, but no," Mr. Stone said. "I am speaking of the Carnevale in Venice.

"Venice." Nikki perked up, sounding too intrigued for my own good. "So not only costumes but masks as well. And dancing. And Italian food."

"And rats," Brody put in, eyeing the far corner of the room.

"Why is he there?" I asked. "Has the festival even started yet?"

"Its first official day isn't until Saturday, as it happens," Mr. Stone said. "However, much as in the days of the original Carnevale, some level of celebration has been going on in one form or another since Christmas. As to why we suspect the Red King is there, that bears some explanation. How well do you know the original story of Carnevale?"

"Well enough. It was a festival that began during the Middle Ages, I think? Marking the time between Christmas and the beginning of Lent. But unlike in other parts of the world, it developed a secondary theme, which was the use of masks to allow the rich and poor to mingle without any disruption of the social order."

"An excellent summary." Stone nodded. "Though masked interaction did exist outside the bounds of the festival, and their use was not so much to muddy the class distinction between the rich and the poor as between the nobility and the bourgeoisie. At that time, the merchant class was rising in leaps and bounds, as was the scholarly class. But these individuals were kept in their own silos, if you will, unable to share their knowledge and experiences with the noble class, except in highly controlled situations. Not surprisingly, this proved to be a very unsatisfactory situation for members of the noble class, who sought to intermingle with men of letters who were not of their station, but who far surpassed them in intellectual richness."

"Only men?"

Stone smiled. "In order to get the dictate to pass and ensure the openness of the event, men did lead the way, but in short order, the fairer sex found ways to utilize the festival for their own interests. Noble-born women were able to socialize in public with their friends and paramours of any station, and many a commoner sought to catch the eye of a potential patron, whether male or female."

Nikki snorted. "Tinder with masks."

"In its way. But the licentiousness of the event was also a cover for far deeper entanglements. Which takes us to the Red King—or a villain masquerading as such."

"Armaeus said it was some sort of honorary title of a great magician."

"It was accorded to whoever claimed the position as the strongest magician in Italy, from about 900 AD on." Stone nodded. "But it's a title that took a decidedly gruesome turn before disappearing altogether during the Renaissance. And it was tied to a figure from Venice's dark past who has also recently reared his unfortunate head. Are you familiar with the butcher of Venice?"

I made a face. "I don't think I'm going to like his story."

"Undoubtedly not. In brief, the butcher Biasio Cargnio lived in Venice in the mid-1500s, and gained some modest renown for his stews, sausages, and pies, like many a butcher of the time. He grew in fame and success until one regrettable day, when the finger of a small child was found in one of his concoctions."

"Sweeney Todd, the opera," Nikki muttered.

"Exactly so." Stone smiled somberly. "Definitely a horror for any Italian, but most especially in Venice, which billed itself as the playground of Europe even then, its residents growing rich on its tourism and trade. The butcher was, of course, brought to justice, and the magistrates of the time determined to make an example of him. Rather than a simple execution, he was jailed, tortured, his hands were cut off and tied around his neck, and he was eventually beheaded in the Piazza San Marco. After that, his body was chopped into four pieces and displayed on pitchforks around various parts of the city."

"Ah…that seems thorough."

"Indeed," Stone agreed. "Less well known is the fact that Signore Cargnio was then cremated and baked into earthenware jars, which were promptly hauled out of Italy and shattered by agents of the city's government. His butcher's shop was also burned to the ground within the week."

He smiled at my startled expression. "Regrettably, if the authorities' intention was to bury his memory, their attempts were in vain. To say Biasio left a lasting influence is an understatement. To this day, nearly all the stops along the Grand Canal in the city are named after one church or religious icon or another, all except for the Riva de Biasio, which is named after none other than the butcher of Venice."

"And so, what—this butcher was actually the Red King?" I asked. "And now some modern-day dark practitioner is roaming around Venice claiming the title as the new Red King?"

"Perhaps. As you know, there's been a recent expansion of magic in the world."

I grimaced. "I noticed."

"That expansion has, perhaps not surprisingly, led to a resurgence in interest in the dark arts, and more frenetic activity by the dark practitioners. Particularly those who believe that the surest path to psychic enhancement lies in the leveraging of organic components, for example."

I'd heard this song before. "You're talking human sacrifices. The dark practitioners are using body parts to make technoceuticals. You think that's what the butcher of Venice was doing back in the Middle Ages?"

Even as I asked the question, I knew the answer. The harvesting of body parts, particularly those of children, had become almost a time-honored tradition among dark practitioners of the Connected community. In recent years, much of the human trafficking that had taken place among the Connected was not for the sex trade, although that certainly was part of it, or even for the service trade. It was for the simple harvesting of a kidney, a femur, an eyeball.

The atrocities committed against the youngest and most vulnerable of the Connected community on a daily basis had been what'd drawn me to take a stand with my work as an artifact hunter. I'd made bank selling arcane artifacts, then I'd passed the money along to a trusted partner who did everything he could to save the children.

I couldn't let my thoughts go down that path, though. Not right now. The recent death of Father Jerome, the man who'd first shown me how much I could help the weakest of the Connected, was too sharp, too present. In many ways, I didn't want to heal from his death, because in healing, I would begin forgetting him.

I didn't want to forget.

Here I was, an immortal, while he'd been stolen from this life far too soon.

Beside me, Brody shifted, craning his neck and staring hard at another set of boxes, this one closer to us.

"Human sacrifices, yes, particularly of children," Stone continued, recalling my attention. "That is what my colleague is hearing tales of in the back alleys of Venice. The return of the butcher—who was possibly the Red King—and with him, the return of the darkest of magic to the city. The villain's timing is most propitious too, I'm sorry to say."

"Venice will be crawling with people," Nikki agreed. "If this nouveau serial killer is looking to find easy marks, he won't have to look far."

Stone sighed. "The problem is worse than that. Carnevale is traditionally known as the time when the rich walk with the poor, but the truth is not so simple. It's where all walks of life may mingle without fear of discovery. The rich and the poor, the pious and the depraved, the agnostic and the believer—"

"The Connected and the Unconnected," I finished for him, standing straighter. "You're saying that the magicians and sorcerers out there can walk freely in public without being identified by either friend or foe."

Mrs. French served tea, and as she fussed, Brody stood. He strolled to the nearest set of boxes and checked behind it, casual as all hell. Then he scowled. Clearly, no one was there.

Stone picked up his tale. "During the Renaissance, it was the only time of year when gatherings of the greatest magicians could take place without drawing undue notice. If you knew who to look for, or you knew where to meet, you could turn Carnevale to your greatest advantage. If you saw nothing but masks and gowns and feathers, then you could enjoy the festival to the fullest, never knowing what dark designs lurked beneath the surface."

"And now?" I asked.

He set his teacup down on its delicate saucer. "I am in a unique position to know the movements of some of the darkest practitioners of the Connected community, as well as some whose light burns with the purest of intentions and the most wholesome of acts. I will tell you this: They are *all* planning to attend this year's Carnevale."

"Because there's been a change in the world," I said.

Stone inclined his head regally. "A change which you and your compatriots have wrought."

"And how's that going over?"

"In the main? Remarkably well. You, I suspect, are regarding the situation with a rather focused lens. I'm sure you're struggling with the more negative ramifications of the end of the war on magic—the growing awareness of governments and multinational organizations of the size and scope of Connected ability, the release of demons into the world, and the ascension of two high-grade sorcerers to the Arcana Council, which has rendered it powerful to a level unseen in modern times."

I grimaced. "That does sound a lot like my lens."

"For the general practitioner, however, the fallout from the war on magic has been nothing but positive," Stone said. "The wellspring of magic appears to be refilled. Raw materials containing positive charges—stones, metals, even sacred objects buried in their crypts which had no exposure to the war or its players—have increased in their strength, and there are more of them. There is talk of returning to previously looted tombs, as belief is running high that new discoveries will be made."

"Okay, so—" I began, but Stone raised a hand.

"That's not all," he said. "Unexpected advances in the technology sector are only now coming to light. Talk of inspiration, divine intervention, dream design, mathematical proofs that have stymied practitioners for years being solved—it's all over the back rooms and private clubs of the intelligentsia. There's not been much crossover between these disparate groups, but again, I am in a unique situation to find myself at the center of several strands of conversation."

"Scientific advancements," I said thoughtfully, my gaze tracking Brody as he glanced behind another stack of boxes. Behind him, a small figure, barely more than a shadow, darted beneath a chair. I smothered a smile, unreasonably heartened by the resilience of little boys. "That would include technoceuticals."

"It would indeed. Perhaps not surprisingly, those advances have been kept far quieter, but you can rest assured they're out there. Rumors are running riot in the arcane black market."

"Black Elixir," I murmured, recalling Ricky's words. *All the way to the Red King.*

"Oh, c'mon, that shit's been out there for longer than a few weeks," Nikki countered.

Stone shook his head. "It's called different things in different countries, but what has changed is the intensity of a given dosage for what is essentially the same amount of product. Up until a few weeks ago, the legend of the fifth hit being a path to transcendence was merely that, a legend that had sprung up to justify the loss of life the drug was indisputably causing, to add mystery and allure to what was a simple lethal drug overdose, no different from one too many hits of heroin. Now, however…" He shrugged.

"Now, what?" It was Brody who asked the question, turning from the far end of the room. So he had been following along, despite his distraction. "We're up to our eyeballs in the drug trade out here, and this Black Elixir is the newest pain in my ass. If you're telling me that the drug is now more potent because of some weird disturbance in the Force, I need to know that like right now. And if this Red King, whoever that's supposed to be, is the guy making it, we've got to get out ahead of him too."

Stone didn't bat an eye. "I'm telling you that yes, all forms of Black Elixir, as well as other drugs created from magical composites that have been produced since the recent influx of magic in the world, are more potent at similar doses than previous iterations of the drug. The effects are more powerful, longer lasting, with greater side effects."

Brody hissed a curse under his breath. "You mean the new stuff that's coming out of production, or everything that's in circulation already?"

"An interesting question, Detective Brody, and one to which I do not have the answer."

I lifted my brows slightly. Out of all the crazy that Stone had been dishing us, this was the first time I was almost certain he was lying. But why ever for? Brody had no jurisdiction over the organization that Luca Stone fronted, and anything that could trickle out from the international drug trade all the way to Las Vegas was following a trail far too difficult to track.

"I need something stronger than tea," Nikki announced. She stood and stretched, catching Stone's appreciative eye, then sauntered over to the bar where Mrs. French had assembled tea. "Sara? Brody?" she asked.

"I'm fine," Brody said, his irritation plain.

"Glenmorangie," I said, glancing to Stone. "If you'd be willing to join me?"

"I would be honored to share a drink with you, Madame Wilde—or Justice Wilde, I should say."

"Excellent." Nikki prepared the drinks and brought ours over to us first. She handed mine over, then turned to Stone, grasping his hand as he reached for the tumbler, the handoff at once elegant and secure. As she did, her eyes flared wider for the barest instant, the only indication she was using her abilities to read his memories. I gamely hid my grin.

Nikki had been a moderate-level Connected when I'd met her, but extended exposure to my crazy had amped her up several times over since then, making her native abilities that much stronger. She couldn't exactly read minds, but her ability to pick up on a target's memories was every bit as useful. Most of the time, the two were the same thing, but not always. Sometimes a person's memories weren't exactly the way things really happened, especially if any amount of time had passed or if the person was under a great deal of strain, though those kinds of influences still helped us create a complete picture of what the individual *believed* he'd seen. But we didn't have to worry about stress or fear with Stone. He wasn't under any influence but an abundance of caution.

Nikki smiled widely, then swerved back toward the sidebar. I didn't think I'd have to wait long.

I didn't.

"Well, then allow me to share what *we* know about all this, and maybe it will help you," Nikki said, sipping her drink. "Word on the street here is that the biggest influence of the magical surge was on whatever product was still in its raw state in December, when it was going through the manufacturing process. Anything from that time and after is affected. What's out there that was in circulation before has also been augmented, but not anywhere close to the levels that the new stuff has been. So basically, it's going to get worse before it gets better. Depending on your perspective."

Stone lifted his drink as well, visibly surprised and relieved, as Brody swung around to Nikki. Something in her face must have allayed his confusion as to how in the hell she'd known all that but had only now shared it with him. Nikki was excellent at allaying confusion.

"I need a drink after all," Brody muttered. As he went to the sidebar, I considered Stone. He hadn't wanted me to know that the December batch of technoceuticals was where all the crazy started. Everything in process then or after was affected. But why? It's not like I didn't know that I was one of the biggest reasons why magic had gotten jacked up in all its forms. This influx was partly my fault. Maybe mostly my fault.

I took another long drink, then refocused on the problem at hand.

"So if that tallies with what you're seeing—either now or what you might find out as information becomes available—where does that leave us?" I wondered aloud. "Ideas that were in their nascent form are more affected, inventions, ongoing projects, existing drugs or new drugs in the supply line..."

"Unborn babies," Nikki put in.

"I don't even want to think about that." I swung my gaze to Mr. Stone. "Tell me that's not part of your friend's concern."

"Fortunately, no," Stone said. "In fact, as important as the distillation of raw material is to the dark practitioners, there's now a growing conversation around harvesting organs from a fully mature psychic, such as a Connected who has leveled up as a result of recent events. My friend believes, with some measure of certainty, that the victims of the current incarnation of the butcher of Venice will include some of the most powerful magicians that currently walk this earth."

"They'll make mincemeat out of full-grown Connecteds, because they figure they were already much further down the path than your average child could be, even a Connected child," I mused. It sort of made sense, as did Stone's reticence to discuss it. He'd just painted a target on the back of every high-level Connected on the planet.

Nikki frowned. "And those magicians are all heading to Venice. Wouldn't it be easier to simply warn them?"

Stone sighed. "My friend's request of me was to ensure that *nobody* stays away from Venice, in fact. It's the key time of the year for magicians of a certain caliber to meet and mingle, to share their knowledge and advancements. If they miss out on this opportunity, particularly in the wake of such a powerful surge of magic, my associate feels the collective will never reach the heights they would have otherwise. They will never maximize the impact of the magic, and they will continue to remain at an imbalance with entities such as, well, the Arcana Council. My friend is quite highly placed in the senate of magicians in Venice, and parity with the Arcana Council is a coveted goal for the organization. If the senate is ever to have a chance at establishing their own base of strength to rival both the Council as well as their Unconnected opponents, they have to act now, both for themselves and for the Connected community as a whole. But the senate can't move forward if their members are too afraid to meet. With rumors of the Red King and/or the butcher returned to Venice, and possibly stalking magicians, it is entirely possible that they will miss their chance. With your intervention, however..."

I nodded. Truth was, I didn't mind taking on Stone's job. First off, I liked the guy, and he'd already proven to be helpful to me. Doing him a favor was only to my benefit.

Secondly, I was already annoyed by the Red King, whoever he was—especially if he had something to do with Black Elixir. Taking him out would be a personal pleasure.

Thirdly, after tonight, I didn't have much interest in poking around the library until after it was cleared of miscellaneous weaponry...and until I figured out how to open up cases without going crazy.

Considering how much my head still throbbed from my altercation with Mak'rep the Magnificent, working anywhere that wasn't here sounded good.

But I still wasn't clear on why Stone was dancing around the timing issue. And I'd never been very good at dancing. "What are you worried about in all this?" I asked Stone directly. "What am I missing?"

He leveled his gaze at me. "I don't want to give too much weight to something that is only a theory, but it's a theory that I'm beginning to see play out all over the world: the world of the Connecteds didn't merely shift with the influx of this new magic, it was *reborn*. And with the gathering of the magicians in Venice—especially if they're being hunted by the Red King—we will be able to take our first measure of exactly how powerful this new infant community is, and how dangerous it may become. We could be on the precipice of the most extraordinary era for magic that this world has ever known...or we could be an eyewitness to the annihilation of all things Connected."

"Oh," I said. Suddenly his reticence about laying the blame for the shift in magic at my feet made more sense. "Is that all."

"There's no way of knowing yet which way it will go, until you see what's actually happening in Venice." He grimaced, and raised his glass. "So here's to you, Justice Wilde."

Our gazes locked, and in his eyes I saw an ally, a supporter. Maybe even a friend. And friendship from someone like Luca Stone was a high honor indeed.

Nodding, I lifted my own glass to return his salute. "And here's to Carnevale."

CHAPTER EIGHT

Nikki and I landed in Venice in the late afternoon on a cloudless day. The City of Bridges stretched out before us in startling splendor, a jewel perched on the water's edge. I'd been to the city only once before, traveling by boat in the dark of night—and I'd been gone by the following morning. My memories of the floating city centered on dank, grimy gondolas, heavy-browed thugs, and the reek of seawater.

Not surprisingly, I'd never returned.

But now, seeing the city laid out before me, I better understood the breathless passages in the travel blogs I'd read on the flight over. The city seemed on the verge of sinking into the lagoon that surrounded it—more of a threat than it used to be, arguably—yet it was a place teeming with light and color. Color had been the operative word in the travel guides, the anchor for the art world to categorize the unique flair of the city. Florence focused on the linear beauty of artwork, Rome was all about form, but Venice insisted that it was the celebration of color that created true beauty in art.

"Is that our ride?" Nikki asked dubiously.

I glanced over. We were fairly well hidden by a profusion of potted bougainvillea plants that had been placed near the windows of the baggage claim area, offering us convenient cover to squint at the small man who hustled up to the line of chauffeurs, holding a sign that simply said "Wilde" on it.

He was dressed like a boat captain, but we were in Venice. Everyone was dressed like a boat captain, it seemed. "Seems likely. Didn't Stone say that the Palazzo Gioia was off the main canal, down some waterway or other?" The palazzo, owned by Venice native and senate of magicians member Count Vitorre Valetti, was to serve as our base of operations in the city. Luca Stone had arranged everything within minutes of me agreeing to take on the job.

"Right, but…I don't know about this. The guy bugs me." Nikki looked around, blowing out a short breath. "Too many people with masks already. We should've waited for backup."

I hiked my shoulder bag higher on my shoulder, reconsidering our hasty flight path. Armaeus had insisted he'd arrange for bodyguards to meet us at Palazzo Gioia, and I hadn't wanted to wait around for another canister of crazy to shoot out from the Justice intake system. Brody couldn't break away from Vegas, not with the newest issues in the drug trade, and I didn't want him along on this adventure anyway. He tended to hover. Maybe it was a holdover from his time serving as my chaperone when I'd been "Psychic Teen Sariah," but that'd been over ten long years ago and several lifetimes of pain. I didn't need hovering.

A bodyguard, however…

"Miss Wilde?" I blinked up, then up still farther, as a man strode quickly toward us. Lean and tan, the guy was wearing a crisp white shirt, open at the neck, above tailored black pants, but I was more impressed with his sculpted cheekbones, his generous mouth, and his sensually dark eyes, the combined effect of which was…distracting, to say the least. Now this was my kind of Italian.

I didn't need to mask my reaction, of course. Not with Nikki beside me.

"Sweet Mother Mary on a gondola," she declared with a broad smile, drawing the young man's attention. "I do believe I'll faint."

"Miss Dawes. I am so glad you have both landed safely. Monsieur Bertrand advised that you'd be landing, but that your travel arrangements have been disrupted. I'm to take you to the city center by a circuitous route, if you would. From there, we'll secure additional transportation to your accommodations."

I frowned at him. Apparently, Brody wasn't the only one who hovered. "What's wrong with the guy sent by Palazzo Gioia?"

"Nothing at all," the young Adonis said with a smile. "But that gentleman waiting over there, he is not from Palazzo Gioia. The water taxi driver who originally was to pick you up was…assaulted, it appears. He could not make his appointment. When we learned of this, we decided to see who did."

"And it was that guy." I didn't bother glancing over to the squat Italian.

"That guy," the bodyguard agreed. "So that, of course, led to our second decision…"

I blinked as I followed his relaxed gesture. Emerging from the airport gates was a woman who—well, she could have been Nikki's twin.

"Oh, who is that gorgeous girl?" Nikki breathed, and she wasn't wrong. The woman towered well over six feet and was dressed in an outfit that defied every airport convention: platform pumps, a skintight mini, and a soccer jersey that looked like it'd been painted on. She had a pile of red curls that trailed down her neck, and she waved in utter delight as she saw the man with the placard. Only then did I notice the young woman beside her. My doppelgänger was decidedly more…drab.

"Yoo-hoo! Yes, you!" the fake Nikki announced as she marched up to the water taxi driver. "Oh, I'm so delighted to see you, I cannot even tell you how my feet are absolutely killing me—"

The man moved with a speed I wouldn't have been able to track if I didn't have enhanced abilities of perception. One second he was holding the placard, another and he'd dropped the card and both hands came up, each with a gun. Before I could gasp out an alarm, he'd shot—and fake Nikki and fake Sara burst into a puff of smoke as the glass behind the apparitions shattered. Then everyone was screaming and running. I gaped, struggling to see as Nikki swore beside me, but our bodyguard was already on point, pivoting with us both on either side of him and walking briskly forward. He spoke, but in an Italian so low and rapid, I couldn't quite follow it.

"That was an illusion?" demanded Nikki. "You just wasted an illusion in broad daylight and you didn't even try to get the guy? We were right there! We could have grabbed him."

"He's being tracked now. To him, the two women merely fell, mortally wounded—to everyone else, he shot at random and no one was hit. It's a difficult illusion to maintain, but we're quite happy with it."

"Armaeus sent you?"

"Well…not exactly."

The man grinned and winked at me. When he spoke next, though he still looked like the hunky Italian, it was a very different voice that came out—rich, rolling, and eminently self-satisfied. "They do say the Devil is in the details. I always did like that phrase."

I tried to stop as Nikki squealed in surprise, but Aleksander Kreios's long strides carried us forward, out of the airport and onto the walkway that led to water transport. He walked past several viable options, slowing his gait to an amiable stroll toward the end. "You'll be going to Gioia as planned, but the diversion was quite necessary, I assure you, for your own protection."

"Apparently."

Kreios reached into the pocket of his long white linen shirt and extracted a photo. It was our assailant, surveying the baggage claim crowd, holding his little sign.

"All this and Polaroids too?"

"My services know no bounds." Kreios winked. "However, this man believes his assignment to be complete, and he has departed. There's some additional information you need to know."

I lifted my brows. Since I'd rescued him from a very confined location in the bowels of the Vatican necropolis nearly a year ago, the Devil of the Arcana Council had become one of my closest confidants. And unlike some of his peers on the Council, I could always trust him to tell the truth, albeit for his own dastardly reasons.

"Information Armaeus couldn't tell me?" I asked.

"For reasons he hasn't shared, the Magician has chosen to distance himself from you on this task. He seems to think you would not appreciate his intervention on your behalf."

"But you don't have a problem with it?"

"I'd never let you out of my sight, as a matter of course." Kreios turned to Nikki. "And any hour with you is an hour well spent, my beautiful Nikki. However, I can't stay. I'm merely the messenger."

That caught my attention. "What's the message?"

"Simply this: In a city filled to the brim with sorcerers, you've now proven yourself as magicians of worth with this distraction." Kreios gestured airily. "You must continue to distract and divert, making everything a sleight of hand until you understand the truth of what's happening here."

"Luca Stone didn't give us the truth?"

"The truth as he knew it, yes. But that's a far different thing from the truth that truly is."

"Roger, that," Nikki said, scanning the dock. There were dozens of water taxis gently bobbing against the pier, waiting their turn. "Can we get to the Palazzo Gioia by water?"

"You can get anywhere in Venice by water."

I turned abruptly as a new man spoke on the other side of Nikki. He bowed as I glanced back to confirm that, of course, the Devil had disappeared.

"It merely takes some ingenuity." The young man bowed. "I am Gino, and I work for Monsieur Bertrand. I'm at your service."

Gray chinos, mock-neck sweater, peacoat, and aviator sunglasses held no candle to Gino's rakish grin. A faint tickle of Connected ability rolled off him as well. Nikki shook the young man's hand and gave me a subtle nod. Gino really was on our side. Good.

Armaeus had an impressive network of assistants, and Gino proved more than up to his task as water chauffeur. With efficiency and easy banter, he loaded us into a gondola taxi and set off for the canal house of Luca Stone's colleague. Though we kept careful watch on both the quays and waterways we passed, no one seemed to be following us. Whoever the squat man in the Venetian airport had been, he hadn't gone to a plan B, but simply disappeared. Which meant our intended demise hadn't been very well thought out.

Nikki and I studied the photo Kreios had left with us, but it didn't offer us much help. The man looked harried and intense, but not particularly Connected. "A magician?" Nikki asked, doubt in her voice.

"If so, not a very high-ranking one. I can't imagine he'll be difficult for Kreios to find."

"He did seem enthused about the search," she observed.

"Everyone needs a hobby."

We stepped out of the water taxi onto a tidy pier, and a short man in a linen suit hurried down the walkway, his face florid underneath the midday sun. As he approached, a flash of sunshine seemed to surround him with warmth, and I was struck by the man's broad smile, bright eyes, and boisterous energy. "Signorina Wilde! Signorina Dawes, welcome, welcome. I am Count Valetti, and I am so very glad to meet you. But what is this? You take your own transportation to reach me? Where is my man?" He looked to the canal. "More importantly, where is my *boat*?"

"Was this your taxi captain?" I asked, showing him the photo I had of the imposter holding up the Wilde sign.

"Him? No! I mean, the sign is correct, but I thought, well, I thought…" Valetti frowned again. "Why is that man carrying a sign with my insignia? A moment, I beg you."

While he pulled out a phone and spoke in rapid Italian, I glanced at the photo. There was no insignia on the sign that I could see, just WILDE written in stylized letters, the I and L slightly longer than the others, one bar of the W slightly shorter. Was that what he meant?

"Alessandro left an hour ago, and he has not returned. My crew tells me you have not appeared at the airport, but there was a shooting, a frightening shooting. No one hurt, thank God, but no one caught either." Valetti's expression of overwhelming good humor had been replaced with one of grim resignation as he pocketed his phone. "It is already beginning, this cloud the dark practitioners would put over my Carnevale. It is not to be borne. You will fix it, though. You will fix it."

He spoke these last two lines as a mantra, and I wondered how many times he'd said it to himself in the last few weeks.

"Maybe you could fill us in on what's going on?" I asked.

"Of course, of course." Rallying, Count Valetti led the way up the pier. I tried not to stare at the sumptuous three-story canal house that rose majestically from the waterway, but it was impossible not to be impressed. Made of white-painted stone with the faintest yellow trim, the building caught the light of the late afternoon sun and seemed to glow with an internal flame.

"I wish I could welcome you to Palazzo Gioia under more relaxing circumstances," Valetti sighed. "Venice is a place of magic and joy, not the site of a potentially deadly assassin come back from the dead to haunt the living."

I shot a look to Nikki, who appeared equally startled. "That's what you think is happening here?"

"Ah, my manners. I'm too distracted, forgive me." The man strode ahead, calling out to an unseen steward. The door opened, and we were herded inside. The interior of the palace was, if possible, more breathtaking than the exterior, with what seemed like miles of marble and gilded edges stretching off in all directions.

"I had such a lovely dinner planned, and it is all ready for you. You haven't eaten, no? Of course you haven't eaten. You should eat! We will eat."

"You need to find your man, and your boat," I said. "We're happy to wait, or start without you if that will be less stressful, but what's most important is that you make sure your people are safe."

Valetti spent the rest of the walk through the sumptuous mansion alternately apologizing and thanking us for our understanding, so that by the time we were left alone at a beautiful table on a veranda overlooking the water, I was nearly mute with exhaustion. He left, taking his frantic apprehension with him.

Nikki waited until the servers had deposited our food and swept back out before picking up her glass of wine. She eyed me over the glass. "I can't decide if this is a promising beginning or not."

"Remember, so far, it's all been an illusion. This looks good, though," I said, poking at something I was pretty sure should be called a crostino.

Everything on the table looked and especially smelled extraordinary, and the sun was warm on my shoulders. I looked out over the water and spied the gondolas far below. Not counting my midnight excursion in the city's backwaters, what I knew about Venice was solely from guide books and postcards, but so far, the city was surpassing my expectations. Aside from today's attempted shooting, anyway.

"What do you think was the point of that?" I asked, and as usual, Nikki had followed my thoughts. She and I had been together in such close quarters for long enough that she didn't need to touch me to piece together my memories. As long as I wasn't blocking her, we might as well be sharing the same brain.

"I'm not sure, to tell you the truth," she said, picking up a wedge of bread laden with figs and honey and some kind of cheese. She aimed the wedge at me and poked the air with it. "If they know who you are, then they should've known random Capper Ken wouldn't get it done. But if they didn't know who you were, why bother with the attempt?"

"They could've been set to tag whoever showed up for Gioia? So maybe they knew I was coming but not anything about me?"

"Other than your name, of course, since it was on the sign."

"But even that—could be they didn't know it before, but were simply looking for whoever Valetti sent. Remember, Valetti said the sign had his signature on it." I pulled out the photo again, eyeing it. Still no signature.

"Insignia," Nikki corrected me. "Maybe how he forms letters? Sort of a calligraphic secret code with his I's and L's?"

"Really? Something that obvious?" I made a face. "That seems…kind of pointless."

"Think about it from their perspective. These guys used to be able to go around half the year in masks, seen but not seen. Maybe the lettering thing gave them a way to make their mark stylishly, in a way that only the few who mattered would notice. Having a super specific lettering style probably made them feel all special—at least until, you know, texting happened."

I snorted as Nikki leaned back, thinking it over. "So let's recap. Luca Stone got word from his buddies in Venice that the Red King was chafing their chaps, not to mention some five-hundred-year-old butcher with questionable recipes, and caught wind of your interest in the Red King as well. Knowing you'd also recently become Justice, he figured he'd kill two birds with one stone and brought you in."

"Which begs the question, how'd he know I'd ascended to the Council?"

She shrugged. "I get the feeling you're more of an open secret than you used to be."

"Yeah, maybe." I frowned. "But that brings us back to the problem with today's attacker. If he knew who I was, do you really think they'd mess with me?"

"I'm afraid it's not you they were taunting, Signorina Wilde."

We turned to see Valetti at the door. He was white as a ghost.

I half stood, but he waved me down, walking out onto the terrace. He paused at the head of the table and reached for the bottle of wine there. With a trembling hand, he poured himself a glass as Nikki and I exchanged looks.

Right as I was about to press, he spoke again. "My man was found by the main canal a few minutes ago. I apologize for not returning to you sooner, but—there were questions I needed to ask, and those I needed to answer."

"Found," I repeated. That didn't sound good.

"He had been decapitated, with his hands cut off, and his torso had been marked with a heavy ink, his naked body diagrammed with…" Valetti took a longer drink. "Meat sections. Like you would see on a cow or a pig that was being made ready for rendering."

I stared at him. "The butcher of Venice."

He winced. "It would appear I am too late in sounding the alarm. Carnevale begins in earnest tomorrow night. The magicians are all in place. There will be two weeks of balls large and small, and the streets will be filled with revelers, tourists and residents alike. Unlike many cities whose natives flee during their key events, Venice is different." He took a deep sigh. "In so many ways."

"We're here to help," I said, taking in Valetti's bleak expression. "I'm very sorry about your man."

"He'd served me since he was a boy." Now Valetti was speaking more quietly, almost ruminative. "He didn't know—any of this." He waved his hand, though I wasn't sure exactly what the gesture was supposed to encompass. "Venice today is different."

"Ah…true. Maybe you could start by explaining what you want us to do."

Valetti breathed out a long sigh. "It is not entirely my story to tell, but I can say this much—and tomorrow, you will learn more. The butcher of Venice wasn't a mere psychotic, knife-wielding maniac. He was a dark practitioner of the Connected community, and his recipes were the stuff of legends. No one knew his secret ingredients—and he was very careful. It's rumored that the finger might have been a plant by a rival who suspected the butcher's methods, but that was never proven. To say he was outraged at his arrest was beyond an understatement, but even he could not overcome the will of the people. The manner of his death was uniquely brutal, by design. That, of course, was nearly five hundred years ago."

"And now?"

"And now he's back."

I held up a hand. "You mean, he's back, back? Or someone is impersonating him? Like maybe this Red King person?"

"Please." Valetti waved the question off as if it was inconsequential. "That is a rumor not worth your time, an old title of importance to no one. The butcher is what's gripped our beautiful city in a fist of terror. Whether he has returned in the flesh, possessed a mortal soul, or another has taken up his mantle, the result is the same. A slim bound packet of medieval recipes was delivered to my door two weeks ago, clearly some sort of spell book. In all the recipes but one, key ingredients were stricken out with a heavy pen. In the last…" He swallowed. "It was a healing tea. And it required the ground finger bones of a child—a strange child, was the actual term. By the terms of the day, the inference was a psychic child."

Nikki muttered something under her breath as nausea rolled through me. "That's…super gross."

"It's more than that," Valetti said. "I wasn't the only one who received the book."

Chapter Nine

Valetti's phone rang. He answered and turned away, speaking in low tones that began with urgency and ended in resignation. When he hung up, he poured himself another glass of wine. By unspoken accord, the three of us took our drinks and moved a few steps down the terraced balcony, closer to the water. I looked over the edge and gave an experimental sniff. No rats, despite what Brody had warned. Maybe this part of Venice had better exterminators.

Certainly they had an army of gardeners at their beck and call. Surrounding Valetti's palazzo were dozens of other townhomes that marched up alongside their neighbors, cheek to jowl. It would've been claustrophobic except for the cascades of greenery that spilled over nearly every deck—bougainvilleas to ferns to oleanders to a dozen more flowering somethings I had no hope of identifying. And, I suspected that Venetians, like the rich in many great cities, mostly avoided the proximity of their neighbors by training themselves not to look.

I wasn't Venetian, however. And my training was in finding things, not ignoring them. So my biggest takeaway from Valetti's palatial spread was how easy it would be to travel from one overdecorated palazzo to the next without ever setting foot on the ground, let alone having to deal with a gondola.

Valetti cleared his throat, drawing my attention back. "I'm by no means an expert on Venetian history, I'm afraid," he said, with the false modesty of someone who'd made their village's history their life's work. "But I am justifiably proud of the magic of this city and the great sorcerers who have traveled to its shores, filling its streets with mystery."

"It seems like an ideal place for them to meet. It's very beautiful," I offered, watching him.

"It is that." He nodded. Valetti wore his grief about his houseman like an uncomfortable suit, shifting this way and that beneath its weight. I recalled what I'd learned about Valetti's background from Stone—a widower whose wife had died years earlier, leaving behind three children, none of whom lived in Venice. This palazzo was his second home and had served as his exclusive retreat during the marriage. Valetti had apparently needed a good deal of retreat too; he'd lived here almost full-time since his wife's death.

Nikki had later looked up the specific details of the wife's death as well. Cancer, with a family history of the same. So Valetti was technically not responsible for that. Always good to start off a relationship with a new client without any obvious murders on the table.

"How many recipe booklets were distributed?" I asked when Valetti appeared content to sip his wine and watch the sun edge closer toward the horizon. "Did everyone in this senate of yours get one?"

"Not everyone," the count said. "A dozen have come forward, but not all of them have produced their books, though they'll be expected to eventually. Still others seem unhappy that they weren't chosen to be terrorized." He chuckled ruefully at my expression. "It's the way of magicians, I'm afraid. To us, everything is power of some measure or another."

"And you haven't called in the police." It wasn't a question.

Valetti shook his head. "No. We could not risk their involvement. Some things have not changed for magicians, no matter how many centuries have passed. Plus, all our members are accounted for, so far." I heard the unspoken distinction in his words. Someone had been hurt, but not one of their own.

Nikki heard the same thing I had.

"What about the magicians who're in town but aren't members?" Nikki asked. "Have you kept track of them?"

"Of course. But not all of them know about this…concern, shall we say. Our top priority is to contain the fear that's growing, not add to it. We have a long and honored history of serving as sanctuary to magicians. That the butcher is undermining that…" He set his jaw, his jovial attitude flashing to one of outrage. "It is not to be borne. We have been too weak for too long."

The edge to his voice made me straighten carefully. This man was a magician, I reminded myself. Even if he was merely a gentleman conjurer, I needed to respect that. To him, this affront to his senate and his city was very real. "You have the book now?" I asked. "The one you received."

"I do not." Valetti pressed his fingers to the table, as if forcing himself to regain his equilibrium. "I gave it to the head of our order, as I was asked." He lifted his gaze to mine, his eyes once again steady. "You'll meet him tomorrow. I hope… It's my hope that he will have learned more by then so we can track down the imposter who's trifling with us."

"Fair enough." I turned my questions to what I hoped was less troubling territory. I needed to know as much as possible about the senate and its history with Carnevale. "How long have magicians been meeting here, exactly?" I was pretty sure Armaeus had never come to this little *Magic: The Gathering* experience, but then again, I hadn't asked him specifically.

Valetti visibly relaxed, clearly eager to play the part of Venetian docent. "Unofficially? Since the city's earliest beginnings. Venice has always been, at its heart, a refuge from the world around it. It was a collection of small islands separated from the mainland by two miles of murky water, water far too shallow for any serious boats to attempt the crossing, yet deep enough that you needed some knowledge of seafaring to navigate its channels correctly. But still people came—first for protection from looting barbarians, and eventually simply because it was an island unto itself."

He smiled fondly, as if talking about an old, licentious friend. "Oh, there were the rich and foolish, the lusty and bold, and the corresponding religious ascetics bent on saving them all from certain doom. There were the breathless artists and the sharp-eyed merchants who built this city brick by brick. But that was merely Venice at first glance. It was the second and third glances that revealed the mysterious allure of the city, and that's what drew the Connecteds—still in secret, of course, but they came. They assembled. In between the shadows and the lamplight, down all the strange little alleys of this city and over its canals."

"And that assembly kept growing?" Nikki asked. "Or did the magicians also decide to stay here full-time?"

"Some did, of course. Most did not. There is a far cry from a safe haven for a retreat or a creative rejuvenation and a place you want to live. Venice is crowded and swimming with people, vermin, disease—and it has its share of crime. The butcher made his terrible sausage stew in the 1500s, but though he was by far one of the most notorious of our criminals, he was not alone. And our collection of low-lying islands mired in a salt marsh has made it easy for both airborne and waterborne illness to find us. Even before the bubonic plague swept through and nearly knocked Venice off the map, there were other outbreaks, other great ills to combat. The smart sorcerer made his money and connections in Venice but his home elsewhere. And by the late 1600s, after the plague, there was a time when only the hardiest souls would venture here. That marked a turning point."

"A new elite," I murmured. As I stared over the terrace wall, I picked out a couple walking down the narrow alleyway. Even at this distance, I could see they were dressed for a party—what I assumed was a party—in feathered robes and white masks that gleamed when they caught the sun. "Venice became the symbol of the strongest magicians anywhere."

The couple turned into a home several houses down from Valetti's palazzo, disappearing into a doorway to enter a space that I could see was some sort of spacious courtyard filled with trees. An indoor, outdoor party?

"Exactly so. Which is why we must keep it that way."

I glanced back to him, once more picking up on the edge to his words. "And you really think your little recipe booklet of doom is an indication that the magicians are in danger?"

"I do, and perhaps more importantly, so do certain members of the senate, for whom I serve as head of security." Valetti grimaced, looking uncharacteristically abashed. "I confess, when the booklets first appeared, I attempted to solve the issue myself. In Venice, we value our privacy very highly. We are loath to bring in the outside world unless we have to. But my attempts met with no success."

"People died," Nikki guessed.

I could tell from Valetti's face she was right, even before he spoke. "People died. No one close to me, not then. These were magician assassins hired for the job, who knew the risks. They were well compensated, and their families well compensated after their passing, as per protocol."

Magician assassins? That was a thing?

Then again, Luca Stone was involved. If anyone knew about magician assassins he did.

Still, I kept my expression neutral. Policing or protecting the Connected underground had always been a dangerous game. One that paid well, but one that played for keeps. "And you think this butcher was behind their killings?"

"That's where it gets a little trickier." Valetti pursed his lips as if considering his words. "They died by poison. And the booklet I received contained recipes specifically intended to poison Connecteds, with the clear directive that with each death, the poisoner would grow in power."

"And so if you're the bad guy and you've got assassin Connecteds running around, who better to practice your poisoning skills on?" Nikki mused. "But that means anyone who got the books could be the killer—or the guy who distributed them could. That gets us nowhere."

"Precisely the problem, though I would like to believe no one among our ranks of magicians would stoop to murder."

From Nikki's face, she wasn't willing to extend that courtesy so easily. Came from being a cop for so many years, I suspected. Either way, I was right there with her. At this point, anyone in the city could be a suspect.

Valetti continued. "Nevertheless, do I honestly believe that the butcher himself walks these streets once more, resurrected from the dead? I, personally, do not. For one, even if he was a great magician, he was killed by great magicians who knew what they were doing. The removal of his hands, the specific torture Cargnio endured, the quartering of his body, and the baking of his ashes into earthenware that was then smashed was all quite deliberate. It seemed like a spectacle to appease a horrified public, and it was that too, I suppose. But it was specially designed to ensure that never again would magic reside in the host of that body."

"Which means that someone else has assumed that magic, either legitimately or solely for appearance's sake." I tapped my chin. "Did Cargnio have any children?"

"If he did, they were lost to history. More than likely, they were lost almost immediately, in the waking hours after Cargnio himself met his grim end. However, magicians are not known for their familial ties. It's my personal belief that if he had any of his own issue, they quickly found their way into his stews."

"That is still completely gross," Nikki muttered.

"He didn't have to kill his own flesh and blood," I said. "He may have considered them entirely separate of his potions."

Valetti shrugged. "Perhaps. Yet there is no mention of his own children even in the most thorough annals of

Venetian history. Which, by the way, brings me to the next part of the story. As I said, I do not have any claim on the history of the city, but there are those who do. Especially those steeped in its darker lore. I have arranged an audience with the prelate tomorrow. He will give you more of the answers you seek."

"The prelate?" I frowned. The sun was now edging perilously close to the horizon, and a movement down the alleyway caught my attention again. Another knot of feathered and masked individuals made their way down the passage, more unsteadily than the first. They stopped in front of the door to the party house's courtyard and paused, appearing to argue among themselves. Then one turned and lifted his arm, knocking smartly on the door. It opened, and the three seemed to fall inside the space, the door once more shutting behind them. That must be some party down there.

But Valetti was talking again. "—Casino of Spirits," he said, and I blinked as Nikki sat up.

"I've heard about that place," she said. "It's owned by a couple of different churches now, right on the water, part of a larger compound of old buildings. Pretty gardens, manicured walkways, the whole thing. And, it's haunted."

Valetti smiled. "In the beginning, its name was merely tribute to the raucous parties that were held on its grounds. It's only in more recent times that its reputation has turned dire. Still, it serves as a fitting location for the arcane library of Venice, which I presume you will want to explore. Alfonse is the titular head of our order, whereas I serve as head of security."

I wasn't making any presumptions yet about avenues of exploration, but I was happy to go along. I needed to talk to another member of the senate at any rate, if only to confirm Valetti's take on events. He seemed perfectly earnest, but he was also determined to protect his senate, the honor of Venice, and the sanctity of magicianhood. And if his job was security for the senate, then I definitely needed more sources to understand what was really going on here.

Still, I couldn't get the image out of my mind of what I'd seen below. "Carnevale starts tomorrow night, you said?"

"Yes," Valetti said. "But as I'm sure you've seen, there are those who have begun the celebration early. It is always that way, the storm before the storm." He smiled indulgently. "In Venice, we would have it no other way."

"And your neighbors here? These look like pretty nice homes. I assume they're all residents, not open for tourists to rent?"

Valetti assumed an expression of patrician distaste. "You're correct. These are some of the oldest families in the cities, and we are all quite protective of our privacy. And, of course, that is the point of the masks, you see? To allow even the most private of souls, the most powerful, to mix among the dancers and the revelers without fear of being known. To laugh, to love, to dance, to mingle. It's what makes Venice, Venice." He sighed almost romantically. "It must remain a place of safety for those who have given so much to it. All would be lost otherwise."

I nodded, my eyes once more on the alley. No one else approached.

"Ah!" Valetti's exclamation drew my attention. He stood, almost like a soldier at attention, his eyes fixed on the western horizon.

"The sun is setting on the city, on the eve of Carnevale," he all but whispered, his words rapt. "All the magic in the world has come to dance in the streets once more."

Chapter Ten

It was another two hours before Valetti finally retired for the evening, and Nikki waited approximately four seconds before she narrowed her eyes at me. "It's a bad idea."

"Nearly a dozen people have entered that courtyard this evening. Only three have come out. Three. And the ones who did looked like their next destination was a detox clinic."

"It's the night before the mother of all parties in the city. Maybe they're pregaming."

"I don't think so. Valetti said that this area of the city was filled with residents, and judging from the state of these palazzos, they're residents with a lot of money. You really think they'd open their doors to carnival goers out of the goodness of their hearts?"

"Airbnb?"

I sent her a withering glance. "The only way you'd rent out homes like these to strangers was through a service that hooked you up with the rich and famous. I'm not saying it doesn't happen, but I don't think that's what was going on down there."

Nikki sighed. She'd seen exactly what I had, because the moment the images had passed into my memory, she had access to them. A process which, of course, was nearly instantaneous. “Fine. It was a mix of men and women, but no way to tell any other details about them. Other than that they didn’t look like this was their first party of the day,” she agreed.

“And none of them were fall-down drunk, though they were working on it. Dutch courage?”

“Maybe.” She made a face. “I know I’m definitely going to need another drink if you expect me to help you astral travel, though. That shit always gives me the willies, I don’t care how many times you do it.”

“Yeah, well. The sooner we start, the sooner it’s over.”

“If you’re sure—”

“Here. We’ll get celestial approval if that makes you happy.” I reached in my jacket and pulled out a card from the deck, flipping it around to show her, certain it would be the Magician, the High Priestess, or even Justice.

It wasn’t.

She peered at the card and rolled her eyes. “The Red King. Great.”

“I don’t make the news, I just report it.” I grinned. “Plus, the King of Cups is above all else a guy sitting on flowing water. That certainly describes where we are.” I tapped the card on the table. “In fact, the Red King could be at that party right now.”

“Uh-huh,” Nikki said, still patently unconvinced. “Or it’s some nice old man hosting a pre-Carnevale get-together.”

“It could be,” I agreed. “It isn’t, but it could be.”

“Fine.” Nikki scooted her chair over to me while I pushed my wineglass farther away on the table. No point making a mess.

Astral traveling was a skill I'd never really much cared for, but it had come in handy, particularly as I'd begun doing work for the Council. It wasn't always convenient for me to bodily transport myself halfway around the world to report on something for the benefit of the Magician or High Priestess. Granted, I wasn't the best traveler, especially on Psychic Airlines. I usually ended up hurling my guts if I had to fly the spectral skies for any significant amount of time. But it did make for soothing one's curiosity in a hurry.

Nikki sighed heavily, clearly put out, but began the words I'd almost learned by heart, for all that they were in no formal language that still existed on the planet. I felt myself sinking further and further into the self-hypnosis necessary to begin any astral travel journey. I slumped forward in my chair, then felt the lift of my body as my spirit broke free from the…

Only, there was no breaking.

No freeing. No nothing.

"Um…" I slitted open one eye, giving Nikki a sideways glance. "It sounds like you're doing it correctly, but nothing is happening."

Not breaking her chant, Nikki waved at me to shut my eyes again, then repeated the words with more vigor. She leaned closer, in case there was some directional issue with her words hitting my eardrum. I winced at her loud voice, grimacing.

"Focus," she hissed.

"I *am* focusing. Nothing's happening."

Typically by this time in the process, I was already out of both my body and whatever building I inhabited and soaring over the city. The queasiness would come later, but the initial hit of leaving my physical form and floating in space was something I could never fully articulate. I'd experience pure weightlessness, and my vision would transform into something supernatural, as if it were made up of a thousand different satellites whose cameras were all pointed at the same location. In other words, I didn't see a single image, but the same image magnified and replicated dozens and dozens of times. It was unnerving, but it was also awesome.

And it in no way, shape, or form was happening now.

"Forget it," I said, leaning back in my chair in disgust. "It's broken. I'm broken."

Nikki watched me with wide eyes, her mouth tight. "Has this ever happened before?" Her lips twisted with grim humor. "I feel like we're on an erectile dysfunction commercial."

"Imagine how I feel," I muttered, more than a little unhappy. As much as I wasn't a fan of astral traveling, I was even *less* a fan of things not working when they were supposed to be working. First there'd been the library brownout at Justice Hall, now this. Before I even knew what I was fully doing, I reached out mentally and rapped on the cosmos's door.

For once, Armaeus was home.

"Miss Wilde," he murmured, his voice less concerned than curious. I knew the man loved me. I knew he'd moved heaven and earth for me. But there was something that ran even deeper than that love. The Magician's eternal fascination with my evolution as a Connected.

"I tried astral travel," I said without preamble. Though I didn't need to speak the words aloud—Nikki could read my memories of Armaeus's and my words the second after we spoke—it felt awkward having an entire conversation in my head. "It was a spectacular fail. What's going on?"

"I told you when you ascended to the Council that your abilities would be curtailed in some ways, even as you added others. There was no way of telling which skills would be affected ahead of time."

I blinked. "Are you serious? I can make blue balls of flame, but I can't zip around with my mind? Who made that decision?"

"It's a sacrifice all Council members must make," Armaeus said. *"You get used to it, or you make adjustments. However, when an ability is lost, it doesn't mean it cannot ever be reclaimed."*

"That's beautiful," I said sarcastically. "What skills did you leave behind when you ascended to the Council?"

"None," he replied, and my eyes widened. A second later, Nikki's did too. She could hear Armaeus as well, as soon as his words passed into my memory.

"What do you mean none? I thought this was some kind of rule."

"When I ascended to the Council, I had no skills as a magician. I had the magic within me, the deep wellspring of possibility, but I hadn't begun working any spells. All that came later."

I opened my mouth to utter a witty retort, then snapped it shut again. For me not to know something so important about arguably the closest man to me on this entire planet was more than a little unsettling. "Oh."

Across the miles, Armaeus chuckled, and I battened down my mental hatches. I didn't mind the fact that he could read my thoughts when I allowed him to, I simply minded it when I forgot to rescind permission.

"So where does that leave me?" I asked. "I can no longer astral travel?"

"It's perhaps reasonable that the Justice of the Arcana Council must confront her mark directly, versus spying on them from the shadows."

"I don't think that's reasonable. You ask me, it's downright irresponsible. What happens if I confront my mark, as you so charmingly put it, and they are way more powerful than anything I've been led to believe? I could be knee-deep in serious crap without even knowing it."

"You have clearly retained the power of healing and translation, and you can now destabilize enough to travel corporeally," Armaeus said, his tone only vaguely soothing. *"You also have, by your own admission, access to spectral fire."*

"I've also retained my unerring fashion sense and my ability to find ice cream in any city in the world, but that's not all that helpful when I'm dealing with magicians who're more powerful than I'm expecting them to be."

"You're one of the most powerful Connecteds in all the world."

"Well yeah, I *was*. That was before I got hit with the abilities tax. Now I don't know so much how I stack up."

I was partly complaining to ensure my skill at whining was still sharp, since it was one of my best talents, but a not insignificant portion of me truly was concerned. Based on what Luca Stone had said about the quality and depth of magical ability heightening in the weeks following the recent war on magic, there were now Connecteds out there who were more powerful than they used to be. Conversely, I was apparently weaker than I used to be. I really didn't like the math.

"It would appear you will need to test each ability anew, as well as determine what additional skills you may have

developed without realizing it," Armaeus said. *"As the old saying goes, nature finds a way."*

"Yeah, well, I'm thinking the first skill I'm going to need to develop is to learn how to keep my mouth shut so I don't piss off the wrong hooligan who's hefting a lightning bolt when he should only have a glow stick."

"As always, I remain fascinated to see what you do, Miss Wilde. Now, if you'll excuse me, there is a matter of the demon horde at the Met that I need to address."

"Fine, fine. Go. Don't mind me." I could tell the moment that the Magician broke contact with me and found myself unreasonably glad that Nikki remained beside me. I hated being dis-Connected.

She looked less impressed. And by far less distressed. "So no more astral traveling?" she asked hopefully. "I absolutely hated it when you did the out-of-body-experience thing, especially since I was usually the one stuck with the body. It never did so great."

"Yeah well, astral travel had its benefits. But apparently, it's off the table for right now. Which means we move to Plan B."

Nikki blinked at me. "There's a Plan B?"

"There's always a Plan B."

This wasn't necessarily true, but it was close enough. I stood and moved over to the edge of the balcony, taking a harder look at the side of our own palazzo. We were on the third floor of the structure, and the building had been constructed during the Renaissance era, if not before. As a result, the walls were not hewn into smooth, uninterrupted rock, but a much craggier surface. Add to that the crenelated flourishes of the window frames, and there might as well be a ladder extending down.

"No, no, no," Nikki said. "There is absolutely no reason for you to investigate the neighbor's party. There was no sign of wrongdoing, nobody screamed, no guns were pulled, no—"

"Shh!" I held up a hand as Nikki groaned and stood, quickly striding over to me. My gaze remained on the doorway to the hidden courtyard as it slowly swung open. Three men spilled out onto the sidewalk, swaying together collegially. Two of them stumbled off down the alley, while the third headed our way. "Those three didn't show up together."

"What are you, the neighborhood watch? Since when is it a crime to leave a party with someone you didn't show up with?"

"An excellent point. Which is all the more reason why you and I should make sure this young man makes it home safely."

"Home?"

"At least down to the end of the street." I eyed the squat, wrought iron banister topping the terrace wall. It was intended almost entirely for show, I suspected, but it did make things a little tricky to go over the side. Still, manageable.

"Whoa," Nikki said. "In case you didn't notice, I'm a little overdressed for climbing walls." She pointed to her shoes. "I left my hiking Blahniks at home."

"Fair enough." My grin widened as something else occurred to me. "I'm Justice of the Arcana Council, and I can teleport at will. That means I can travel with anyone to a new location, so long as I've seen that location. Did you know that?"

"Ummm…"

I pointed to the sidewalk below us. "I've totally seen the sidewalk. So it stands to reason that I could get us both down there without the whole wall-climbing thing. Purely to protect your heels, of course."

Nikki made a face. "Are you serious? Do we really have to do this?"

"Choppity choppity. Dude is walking slowly, but he *is* walking. I need your help."

For the second time in the space of ten minutes, Nikki let out a long, heartfelt groan. But she didn't flinch more than a little when I put my hand on her shoulder.

"Is that the best place for your hand?" she protested. "Shouldn't you hold on to something a little sturdier? Like all of me?"

"Stop being such a baby."

I didn't close my eyes, but I did tense up as I felt the energy surge over me. As always, I simply imagined myself in the other space. Which was why I needed to see a given space before I attempted going there.

It worked like a charm. I could feel myself becoming less corporeal, Nikki right along with me. My fingers sank more deeply into her muscled shoulder. This was going to work, I realized. I might not be able to astral travel, but I could legit travel from point to point on demand. I could get used to that. Certainly, it'd make getting home easier. In fact, the only downside was—

I jerked with sudden realization, but there was no way to reverse the shift once I'd started it. At least no way that I knew of. That meant I was going to have to go through this no matter how awkward it was. And Nikki was too. She realized that two seconds later.

"Does it feel a little hot to you?" came her alarmed question.

We flared back into existence a second later at our destination, both of us slightly charred, but fortunately the conflagration hadn't come with us. I was a little concerned that I'd manifested fire several times in a row now as my transport add-on of choice. Of all the ways for me to expedite the traveling process, it seemed like I could come up with something a little less hazardous than fire.

A little less noticeable too. As we straightened and gained our feet on the narrow cobblestone alleyway, I realized that the inebriated guest from the hidden courtyard was standing right in front of us. He stared, his dilated eyes open wide, his mouth gaping. I wasn't sure if he'd seen any of the flame throwing, but he'd certainly made note of the two strangers that'd suddenly appeared in the space before him where there hadn't been anyone before.

Nikki and I didn't give him a chance to get his bearings. Swaying against me with a rough and boisterous laugh, Nikki swung around to the man and staggered forward, crashing into him bodily. Drunk or no, the Venetian had been raised correctly. His arms immediately went out to steady Nikki, his face tight with concern.

"What—who? How?" he asked in Italian.

It only took the briefest touches for Nikki to get what she needed.

CHAPTER ELEVEN

We sent the man on his way with a minimum of fuss, and Nikki turned to me, making a show of checking her outfit.

"Next time I tell you I'm smokin' hot, please do not take me literally," she groused.

Belatedly, I glanced down to my own outfit. Like Nikki, I was a little crisp around the edges, but not to the extent that anyone would notice.

"So maybe I had to trade the astral travel for the real teleporting," I said. "I guess that's a fair trade."

"Except for the fire stuff, yeah, and the part about needing to have seen a place first before you can go to it," she pointed out. "That sort of makes it difficult for the search part of search and rescue."

"True, but I could get close, right?" As we talked, we naturally had started walking down the street toward the party palazzo. "Let's say that something was most likely holed up in Carnegie Hall, and I've never been to Carnegie Hall, but I've been to New York. So I can get close."

"And maybe…" Nikki snapped her fingers. "I can do you one better. What if you saw a place on Google Earth? So you know that you need to be inside, say, a palazzo in Venice. You can't get into the home on your own, but you could line up right outside the front door. Assuming, of course, nobody was standing there at that exact time, because then they would see you poof into existence. Which can be awkward."

"That wasn't all that awkward back there."

"You weren't the one practically landing on the guy."

"Fair enough. Speaking of..."

"Speaking of, he was lit up like a Christmas tree. From what I could tell, nothing technoceutical, just garden-variety hallucinogens. They were already wearing off, which was why he decided the party was no longer any fun, so he was off to the next gig. This is interesting too: even his whack memories were starting to fade, and dude had only been out of the house for approximately what, three minutes? By tomorrow morning, he won't even remember he was here."

I frowned. "Like he'd been roofied?"

"That's one possibility. On top of whatever he took himself, he could've easily had something slipped into his drink behind door number one. But I'm telling you, dollface, there is *nothing* interesting in a metaphysical sense about this party, at least not from boyo's perspective. Everybody's in feathers and masks, granted, but I think that's going to get pretty commonplace here in the next day or so."

I frowned, then squinted up at the house. "Well, we're already here. Should we knock?"

Nikki shrugged. "We're not exactly correctly dressed, and Valetti is this guy's neighbor. So it depends on how noticed you want to be."

"Since when did you become the voice of reason?"

Nikki pointed down again. "Blahniks."

"Fine. We'll go around to the back, if there is a back. These row houses are kind of creepy with no space in between them."

"Agreed. But one block over…" Nikki glanced down the street from where we came, then back the other way. "More of the guests seem to be arriving from that direction," she said. "All of them on foot. Gotta be some sort of public water taxi stop, since Casa Crazy here doesn't have its own pier."

"So to get behind it…"

"Up the street we go." We retraced our steps to follow the young man we'd interrupted, and went another block up, then down again. Logic dictated we'd see a house built of the same pink stone we'd seen on the front courtyard.

Logic was with us, but backward.

"They were going in the back garden door." Nikki craned back to get a better look at the façade. It was worth the effort. Like Palazzo Gioia, this building put the "whoa" in row house. Three stories of flawless pink-tinged stone would've been impressive on any street, in any city. Here, however, it was merely the fifth house down. All of its neighbors were equally majestic, if not quite as pretty.

It also was not a place I'd expect people to be dropping acid. "This seems a little staid for a drug party."

Nikki nodded, then grinned. "All business in the front, a party in the back. It's a Venetian mullet."

"And it's locked, no matter what." I shook my head. "I'm changing my mind. Astral travel was better."

"Unless…" Nikki pulled me along until we reached the top of the street again, and we wound our way back toward Palazzo Gioia. "I've seen the inside. I mean, our drunken friend did, and he remembered it, mostly."

I frowned at her. "But you're not the one driving, right? It's not like you can put your memories in my head."

"But if you trusted me? Would that work?"

"Well, maybe. Or maybe we'd end up in the middle of a wall. On fire."

Nikki considered that. "Okay, so possibly not the best idea. Which leaves us where?"

"Which leaves us..." I paused as the door at the far end of the lane opened. Four guests nearly fell on their faces in the alley, and I glanced up. "How is it nobody is complaining about this? Are there seriously not enough nosy people in this town to see what's going on?"

"I get the feeling this crowd only looks up," Nikki said drily.

"Yeah, but—cameras? Busybodies? Maids or manservants? Surely someone's got the time on their hands to check this out. All I had to do was look over the side of the wall."

We paused as another set of revelers came up the alley in grand feathered gear, only they were entering, not leaving. I watched them until they disappeared behind the door. "At least we know the party's still going strong."

"I still think you should give my idea a try," Nikki said. "I could describe the courtyard to you. We could hold hands or something."

"No," I said again, more firmly this time, in case she'd forgotten the meaning of the word. "I think that's... Wait, here's more."

Two new revelers, one large, one of medium build, drifted out of the doorway, hand in hand. They stopped on the side of the alley and embraced, clearly entranced with each other. They fumbled and laughed as their masks clicked together, their hands bunching up their heavy feathered robes. I stared, not proud of the thought forming in my mind.

Nikki of course, had no such issues. "Two capes, two masks. And those costumes are clearly getting in their way."

We moved quickly to the main street, loitering under some trees in front of another house. It didn't take long for the couple to give up on trying to make out in costume, and we let them pass us as they exited the alley. They were heading for the water taxi stand, hand in hand.

"Hit them or pay them?"

"They seem nice enough…"

"Drunk enough too," Nikki observed. Without giving me time to consider a more thoughtful plan, she bounded forward, her bright voice startling the couple, nearby residents, and several birds. But when she pulled out a thick wad of American bills, she managed to convey what she wanted to the Venetians with startling ease. It took only a few minutes for her to return, burdened with masks and feathers.

"Knockoffs," she said, sniffing the ensemble. "And they reek of booze and cigarettes."

"Then we should fit right in." I pulled the smaller of the two costumes from her. In five more minutes, we were dressed and practicing our best flamboyant strolls, Nikki continuing to fuss with her costume as we walked.

"These guys were more with it than the other one, more drunk on love than narcotics, but they saw the same thing the first guy did. Courtyard, open-bar setup, chatter, laughter, trees with lights strung in them, pretty girls handing out drinks and pills."

I glanced up toward the courtyard walls, and sure enough, there were lights in the trees. They were more noticeable now that the sun was officially down. "Any idea who the house's owner is?"

"I've got a first name, but it's not all that helpful: Fabrizio. There are undoubtedly a thousand Fabrizios in this section of Venice alone."

Fabrizio, I thought. Was he the Red King? Maybe. But even if he wasn't, the King of Cups in traditional card readings was also known as the God card. How could I say no to going inside if God was on our side? "How'd they learn about the house party, in case we're asked?"

Nikki grinned. "I knew you were going to pose that very question, so I poked around their earlier memories. They decided to check the party out this afternoon. They already had costumes left over from last year, though they weren't pleased with them."

"Explains why they were so willing to part with them."

"That and the ridiculous amount of money I shoved at them, yep. Once they took the water taxi here, they found the place with their phones, walked in, handed over said phones, and signed their names in a ledger."

"They gave up their phones?"

"What can I say? They're Italian. The phones were left in plain sight, in a bin behind the bar, but the owners didn't want any pictures. Apparently, this wasn't a surprising request to any of the partiers."

"Interesting."

"I thought so too. But no one confronted them, no one talked to them, other than a cocktail girl shilling drinks. Which were free, along with an assortment of designer drugs."

"And the point of all this?"

"Drugs and drink tastings, market research. They'd seen a flyer in a local park. They sampled the booze, declined the drugs, and there was no muss, no fuss. They left soon after, not even embarrassed. What I suspect ol' Fabrizio is doing is testing out some new strains of woo juice he wants to put out in circulation, but he needs to make sure he doesn't blow anyone up first." Nikki continued manipulating the feathers of her costume as she walked, in a futile attempt to get the feathers to lie straight. "You'd think—whoa, whoa, whoa."

Nikki's long fingers dived between two feathers, and she came away with a small metallic device. "This is interesting," she said blandly.

"Very interesting," I agreed, peering at the bug. "Do we care?"

"If it's a tracking device with history, they'll know the capes were at the party twice. If it's a tracking device without history, and they haven't started tracking, then no harm, no foul."

I thought about that. "How would we know?"

"We wouldn't. I suspect they simply want to make sure no one ups and dies on them. Would kind of put a damper on the whole market research angle. I'm thinking we move the bugs but keep them on us, then ditch the costumes as soon as we're done doing whatever it is we think we're going to do in there."

"Agreed."

We approached the doorway, and Nikki reached out, knocking authoritatively on the unadorned wooden door. It opened almost immediately. We were ushered into an incredibly lush courtyard that looked like it had played host to parties since the Middle Ages. Stone benches wove in and around fully grown trees and plants, all of them dripping with twinkling lights.

A modern bar stood at the far corner of the deceptively large space, and we hadn't even walked three steps toward it before a woman whisked in front of us—wearing a half mask and a wide smile above her feathered minidress.

"You're American?" she asked.

I stared through my mask, and Nikki put her hands on her hips. "How is it that obvious?"

"Because of you." The woman laughed, pointing at Nikki. "You are no Venetian. You will be a delight at every party you attend."

"It's a particular skill of mine."

"You wish drinks?" The woman offered us the tray, but in addition to the drinks were several small plastic cups with two pills each. I itched to pull the pills off the tray, but I felt the attention of several sets of eyes in the room. What we lifted from this tray, we'd be expected to consume. The booze hadn't harmed anyone, at least not from what we'd seen. The pills were an unknown quantity.

We both reached for the glasses, but I couldn't help a growing sense of unease as I stared around the courtyard. This was all wrong. These people were too happy, too relaxed. They'd done this or something like this before. To them, there wasn't anything inherently creepy about it. And, bonus points, no one seemed particularly Connected. Not the bartenders, not the waitstaff, and definitely not the guests.

So why had I felt so sure I should investigate?

An excited murmur started at the front of the room, and Nikki looked up, her body suddenly tense.

"What is it?"

"Something's wrong. Energy's changed," she said in a way that wasn't so much psychic smart as cop smart. Before her stint as a Vegas psychic, Nikki had spent a lot of years on the Chicago police force to hone that kind of instinct, and her eyes had gone flat and hard. "We need to go."

"But shouldn't we— " I didn't have a chance to finish my words before the first startled shout went up. Even in their pleasantly impaired state, the crowd darted away like startled fish as a man half staggered, half fell out of the house and into the courtyard. He was enormous, wearing a luxurious feathered cape and a long beaked mask that showed his mouth beneath it, but that mouth was now open in a horrible grimace. His arms were stretched wide, his body writhing. He chased away any who came close.

"Dollface..." Nikki said quietly. She was already edging toward the door, which was an open maw to the street, with frightened partiers spilling out. No screaming, no shouting, no chaos, just a party gone very badly wrong and everyone wanting to cut their losses. The official staff were mostly frozen in place except for some of the bouncers, who were circling in on the feathered man with a mixture of reverence, fear, and, worst of all, surprise.

"We can't go," I said tightly. "He's been drugged. Like, a lot."

I stepped forward, and the man looked up, apparently watching me through the mask. It was an unnerving experience because though I could see his mouth, I couldn't see his eyes.

"You!" he gasped, his entire body stiffening. "You were—supposed to come! To save me! It wasn't...it wasn't my time!"

He doubled over in a fit of the shakes, and I reflexively looked for the slash over his right temple, gleaming in silver. Only...it wasn't there. Instead, his head was surrounded with a faint corona of glowing purple light—which was *definitely* not the same thing.

The guy might be a technoceutical pusher and a dirtbag in his own right, but he wasn't marked for Justice.

Crap.

Chapter Twelve

I didn't waste time parsing the particulars. With a dozen more strides, I was right up on the guy, jerking one of the bouncers out of the way. Said bouncer apparently hadn't been expecting me to be so strong, because he crashed into several other staffers with a curse I couldn't quite translate. Nikki stepped in right beside me, shoving another two men back. In my peripheral view, I noted that the revelers who'd been hardy enough to stick around were still sticking, all of them watching. There was something else wrong about this scene, and it hit me as I rolled the heavy man over to his back.

"Where's the ambulance?" I snapped. "This guy's been in trouble for at least ten minutes, probably more."

"His personal physician is on the way." The voice spoke from above me, sharp, worried, but firm. "There will be no ambulance."

Freaking great. The big guy's breathing was coming in short, shallow bursts, and his skin was pale and waxy. I reached down to rip the mask off him, but he struggled, his hands coming up to hold the mask on.

"Nooo," he gasped. "No."

"Everybody's a drama queen." Without waiting another beat, I stared down at the man, allowing my third eye to flick open.

Instantly, the world around me was no longer merely a construct of form and color, but dancing electrical circuits, weaving in and around and through the humans and plants and other life-forms that were occupying this space—and all of it was a life-form of some sort or another, none of the figures truly inert. Not even the guy passed out at the far edge of the bar. Somewhere deep inside me, I breathed a tiny sigh of relief that this was one skill I'd managed to retain. I should probably start a spreadsheet.

For now, however, I needed to focus on the soon-to-be-dead guy in front of me. With the vantage point of my electrical sight, I could see exactly where the problem was: everywhere. The man's life force wasn't so much shutting down, it was already well into ghost. His heart was pumping, his brain was firing, but both processes were operating at well below optimal levels. It was as if he were trying to push his body through a tub of Jell-O with his feet tied together. There were so many things going wrong at the same time, I didn't know what to hit first, his withering heart, his darkening brain, his collapsing lungs, his sluggish blood, or his misfiring nerves.

So I went with option F and hit everything at once.

Focusing my own energy into a massive bolt, I released an electrical surge into the man's body at chest level, the trailing ends of fire moving both up and down his form. I watched carefully to see where, if anywhere, the energy pooled, and I wasn't disappointed. The point of entry for the poison wasn't the guy's stomach or, more appropriately, his mouth, as would've been reasonable, but an injection site directly below his left ear. He'd not only been drugged, he definitely hadn't been the one doing the job.

I clapped my hand over the injection site, and the man jerked again. By this time, the onlookers had given us a wide berth. I got the sense of a man in a dark, subdued suit hustling up. But he made it no further than Nikki, because I wasn't done here, not by a long shot. I'd immediately recognized the energy signature of this drug—sort of. It was Black Elixir, only a strain of the technoceutical that was a million times more potent than any I'd ever encountered before. Infused with powerful organic compounds I didn't recognize, the drug hadn't augmented the feathered man's natural magical ability, which was fairly high, it'd turned that ability into a self-destructing weapon. I saw now that the man's brain hadn't gone dark, exactly. Instead, it had taken on a wasting energy that was billowing through his body like an insidious army of ants, eating everything in its wake. With a slash of my own energy, I halted the oncoming tide, and the man's cells responded. His synapses began firing again, his heart started beating, and his nerve endings stopped their frantic dance. But something was still terribly wrong. Even as I pushed back the malevolent wave of energy, I realize I'd already lost the battle. At least the battle that would have meant anything to this man, if he was as Connected as I thought he was.

He'd lost his magic.

"Signore Balestri, no!" The slender man in the dark suit managed to duck beneath Nikki's outstretched arms keeping everyone away. He dropped down beside me and started speaking in a rush of Italian. He was a doctor, Signore Balestri's doctor, this was an overdose, and apparently not a surprise. This was something he understood and knew how to handle, and there was absolutely no need for alarm.

Beneath us, the feathered man had rolled over on his side and started throwing up, lending credence to the whole overdose concept. He was breathing more easily now, his heart pumping at a normal pace, his adrenaline level receding. His brain was even firing normally. But that was the problem. It was firing *normally*. The element of this man that had made him a psychic was no longer there.

As if in response to my assessment, the man groaned, saying something in a low tone to his doctor, who stiffened at the request, alarm spreading through him.

"Signore—" the doctor began again, his face tight with alarm.

"Not on my watch, buddy."

I flipped the man over again, scowling down at him as he looked up at me through the mask, his eyes finally discernible through the holes cut into the gleaming white surface. Balestri knew already, he knew what he'd lost. But I wasn't going to let him administer the fatal dose of whatever toxin he'd requested from his doctor. I had enough deaths piling up at my door.

"You were supposed to *save* me," Balestri said again in garbled Italian, his voice morose.

"Who did this to you?" I asked. "Who'd you let get close to you, close enough that they could stick you with a needle behind your left ear?"

But the man was shaking his head as if I had missed something terribly important. His next words confirmed it. "You don't, cannot understand," he muttered, his words half-coherent syllables, half groans. "He has agents—everywhere. The very breeze whispers his commands."

"That's beautiful, but let's try this again. Who was close enough to you to stick you with a needle? Because unless it was delivered by blow dart, there's no other way you could've been hit with this toxin."

"Toxin," said Balestri. He coughed up phlegm and spit to the side, patently disappointed that it wasn't blood. He was going to survive all right. The shock of the drug in his system might have killed him if I hadn't been here, but that hadn't been its primary goal. In fact…

"What do you mean I was supposed to come?" I demanded. "What did you see about me? How long have you been taking Black Elixir?"

That brought his head around.

"I don't need a *potion* to predict the future," Balestri retorted, as if I'd delivered an unforgivable insult. By now his physician was helping him to a seated position, and one of the bouncers was bracing his back with a broad arm. "I've been doing that since childhood."

His eyes widened even as he spoke the words, and I watched as realization hit him again, his face going positively gray.

"Stay with me, buddy. We'll figure it out. So, okay, you saw me all on your own. Good for you. Why? What'd you see exactly?"

"That you were coming for me," he said morosely, a self-mocking smile creasing his face. "That you would see me and judge me worthy."

"Not my department," I started, but the man wasn't listening anymore.

"I moved up my timetable because I knew your arrival would throw everything into a panic. I needed to get the last market test completed, then prepare for Carnevale—but there was too much to do. I knew you'd been drawn here, and I knew why. Valetti and the others' old-woman concerns about the return of the butcher. Foolishness." He shook his head. "Still, you were supposed to protect me. To keep me in the game."

"The game."

"The senate has reached a point of power never before achieved." A burst of animation infused Balestri for a moment, and he stared at me with mirror-bright eyes. "All the magicians in the world of any merit have gathered here, will gather here, and the competition for a guiding role of the senate will be the stuff of legends. I *deserve* to be one of those guides."

I eyed him in disbelief. "This is about serving as a committee chair?"

Balestri sagged. "But you didn't come in time," he said dully. "He came first."

My head was starting to pound. "You predicted I was coming. So you busted tail to get your last bit of drug data before closing up shop and partying, but you weren't fast enough. One of your other enemies got you first."

"Firrrst..." the feather man was overcome with another paroxysm of trembling, and the doctor shooed me away, opening his bag.

"He's going to be okay," I said, because I couldn't help myself. I'd be damned if some doctor thought that his injection of goop was going to do anything to save his patient beyond what I had already done.

"He's *not* going to be okay," the doctor said in tight Italian. "You have restored the body, you may have even restored the brain, but you have not restored the mind. And what are we without our minds?"

I opened my mouth to protest, but the man rushed on. "He needs to be stabilized, you need to go, and then he needs to go deep inside himself and see what there is to be seen. After he does, with some luck, he will do everything he can to restore himself. That I can handle." He shook his head, looking at the feathered man with something that was almost like affection as he slumped in the bouncer's arms.

"Wait, you know what this drug is? How it works?" Because I didn't. I couldn't stop what I didn't understand.

"I don't, no," the physician sighed, then bent down to rummage in his bag. "But I also cannot allow Signore Balestri to take his own life out of despair for what he has lost, until he has at least explored the possibilities of finding it again."

Nikki clasped my shoulder. "Somebody will report this, dollface. I don't think we should be here when that happens."

The sound of the distant sirens finally broke across the quiet night. But I couldn't help staring at the doctor. I took a gamble.

"How much do you know about the Red King?"

"The Red…" The man frowned in what seemed to be genuine confusion, then he shook his head again. "If that's some new drug on the market, I've not encountered it yet, and to my knowledge, Signore Balestri was not under its influence. He prided himself on being a producer, not a taker of technoceuticals."

"What a champ," Nikki said drily.

"Not true," I objected. "He was under the influence of more than just a healthy self-image, even before this new toxin was injected into his system."

"You mean wine, you mean cocaine, of course. I suspect when I check, I'll also find the fentanyl patch supply has dropped since last time I was here as well."

"But you said he didn't take drugs."

"He didn't take *technoceutical* drugs. He was—is—pure-blooded. A magician of the highest order, who has never fallen prey to the siren song of any augmentation he hadn't earned through his own strength and study, even though his natural power was not nearly as strong as he wished it to be. There are very few true magicians in the world that can claim to be truly pure-blooded, and Fabrizio Balestri is one of them. He is also an honorable man."

The doctor straightened, turning to me. In his hand was a small red leather-bound journal, wrapped tight with black leather cords.

My eyes popped wide. "Is that what I think it is?"

"Signore Balestri received this two weeks ago, but he knew his history. He was no fool. And as for the drugs he made…" The doctor shoved the book at me. I took it. "No one died. He did not deal in Black Elixir or anything like it. He was an alchemist, and devoted to the cause of augmenting Connecteds safely."

"And making money from it," I pointed out.

"There is no crime in that," the doctor said severely. "He was pure-blooded. Magic to him was life. Everyone knew it, and they were all coming here, to Carnevale, where he would finally make his stand."

"Well, not anymore," I said grimly, looking down at Balestri's crumpled form. "So what's next for him?"

"Next you will leave, and Signore Balestri will heal. And then I suspect he will break his vow of pure-bloodedness and rely on the augmentation drugs so favored by the weakest of his kind. His pride will take a hit, but better that than living even a day without the powers and psychic abilities that have defined his whole life. Unless, of course, you could restore him?"

I considered that. I honestly didn't know if I could, given the destruction I'd seen along his neural circuits. And the man still was a drug dealer. Then again, if he could be of greater help to me later… "You know his crimes?"

The doctor's face shut down, and he glanced away. "We all have our crimes. Yours is that you came too late to be of any use to us, Signorina Justice."

Yet someone else who knew who I was. "I'll add that to my performance review."

"Dollface," Nikki said again more urgently.

"Yeah, yeah." I stood up and stepped back from the doctor and his patient, pulling off my feathered cape. By now, the sound of sirens had chased away most of Balestri's employees, and the ones that remained didn't look too happy. I moved with Nikki across the courtyard to a shadowy alcove, and she removed her cape as well. We dumped them by the wall. Both of us still wore masks, as did most of the people left in the courtyard. It was an odd sensation of feeling completely hidden and protected while still being exposed in a crowd. Maybe that was why the masks had become so popular.

"You got a fix on Valetti's balcony?" Nikki asked. "I don't think it's a good idea for us to head back down the alley. Somebody will definitely be watching at this point."

"Agreed." I'd no sooner placed my hand on her arm when a sudden commotion behind us drew our attention once again. A half-choked scream broke off as Balestri lurched to his feet again, wheeling around toward me. He had a gun in his hand.

"Gun!" Nikki shouted, shifting in front of me to block the bullet. Never mind the fact that I was the one who could heal myself.

When Balestri saw me, however, he stilled, his mouth gaping open beneath his mask. He tried to speak, but his mouth seemed to have difficulty forming the words.

And then it didn't.

"The Red King will be the strongest in all of Venice!" Balestri intoned in a terrible voice that was nowhere near his own. Beneath his half-mask, his face seemed to morph as well, as if a hive of bees swarmed beneath the skin, and his lips parted in a terrible grimace as he groaned his next words. He looked for all the world like a man possessed, but how? "And as it goes in Venice, so goes the world. If you seek the path of the Red King, follow the bodies of the greatest magicians in the city—until you reach the one who is greater than them all. I look forward to your hunt."

He put the gun into his mouth, and fired.

Chapter Thirteen

"I cannot apologize enough." Valetti's hand shook as he set his teacup into its saucer. "Police were knocking on doors until the sun was practically risen again. I am so sorry for the disturbance, I assure you this is one of the quietest neighborhoods in Venice. Disruptions such as this simply do not happen in this area. The families are old and well respected. The police, some of them, do not respect the old ways the way they should."

There was an odd note of privilege in Valetti's voice that I hadn't heard before, layered with a genteel outrage, as if the normal course of business for the police was simply something not to be borne by this neighborhood in particular. I eyed him over my espresso, my third of the still-early morning. "How well did you know Signore Balestri?"

"Not well, not well at all," Valetti dismissed with a casual wave. "I knew him in the way of neighbors. We were friendly, of course. He was a part of the neighborhood, and we respected each other's position in the city."

"He was Connected," I said bluntly. "A magician."

"Ah, well, we all in Venice are Connected to some degree or another, don't you think?" Valetti's smile had turned a bit condescending. Interesting. "As to being a magician, well… Signore Balestri liked to style himself in the mode of a pure-blooded magician, yes. However, he was more, how would you say, *grandfathered* into the role. His family was one that had long held a position of power in the senate, and that accorded him some measure of respect."

"How many people make up this senate thing?" Nikki asked.

Another hand wave. "We have a long and glorious history of which we are perhaps a bit too proud. But I'm afraid the reputation of Fabrizio Balestri did no favors to his family legacy. He was known as a debaucher who would use what little Connected ability he had to manipulate the unwitting into purchasing a string of designer technoceuticals he'd manufactured in boutique supply." He glanced up, catching my confused expression. "It's become quite fashionable in Europe, and arguably in Venice for quite a bit longer. We do tend to set the trends rather than follow them."

"Of course," I murmured, but Valetti either didn't catch my sarcasm or didn't understand it. He continued on.

"Obviously, setting oneself up as a drug kingpin requires a great deal of work and organization. So even those of us who have the means and the capability of recognizing true magical compounds when we see them, and who could then synthesize them into distributable form, it is too much, you see? Yet it is tempting to step into this scene at least in part, if only to provide a glimpse of what's possible to those who cannot achieve psychic greatness on their own."

"This city is filled with humanitarians," Nikki muttered.

"So, Balestri was one of these boutique suppliers," I said, turning the phrase around in my mind. I had to admit, I liked it. "You make just enough product for a very limited distribution. Your advertisement is word of mouth, and your clientele is very exclusive." It wasn't so different from Leonardo and Rocky Mountain Ricky when I thought about it. They were the end of a very long supply chain, but in their own little neck of the woods, they could run their business however they saw fit. And catering to a group of vetted, proven regulars, was a better business model no matter what the product.

"Indeed," Valetti said. "You can see the appeal, and Signore Balestri proved not to be able to resist it. I cannot fault the man for that. If it weren't for his other flaws, it would have been a benign indiscretion. Nothing more. But he insisted on going further, pushing the boundaries of taste and decorum." He sighed with false regret. "It's perhaps no wonder that he drew the attention of some senior dark practitioner, no doubt irritated that he was moving in on his turf, as they say."

I exchanged a quick glance with Nikki. "Wait a minute. You think this death is a one-off? You don't think it has anything to do with threats that are facing the magicians in the city?"

"Signore Balestri? Oh, I can't even imagine. And if so, then allow me to be the first to say how terribly sorry I am for bringing you all this distance, and how even sorrier I am that I called in a favor from Signore Stone to make it happen. Because if the threat that I believe is stalking Venice's canals and byways is truly so indiscriminate as to strike down Fabrizio Balestri, then it is not only the elite who have the issue. In fact, it is not the elite at all. We have nothing to worry about."

I eyed my espresso with dismay. Valetti was making less sense as the morning went on, not more.

Fortunately, Nikki was still tracking him. "You're saying that if this was the work of the butcher of Venice, he suddenly isn't as scary a perpetrator, because he's not targeting the top-level magicians anymore."

"He could as easily strike a common prostitute next and it would no longer be a surprise. Not that that wouldn't be a horrible turn of events, of course," Valetti said hurriedly. "I merely mean that the method to dispatch such a criminal suddenly would move from a pair of tweezers to a hammer."

One thing about Valetti, he certainly had a distinctive turn of phrase. I debated asking him about the Red King, but hesitated. There was something more to Balestri than Valetti was letting on—the man had been a high-level Connected, even if all those systems had gone dark within him by the time I'd reached him. And he had a recipe book. Why was Valetti downplaying him so much?

Valetti looked up as a new man entered the room, a staffer who held out his phone with a gloved hand. "The prelate, Count Valetti," he said quietly. "He is quite ready for you, at your convenience. He wishes you to call him directly."

"Excellent." Valetti beamed as he rose. He turned to us. "I'm pleased to share we will have all your questions answered in short order this morning and be able to put your mind to rest regarding Signore Balestri's unfortunate death as being any part of our larger question. The prelate is in a unique position to assist in our efforts. We'll go to see him now. If you'll excuse me, I'll make this call and then meet you in the foyer?"

Without waiting for us to respond, Valetti tapped on his phone and held the unit up to his ear, quickly striding away. The phone call connected, and a murmured wave of melodic Italian drifted behind him on the lilac-scented breeze.

"There are so many things wrong with what we just heard, I'm having trouble keeping up," Nikki observed.

"I'm right there with you."

We stood as well, keeping our voices low as Valetti's staff came in to clear away the breakfast dishes. We were already dressed for the day, so we headed immediately down to the foyer. It was a small but elegantly appointed room, and we were more or less alone except for the doorman, who, not too surprisingly, hovered near the door.

Nikki sidled closer to me. Today, she wore a feminine Italian business suit in deep black, the jacket cinched at the waist. On her feet were four-inch pink leather platform heels, or, as Nikki liked to refer to them, walking shoes. "I asked Council HQ to give me the lowdown on this prelate guy. Simon was all over it."

"I can imagine." Simon was one of the newest members of the Council, a former addict and gray hat who had ascended to the position of Fool of the Arcana Council in the late 1980s after he'd cleaned up. In addition to adding a certain looseness of style that the Council sorely needed, he also was a tech wizard of remarkable skill. He kept the Council fully wired and was able to track nearly anyone through the various iterations of the internet that circled the globe, dark web and arcane web included. "How deep did he have to go?"

"Not all that deep. Ol' Prelate Patrick had plenty of information available from the most basic of Google searches."

"Please tell me his name really isn't Patrick."

"It's not." She grinned. "But that sounds better then Prelate Alfonse. Anyway, the prelate has been custodian of the Casino of Spirits for the past decade. It's a quiet job, given over mostly to maintaining the research library and allowing tours every so often. The library is for members of any established religious order, and it contains texts on world religions that are considered to be quite extensive."

"A haunted house seems like an odd place for a library."

"From what Simon was able to gather, its relative remoteness and less than ideal location was chosen quite deliberately. The church didn't want to give the arcane texts more power than they really deserved by outright banning them, and they were too well-known to simply be destroyed. So shutting them up in a tiny little building which is difficult to access, not to mention haunted, tends to cut down on the curiosity seekers. And it became known that those who frequented the Casino of Spirits were put on a watch list by their sponsoring order, which also helped cut down on patronage."

"A watch list seems a lot worse than your standard library fine."

"You're not kidding. It doesn't stop inquiries, though. Most of the searches tend to be along the lines of identifying specific demons in a spiritual practice's deep mythology. And perhaps not surprisingly, there's been a noticeable uptick in those types of searches in the last few weeks. Simon suggested that the prelate might have some questions for you on that topic."

I lifted my brows. "The prelate knows I'm involved with the rash of demons that's hit the planet?"

Nikki snorted. "Honey, everyone north of the equator knows you're involved with that. But bottom line, the prelate himself isn't so much an enigma as boring as shit. Started out as a Catholic priest in the requisite tiny little town in Italy, moved up to becoming an administrator at the Vatican, ran afoul of some church staff realignment—though it seems a benign issue, not that he caught the pope's robes on fire or anything—and he got put on spook duty. That was ten years ago, and he's been here ever since. He's allowed himself to let his freak flag fly a bit more in the subsequent years, but only among close friends."

I grimaced. "That's all Simon could find?"

"That's all we've got so far, yup. Simon texted me some family stuff that might have bearing—Alfonse's family used to live in Venice during the Middle Ages, a fair number of them priests. Then again, a fair number of everybody's families seemed like they were priests in the Middle Ages."

"Beats working in the fields, I guess."

"And you never needed to worry about what to wear."

Valetti chose that moment to interrupt our conversation, and we were out the door and onto his private pier a few moments later, where a small motorboat waited for us.

"It is a beautiful day, and there are so many tourists in the city. This is easier than walking, especially when we get into open water." He smiled with his usual self-deprecation. "And, too, if we are followed, we will know it much more quickly in a boat, yes?"

This made perfect sense, and I certainly didn't mind the open-air transportation. Today, none of us were wearing masks. However, by the time we entered the Grand Canal, I realized that our lack of costumes put us so much in the minority, I began to feel seriously underdressed.

As we left the canals and moved into the shallow Venetian lagoon, I was gripped by an undeniable apprehension. I scowled down at the water, reminding myself that it was only a few meters deep. Deep enough to drown in, sure, but it wasn't like we were boating over the Mariana Trench. I didn't really have anything to worry about. And I could swim, technically, though that was a recent development. I didn't want to test that skill out right now to see if it remained with me.

Pushing those thoughts away, I turned to Valetti. "Carnevale starts tonight, right? The big parade or whatever?"

"The opening ceremony is tonight, and the parade is tomorrow. Piazza San Marco will be overrun for the next two weeks. The balls commence at the same time, both the public ones and the more private ones." He gave me what could only be a pitying glance. "I can get you tickets into some of the events, but some, I'm afraid, are invitation only and quite exclusive."

"I'll try to conceal my disappointment."

Once again, he didn't seem to understand the sarcasm for what it was and instead nodded encouragingly. Beside me, Nikki turned away to stare out over the lagoon, and I watched her shoulders tremble with quiet laughter.

We arrived at the Casino of Spirits a half hour later, Valetti making good on his intention to ensure we were not being tailed. The building itself was not all that prepossessing, a thought that made me smirk, though it was pretty in its own way: a three-story rose-brick row house rising in front of us, with a view that gave way to a private dock and a more traditional church-like building plus several other smaller structures on the far side.

Standing on the dock were two men, both in coordinating priest's robes, both looking like they routinely accepted visitors on the front dock, though we were the only boat venturing close.

"Why aren't the others trying this?" I asked, peering over at the tourists who were staring at us, cameras poised. I turned away, once more regretting that we weren't wearing masks.

"Because their pilots know they will be refused. You come to the private dock of the Casino of the Spirits by invitation only. Otherwise, there is a public entrance at the front." Valetti gave a dismissive wave. I was beginning to think dismissive waves were the Venetian salute.

I turned my attention to the men waiting to greet us. The prelate in his emerald-green robes stood taller and straighter than the black-frocked priest beside him, thin and angular beneath robes that seemed a size or two too big. His face was gaunt and unsmiling as we pulled up, and I waited until Nikki had clambered out of the boat and turned to me before letting myself be hauled onto the dock. When my feet were on more or less steady ground, I turned to the prelate.

"Justice Wilde," he said without preamble, his hard gaze narrowing on me intently. "You've been busy."

CHAPTER FOURTEEN

"Alfonse the Prelate." I stared back at him. "You've been snooping."

A quick, surprised smile flashed across the man's taciturn face, then he was back to his Sam the Eagle routine. "Count Valetti has explained at length his concerns regarding a potential attack during Carnevale, and your potential aid in stopping it. I can shed some light—but only some. I suspect the count's fears are overstated."

I blinked. That wasn't exactly a whole-hearted endorsement of the senate's head of security. "I certainly hope you're right," I offered.

"Alfonse is at heart a pragmatist," Valetti interjected with an almost fatherly indulgence, though from what I could tell, the men were contemporaries. "He is forever debunking our overwrought concerns, even mine, which are perhaps more well-grounded than most."

Alfonse turned his cool gaze on Valetti, then slanted his attention back to me. "We can go inside. It's a far more comfortable place to have a conversation."

We turned and moved toward the great doors of the casino. "I trust Count Valetti has given you the history of our fair library?" he asked.

"The highlights." I nodded.

"Then allow me to fill in what I may." I didn't really need the dime tour, but it seemed like everyone in Venice was one coin slot away from becoming a perpetual-loop visitor's guide. "What we think of as the casino is technically the annex building of the Palazzo Contarini dal Zaffo, which belonged to Joseph Contarini in the sixteenth century. While in its earliest days the casino got its name from being a boisterous house of entertainment, over the years that description morphed into one far more sinister. That the casino is an accursed place, filled with ghosts."

"Are there cemeteries on the grounds?" I asked.

"There are undoubtedly some souls buried within these walls," the prelate said cryptically, because—of course he would. "But Venice as a city was devastated by the bubonic plague several times over. There have been many deaths on this lagoon that could give rise to the spirits that are believed to haunt this building. The most famous ghost we are credited with is that of Luzzo, a painter from the sixteenth century. As the legend goes, Luzzo used to meet in one of the rooms with Giorgione, Titian, and Sansovino. He was madly in love with one of the lovers of Giorgione, a young woman named Cecilia—and she did not return his affections. Some say he committed suicide in despair, but in any event, he returns from time to time, seeking her still."

"Such a tragedy," murmured Valetti. I cocked an amused glance at him.

"Granted, most of the rumors began because of the building's isolated location and the sound of the lagoon water in constant motion, as well as the frequent breeze that whistles along the stones. But the stories add a bit of color to the place."

"Valetti mentioned that there are essentially two sections to the casino," I said, trying to steer the conversation to more useful areas. "Will we be able to use the library, or is it occupied?"

"We always have researchers from one religious doctrine or another seeking answers they cannot find elsewhere in the world." Alfonse nodded. "They won't disturb us, however. And the public tours are finished for the morning. Come this way."

We entered the cool quiet space of the casino, moving down hallways that were largely unadorned. You could tell the space had once been meant for social gathering, but now it looked much like what it was, a haven for study and retreat.

"Do you enjoy it here?" I asked, breaking the stillness that had begun to encroach around us.

Alfonse glanced my way. "It isn't for me to enjoy or not enjoy a mission for the church. My duty is to protect this place and serve those who come here."

"And to keep the lore of the city updated," Valetti cut in with a little more strength to his voice then seemed necessary.

Alfonse, for his part, merely shrugged. "I am happy to serve the senate in the way that also brings the greatest glory to this space and to God. No matter how that may best be accomplished."

He said this last bit directly to Valetti, who continued to eye him with something that now approached suspicion. Apparently unfazed, Alfonse turned back to me. "I am most interested in what *you* would be willing to share, Justice Wilde. I find my information on the history of your organization is severely lacking."

My brows went up, but before I could respond, Alfonse glanced down the corridor. "Ah, here we are," he said. We entered a doorway flanked by two tall pillars, one light, one dark. Then Alfonse ushered us into a room that looked like a party hall for monks. There was a long wooden table with benches on either side, the wood polished and worn to a soft sheen. No artwork adorned the walls, but shelves of books lined the space, most of the titles looking old and esoteric. Three doors were cut into the far wall alongside all the books, and surmounting the doors were carved flowers—presumably the patron flowers of Italy. I could make out a rose, a lily, and some little scrubby-looking flowers. Poppies, maybe.

"You don't preserve any of your history in digital format?" I asked, thinking of Mrs. French and the antiquated though certifiably operational pneumatic tube system in my office. What was it about curators of the arcane that prompted them to err on the side of the archaic when it came to their storage processes? "What if there's a fire?"

"Perish the thought, but of course you are correct. We do have a fully digitized file system of all the artifacts in this museum. Translated into English at a minimum, other languages as befits their origins. That said, the experience of the old texts is as much in their tactile sensation as it is in the content of their scripts. We find that those who come to research here crave the full experience."

"Got it." It didn't explain the group's aversion to email, but at least it made sense in terms of accessing ancient books. It also allowed me to bypass any farce of reading library books while we were here. Simon would be able to download the entire collection in a blink, and we could search the contents at our leisure—assuming they were accurate translations. The Arcana Council had its own library of the mystical and absurd, I knew.

There'd be enough overlapping texts that we'd be able to see if the prelate had been abridging the electronic versions of the sacred texts, and how.

We took our positions at the table, and I noticed that Alfonse didn't offer us any refreshments. Probably a good thing, with priceless books not three feet away.

The prelate laid his hands on the table and stared at them, seeming to organize his thoughts as he regarded his fingertips. Then he lifted his gaze and spoke.

"Valetti advised that your Council has grown concerned about the events in Venice this past fortnight, particularly as they relate to the resurgence of interest around the butcher of Venice."

I glanced at Valetti sharply. He made a gesture as if to say, go with it. I went.

"You know that tale, I'm sure," Alfonse continued.

"The basics," I allowed.

"The basics are all that's necessary. The butcher ran a sausage and stew shop and was known in many circles as a closet alchemist and sorcerer. The general public, of course, had no knowledge of this. Neither did the ruling Council of Venice at the time—neither the magicians' senate, nor the official city government. And so they were all caught off guard when a stonemason found the finger of a small child in his soup—complete with the nail."

I grimaced. No matter how often I heard this tale, it never got any better.

"Upon searching the butcher's kitchens, the authorities found the remains of other humans, predominately children. The butcher was arrested, tortured, dismembered, and ultimately put to death. However, because his crimes were so heinous, he lives on in the popular imagination of Venetians and tourists alike. The butcher's shop was demolished, of course, and there's only the street named after him that can center the public's focus. He should have been forgotten long ago. He's of no concern now."

"Okay, so why is someone distributing recipe booklets with parts redacted and attributing it to this guy?" I remained acutely aware of the recipe book I'd received from Balestri's doctor, which I hadn't shared with Valetti. I'd spent most of the previous night reading it, and I was itching to get my hands on a second one.

"Publicity? Variety? It could be any number of things. But I have examined the recipe booklet that Count Valetti received and a few of the others, and I have found that though they are bound with aged leather, they have been written on thoroughly modern paper, with a modern hand. The directions for the preparation of the stew in question are admittedly written in a more archaic format, but nothing more than it would take anyone with access to the internet or old books to cobble together pretty quickly based on other recipes from the time."

"Alfonse," Valetti said quietly, almost reprovingly. "You cannot dispute that more members of the community than we know received such a book. Even members who have done their level best not to be known outside our number as magicians."

"Where are you keeping the books you've received, anyway?" I piped up. "It'd be helpful to take a look at them."

That reasonable request seemed to catch the prelate off guard. "Why?" he asked. "I've told you what the contents are."

"Yeah, well, this is a library, and those are books," I said, the soul of reason. "Surely you have them here."

"Of course I do," the prelate huffed. Even Valetti was eyeing him oddly now, and I didn't miss the thread of concern that skated across the count's face. These two guys might or might not like each other, but they definitely weren't pals.

"It's a fair request, Alfonse. What have you done with the books?"

"They are safe, there," Alfonse said, pointing to a box that looked like a receptacle for donations at church—very narrow opening on the top, heavy padlock on the side. No one was getting in there without a key. "And despite what you believe, Count Valetti, there have been only four copies recovered. I've only your insistence that there are others out there."

Valetti looked mutinous, and it was all I could do not to toss my own recipe book on the table. But the prelate kept going. "As I've said before, I am less worried about the return of a medieval butcher and far more about the possibility of disaffection within our ranks."

Valetti exhaled with irritation. "I don't know why you are resisting this idea so much. It is getting in the way of solving this problem before another one of our own is struck."

"The magicians of Venice are not getting targeted," snapped the prelate, with more energy than I'd seen him display so far. "The senate has become a bored lot of fools who are searching for meaning outside of ourselves, irritated that other factions of the arcane community have outdistanced us in utilizing their magical abilities to manipulate others."

Something must have flickered on Valetti's face, because Alfonse smiled. It wasn't a good smile. "Yes, Count Valetti, I listen to the murmurs of our members on occasion. I understand the challenges that the magicians of this community face, and I applaud you for holding the line for as long as you have. But even if you cave and enter the drug trade, that's not something you require my assistance for—or the assistance of a hired killer."

He gestured toward me, and I found myself resisting the urge to look behind me, in case there was someone standing there I didn't know about. Hired killer? "Um, I don't typically—"

"Dammit, Alfonse," Valetti growled. "Do I have to spell it out for you? Signore Balestri died last night. In his own house. By his own hand."

"I heard about that," Alfonse said, while I struggled and failed not to stare at Valetti. "But suicide is hardly—"

"I thought you said Balestri's death was unrelated," I interrupted.

Valetti glanced at me, his eyes as cold as a cop's. "It wasn't my place to brief you on the larger plot at hand. It's the *prelate's*. The less information coming from me, the better. That doesn't mean I don't know the information. It merely wasn't my place to share it with you."

He returned his glare to Alfonse. "What's more important, Signore Balestri wasn't the only magician in his house last night. And he may not be the only one who died."

That seemed to get Alfonse's attention. It certainly caught mine. "I wasn't informed of this," Alfonse said. I glanced to Nikki. We hadn't been informed either. And I'd been right there.

"Well, I'm informing you of it now," Valetti said. "Two other magicians of the senate are unaccounted for and were last seen entering Signore Balestri's home yesterday afternoon, the Englishers Greaves and

Marrow. They've not made contact and cannot be tracked by any of our seers. And they'd be noticed too. They wear costumes that echo the Union Jack flag wherever they go. It is the strong suspicion of many senate members that they will turn up again, but in pieces, no doubt as part of a much more modern blend of the butcher's stew, making it even more magically potent."

I frowned. Something about this didn't add up.

"But you see, that is the problem," Alfonse murmured, seeming to agree with me. "That wasn't the nature of the stew the butcher of Venice created."

"Speaking of stews, how about we check out some recipes," I suggested as cajolingly as I could. "I'm Justice of the Arcana Council. I know my way around a book of spells."

Alfonse blanched but didn't make any move toward the locked box, and my temper snapped.

"Okay, enough of this. I've got another copy of the damned book." I pulled the leather-bound recipe book free of my jacket and waved it in the air. Valetti practically lurched for the book, and I stepped back sharply.

"No," I said, shoving the book back in my pocket. "Not if you don't share first. But this book was given to Balestri at some point in the last two weeks, and now the man is dead. And I'm here to tell you, he was *not* augmented. Far from it."

"How can you know that? Who gave you that book?" The prelate whirled on me, his demeanor completely transformed. Gone was the air of perplexed studiousness. Instead he stepped toward me, his manner intent. "Has anyone examined the body of Signore Balestri?"

"No, they have *not*," Valetti said, still glaring at me. "It hasn't yet been released from the police, and his family is clamoring for an autopsy, though eyewitness accounts corroborate suicide as cause of death. Where did you get that book? Who gave it to you?"

"Let's say that Signore Balestri's death wasn't a simple suicide," I hedged. "Let's further say that he was drugged by the same person who sent you the butcher's recipe books and something terrible happened to his brain, which led him to take his own life. How does that change things?"

The prelate blew out a deep breath, straightening. With two quick strides, he reached the lockbox. Pulling a key from his belt, he unlocked the box, and took out four small leather-bound volumes. Their exteriors were identical to the one in my pocket. But what about the interiors?

He turned back to me, his gaze hollow. "If that is the case, then I owe the senate a sincere apology for not acting sooner. Because the information we gathered regarding the butcher of Venice back in the 1500s made it very clear what we were looking at. Biasio Cargnio was no ordinary sorcerer, even if he did seem to aspire quite sincerely to become a member of the senate of magicians. But by all accounts, he was a sorcerer who employed Nul Magis, and one of the most powerful strains of the toxin that has ever been recorded."

"Nul Magis?" Nikki took one for the team and acted stupid so I didn't have to, but I was now staring at the prelate too. I'd never heard the term Nul Magis. Knowing what I did about what had happened to Balestri, however, I could guess the rest.

The prelate didn't keep us waiting. "All of magic is geared toward one thing in the main," he said. "The making of more magic. The Philosopher's Stone, the search for any number of elixirs of immortality, of the Ark of the Covenant, the Holy Grail. The heralded searches for these artifacts were undertaken with the uniform intention to use the power found—at least when magicians were doing the searching. Obviously, throughout the centuries, religious organizations have striven to eradicate all that is magic in the world, at least that magic which was not supposedly generated by their own god."

I grimaced. I'd come up against those kinds of religious organizations. They didn't give up easy.

"But that's not what we are dealing with here. A magician willing to use Nul Magis, a poison created solely to eradicate the magic or cut the psychic thread in a Connected, is a danger of inestimable proportions. The desire to destroy the creative spark is counter to all those who aspire to magic. As diabolical as dark practitioners can be, their aim is always more, more, more. Not less. Never less. An eradication of power serves no one. Magic can be grown, but it cannot be created out of thin air. There must always be a wellspring. Drain enough of those springs, and it has an exponential effect."

Valetti stared at the prelate. "And you mean to tell me you have no idea who this new practitioner using Nul Magis might be, or how he or she is employing the toxin to eradicate magic, specifically?" he demanded, his voice shrill. "We have traditions we need to keep up, Alfonse. Ceremonies. I can't have all the magicians fleeing Venice because we can't keep our local population in check. I'll be a laughingstock, and I'll lose my position on the senate."

Again with the senate. These guys were worse than the Elks. "You want to explain this senate to me, Count Valetti, while we're up? It's not in my tour guide."

"Of course, of course." But it was Alfonse who spoke, not Valetti. "It's the senate of magicians, the highest and most elite organization of its kind in the world. Even your own Arcana Council is not made up entirely of magicians, Signorina Wilde, so you can see the difference."

"Sure." I nodded. A senate full of Armaeus Bertrand wannabes. It sounded awful.

"The senate gathers once per year in the open, as it has done since it was formed in the twelfth century, utilizing the only place in the world it can hide in plain sight."

"Venice," I said.

"More specifically, the festival of Carnevale. Instituted by the first magicians in 1162 to capitalize on a very convenient victory against an abysmal patriarch and the grace of an open-minded public."

"Okay, so you've got everybody who's anybody coming into town, and you've got a killer on the loose who may or may not be a reincarnation of the butcher of Venice, who may or may not be trying to snuff out magic in the best of magicians—"

"Signore Balestri was by no means one of the best," huffed Valetti, but I put up a hand to shut him up.

"And who may or may not be the Red King."

"The what?" the prelate snapped, his gaze sharpening on me.

"Alfonse, Alfonse." Now it was Valetti's turn to put his hands up. We were a walking Christian revival camp, but he turned to the prelate with an unmistakably placating attitude. "That title comes up every few years. You know that."

"It has not come up since I began as prelate," Alfonse growled. Nikki and I glanced at each other, equally mystified.

Alfonse didn't miss our confusion. "Forgive me, Signorina Wilde. The Red King is—well, it speaks to a practitioner who was an abomination to magicians in the senate. Our darkest, most heinous moment in history." Valetti, now mute, watched him impassively.

I took that in. From Armaeus's description, the title had started out as something positive—but apparently, that was a long time ago. "So you're not a fan, I take it."

The prelate's smile was weary. "A fair assessment, and I'll thank you not to share that title with anyone else. Though we should both sit now and compare our books. It would seem that there's more to Valetti's concerns than I have wanted to believe."

He sighed as Valetti reached out to pat him on the shoulder.

"You were right, Count Valetti," Alfonse continued. "We have held this matter too closely between ourselves. It is time we gave it the attention it deserved, so that all might understand there is a powerful and deadly sorcerer in our midst."

Valetti practically preened, and I watched him, intrigued. Clearly, this guy did not get nearly enough attention as head of security.

The prelate swung his gaze back to me. "Tonight, Justice Wilde, you shall join us for this year's opening convocation of the senate of magicians, on the first night of Carnevale."

CHAPTER FIFTEEN

"You guys have your own party?"

It was Valetti who answered. "As I mentioned, there are many celebrations that circle around Carnevale. Some of them are public and some—" another hand wave, "are quite private. I am regrettably not in a position to extend invitations on behalf of the senate, but thankfully for us all, the prelate is."

"Which explains the suddenness and urgency of your visit." The prelate nodded. The look he turned on Valetti was one of new appreciation. "When I heard of Signore Balestri's death, I suspected I would be contacted, but not by you. You've made no secret of your disdain for his tactics."

"Disdain is a bit harsh," Valetti sighed. "And the man is dead, which weighs heavily on me, make no mistake. I didn't approve of his little drug sideline, I will say that. I had no idea it would lead him to this impasse, though. It's simply dreadful."

"You aren't the only one who disapproved of Balestri's emporium," Alfonse assured him sympathetically. "We are old families whose histories have deeply intertwined in this city. It's reasonable to think that the new generations will maintain the decorum of the old. Reasonable, but not always possible. We can't know what troubles haunted Signore Balestri to drive him to such an action."

Valetti opened his mouth as if to respond, then shut it. I had the feeling he knew exactly what had driven Balestri to his actions, his impasse, and his untimely death. They'd been neighbors, and despite what anyone was admitting to, some neighbors knew a lot about each other.

Still, Valetti was also a man of decency in the end. "We will honor him tonight, if we might, Prelate Alfonse. He wanted nothing more than to advance in the eyes of his peers."

The prelate nodded. "We will honor him tonight."

Valetti swung his gaze to Nikki and me. "As I'm sure won't come as a surprise to you, we are an old and storied group, steeped in our traditions. Did you bring a traditional Venetian costume with you?"

I started to respond, but Nikki beat me to it. "What we brought was meant to blend, which I can already see was the wrong idea," she said, shaking her head with such authentic regret that I blinked at her. For one thing, we absolutely hadn't brought costumes. For another, Nikki had never intended to *blend* in her life. "So what we need is a tailor of the highest caliber who is willing to work at the last minute for an unreasonable amount of money. I don't suppose you happen to know anyone who'd fit that bill?"

The prelate, to my surprise, didn't seem fazed. "There are two tailors in the city I recommend for exactly that." He eyed Valetti. "Unless you have a suggestion?"

"When I've had a similar problem in the past, I've gone to Signore Gazie. He is the best in the city, simply the best. And we have an account with him. You can trust him to be discreet."

"Completely discreet." The prelate nodded. "There is also Signorina d'Eauchamp. She's French, of course, but we have come to terms with that over the years. She will serve you well."

I glanced at Valetti, and he nodded his agreement. "They'll both know the requirements for the capes as well."

"Requirements?" Nikki raised her brows. "A costume party with rules. I excel at these."

"You'll find these easy to meet," the prelate said, flashing another of what I expected was a rare smile. Nikki had that effect on people. "The cape itself must be full body, so there is no indication of whether you are a man or a woman. Footwear, I'm afraid, must be a knee-length, flat-soled black boot."

"A riding boot," I interjected, truly surprised. The unisex cape made sense, but... "Are we meeting on horseback?"

"We are not, but the earliest members of our group were prepared to ride at a moment's notice should their convocation be discovered. The style became part of the accepted attire, and is now considered an easy indicator—but not too easy. You'll find many in the streets have black boots beneath their capes to manage the cobbled streets without resorting to athletic shoes."

"Amateurs," sniffed Nikki.

"But the most important element of the costume is the hat and mask. Both are required. For the hat, please select a tricorn with any ornamentation you desire, so long as it doesn't prove a hindrance to you. Where we'll be meeting is a building rife with old passageways that were built on a rather small scale."

"Done," I said. "And the mask?"

"Definitely nothing from the Commedia dell'Arte," the prelate instructed. "Those are all half masks except for the pierrot, and not as steeped in the tradition of the earliest days of Carnevale." Another self-deprecating grimace. "We're fond of our traditions, as I suspect you've already noted."

"Our traditions have saved our lives and made our fortunes," Valetti said, and the prelate nodded as if it was another inalienable truth.

"Bauta is the most prevalent mask during Carnevale, but any of the fuller-face masks will suffice—the dama, jester, volto, or dottore peste. Your mouth and lower face may be exposed, if you wish, but many of these masks do a good job of effectively obscuring detail, which is the goal. Either Signore Gazie or Signorina d'Eauchamp will have these at your disposal. They always keep a certain number back for emergencies, of which there are a surprising number at Carnevale."

"Good enough, thanks. But when we leave here today, we should exit through the public access area, if it's all the same with you. It wouldn't hurt for us to walk our way to the costumers' shops."

"They're quite close to each other. You have a street map?"

"Always," Nikki said, patting her bag. It was a Bottega Veneta, and she tended to pat it a lot.

"I'll give you the street names. Otherwise, we meet tonight at nine p.m. at this address." Valetti rattled off the digits, and Nikki obligingly spoke it into her phone, then tucked the device back in her expensive purse.

Alfonse lofted one of the recipe books, his rueful smile creasing his face. "Shall we compare the books?" he asked. "Sadly, we have enough to go around."

I pulled mine out as well, the moment feeling almost eerie, as if both the Arcana Council and the senate of magicians were holding their breaths. "We should."

We sat down at the table, and opened the booklets…

Which were exactly alike.

Exactly.

Alfonse sighed after reviewing several pages of two of the thirty-page booklets, then glanced at Valetti. "Once again, they are the same, Vittore. Was it not you who told me there were differences in the books?"

"I…" The count looked equally mystified, blinking several times. "I did say as much, but I have never seen two side by side. I was going only by the whispers and mutterings on the street."

"Some could be different, some the same?" Nikki offered. She was standing away from our hunched bodies—me in the center, the two magicians on either side of me. It was getting a little claustrophobic, especially with all the Latin. And there was something about the recipes that were tugging at me, the graceful alternating lengths of calligraphied letters tickling a deeply buried synapse. "Though having five dupes does seem to argue against that."

"Maybe." Alfonse sat back. "There's no denying the key ingredient, though. It appears over and over again." He pointed to a phrase that wasn't what I had snagged on—which had to do with a kidney—and tapped it.

I squinted down. "Tenebrus Sanguine," I recited. "Dark blood? What's that mean, fresh?"

"Most likely," Valetti huffed. "Or the blood of a criminal."

"Or the damned." Alfonse nodded, tapping his chin. "The butcher himself would qualify with the atrocities he committed. And the requirements for each of these recipes were not so stringent that he couldn't supply the ingredient himself."

I didn't even try to hide my disgust as he and Valetti fell into animated conversation over the possibility of the butcher supplying his own blood to his dastardly recipes. Magicians. Always had to take things one step further.

But there were no additional discoveries to be made from the books, at least not that uncovered the mystery my mind kept tugging at. Over the prelate's disapproval, I kept Balestri's copy, and a few minutes later, the four of us wound our way without further conversation back through the darkened rooms of the Casino of Spirits. I was disappointed there wasn't even the hint of any ghostly apparitions. Then again, it was full daylight. I suspected the hauntings of Venice were far more prevalent at night.

A few minutes later, we were back in the bright daylight of the courtyard of the Casino of Spirits, but on the land side of the building. The prelate and Valetti didn't exit with us, still arguing over how much blood a man could drain from his own body without lasting damage. I was happy to be away from them both, frankly. We had our marching orders, and we had our plans.

"So…that was weird," Nikki muttered. "We've got the prelate now convinced that the butcher is a real deal and walking the streets of Venice passing out recipe books, Count Valetti basking in approval over being proven right, and an invite to what's got to be the weirdest costume party on the planet tonight."

"And both magicians were being super creepy about blood—and super dismissive about the title of Red King."

"Yeah, I noticed that," Nikki agreed. "Something bad went down in the Middle Ages around that name, that much is clear, but what?"

"The library!" I stopped short on the cobblestoned street, causing her to lurch to a halt beside me.

"The what?"

"Contact Mrs. French, and have her look in the library for…uh…" I frowned, trying to remember the line of arcane books I'd seen while recovering from my gunshot wound. "Hell, I don't know where they were. But have her look up any dark practitioner cases from the sixteenth century, and see if she can get any hits on the Red King."

"Hits?" Nikki asked, though her eyes lit with understanding. "You know she doesn't have those books digitized."

"She's got to have some sort of filing system—ask her," I insisted. "There's got to be some mention of it if the mere title upset Alfonse that much."

"Totally with you there." Nikki obligingly pulled out her phone, keying in the text. "I'll have her send me any intel via phone."

"Excellent." I watched her type for a few seconds. "You figure out where Alfonse and Valetti wanted to send us?"

She nodded. "I did, but I'm pretty sure Simon can do us one better with an Arcana Council-approved costumer. That prelate gave me the willies."

"He did? I thought you were charmed by him."

"How could I possibly be charmed by anyone who thinks I should be wearing riding boots?" Nikki retorted. "I have never in the history of my *life* had to rock riding boots. They have no heel whatsoever! I might as well be wearing flip-flops."

She continued to grumble as she typed furiously on her phone, then scrolled over to another screen. A moment later, she stopped. "Oh! Well, that'll work nicely."

"What?"

Her phone dinged, and she grinned, waving the device at me. "Platform riding boots. But hold please, more important matters. We've got our Arcana Council-approved costumer." She scrolled down her return text from, I assumed, Simon and chortled. "He even gave me the names of the woman's grandchildren. God love that boy. If he wasn't so damned young, I'd kiss him the next time I saw him."

I slanted her a look. "He's older than you are. A lot older."

"Not in any of the ways that count." She strode ahead as we reached the main canal and ordered us an honest-to-God gondola.

Though only a few people on the banks of the canal were dressed in capes or obvious costumes, half the crowd we passed was wearing masks, but the opening ceremonies for the carnival were still several hours away. Still, it was a little unnerving to see so many blank faces intermingling in the crowd. I began to imagine what it must have been like for the nobility and lower classes alike to be able to don inexpensive masks and go out among each other as equals. I suspected there was a lot of partying going on whenever the masks came out.

Nikki and I kept our conversation light and undirected while we floated down the Grand Canal. It was clearly a popular pastime, but I didn't see any familiar faces. Or, perhaps more importantly, I didn't see any faces more than once. I saw a lot of absolutely identical masks, but their surrounds always varied slightly—from feathers to velvets, to hats to hoods.

We disembarked from the gondola stand a few minutes later and wound our way into the alleys of Venice, taking what I hoped was a deliberately circuitous route.

"You do know where we're going, right?" I asked after I saw the same shop sign three times.

"I do," Nikki said. "This was part of Simon's message. It wasn't so much that we see the shop we're heading into, it's that they see us. It's that kind of shop."

"Oh," I said, peering down the long street. There wasn't a huge number of tourists here, what I assumed were tourists, but they were lingering in front of the storefronts, each more elaborate than the last, filled with colorful costumes and masks of every description. Mostly for show, as the shops appeared to be closed up, but like the two names that the prelate had given us, it seemed there was always an exception that could be made.

"Another thing, dollface, this place we're going to tonight? I checked the addy. Totally on point for the Creepio Brothers back there. Ca Daria. Turn here."

I turned. "I'm not familiar with the place. Should I be?"

"Only if you have a death wish. Gotta be one of the most haunted places in Venice. These guys really have a thing for Ripley's Believe it or Not." She held up a hand, forestalling my response. "Here we are."

I looked up and saw one of the tiny doors had opened, three down from us, the minutest crack. "Are you serious?"

"As a heart attack, but I'll go first." Nikki strode forward and pushed the door open. It gave way, and a rush of cool air tumbled out of the air-conditioned interior, redolent with spices and perfumes.

"I don't even care what's in there, I'm going," Nikki breathed. "It smells better than this entire city."

"I'm right behind you."

No one came out to greet us or shoo us away, so we stepped into the gloom. The moment we cleared the door, it moved, and out of a long habit of self-preservation, I jerked out a hand to stop it. A rod cracked sharply over my fingers with such force, I jumped away, blue fire instantly erupting to encircle my palms. The door slammed shut behind me, and my ball of spectral fire illuminated three wide-eyed children and a woman who looked to be about a thousand years old. She was wielding a measuring stick like she was going to hit a home run with my head.

"No magic!" she hissed with a thick Italian accent, flicking out her unencumbered stick. To my shock, the blue light in my palms vanished.

"Signora Visione?" Nikki asked, her voice overloud in the fraught silence.

"Of course! And look at you, you're built like Venus." She still sounded enraged, but she circled Nikki with a string of compliments she made sound like curses. "Never have I seen such power, such strength, such joy of femininity in a woman! You will be a triumph. We will dress you in red and gold, a dama mask, the most beautiful we have, Beggio!"

One of the boys leapt to attention, and she ordered him to go find something called "La Princessa." He scampered off. She muttered in disgust. "He is the best grandson an old lady could have. My heart, my true, deep heart. Boots!" She glanced at Nikki's feet, then cut around to a second child, a girl who barely came up to my waist, and sent her off at a run too. Then she shooed Nikki over to the bench. With the vantage of a few minutes in the gloom, I found I could see again even without my glowing fireballs. The room was lit, after a fashion, with a thousand fairy lights far above, holes that I suspected had been cut into the ceiling to create a false night.

The old woman caught me looking. "The beauty and the mystery," she said in an angry snarl. "It sweeps around you, creating a cape of stars. You are those stars."

"I'm fine with simple—"

"You're fine with simple. Fine with simple, she says, Mangiana, have you ever heard a sillier thing?"

The little girl who remained eyed me with enormous soulful eyes and shook her head. "Sei fatto di stelle," she whispered. "You're made of stars."

"And stars we shall wrap around you, Sara Pelter Wilde, hunter of the arcane, Mistress of the House of Swords, Justice of the Arcana Council, Su—"

"Nonna!" Mangiana's dismayed interruption seemed to recall the old woman to herself. I glanced from her to Nikki.

Su—? I mouthed to Nikki as the old woman started to mutter and hiss at how beautiful and petite my feet were with the same dismayed voice she'd accorded to Nikki's size thirteens. Nikki looked back, equally wide-eyed, and shrugged.

"We will clothe you with the boots of the Valkyries," the old woman said. "The wings of the raven, the stars of the night sky, and a mask…a mask…"

"Um," I offered, almost afraid to interrupt her. "I don't think we're supposed to let on that we're female, necessarily."

"I have no problem breaking that little rule," Nikki chimed in.

"And you…you. You could, we could, we should, hmm…" The woman pursed her lips and frowned at my face. I got that a lot, but it was still unnerving. "A volto, I think. Or maybe…psht. Men and their rules." This time, her disdain sounded legitimate, and I was forced to rethink everything she'd said about me. "Yes!" she growled, then looked around quickly for a child. They were all gone.

"My hearts!" she snapped, and dashed off into the shadows.

"Supe, maybe?" I said out loud, still wondering at the last title Signora Visione had attempted to assign me. "What could that mean?"

"Supergirl? Super sassy?"

"Supreme Court Justice?" I grinned. "That'd be a twist."

"You'd never get approved." Nikki shook her head. "Supernatural? Superfriend?"

Our suggestions were cut short as the old woman and her charges burst back through the door. With a crack of the old woman's command, the lights came up in full, blinding us momentarily. Then we were assaulted with a flurry of whirling figures, and any other hope of conversation was done.

We were in the capable hands of Signora Visione.

Chapter Sixteen

"Yo, SuperBad. You're looking fine."

"I can barely see through this thing." By the time we walked down the side street and back to one of the main thoroughfares of Venice, night had fallen. According to Signora Visione, we didn't have far to go to get to Ca Daria, but she'd had the same reaction that Nikki had when we told her that was our destination. Except with more crosses.

"You cannot be too careful in Ca Daria, yes?" she'd said. "People who are respectful, who are gentle and strong, they have no trouble there. The prideful, the weak, the foolish. They should be careful. You should be careful too, yes? Because you are wearing my creations and you should be seen by all of Carnevale in them."

With that, she'd shooed us out of her shop, the door slamming shut behind us, only it wasn't yet time for our appointment with the magicians. I had no interest in simply cooling my jets near Ca Daria, but I didn't want to get our costumes dirty either.

"Do we even know how to dry-clean these things?"

"I get the feeling little fairies come and whisk them away when the time comes."

"Nice. So how far do we have to go?"

"Three blocks and two hours," Nikki said cheerfully. "I think we should explore the canal again, maybe hit the old stomping grounds of our friend the butcher."

"You just want to be seen by as many tourists as possible."

"That too." She grinned, or I assumed she grinned. It was difficult to tell with her mask. Then again, it was one stunner of a mask. True to Signora Visione's word, Nikki's attire was fantastic enough to turn the heads of statues. Her hair was topped with a voluminous red tricorn hat that perfectly matched the fiery red feathers tipped with yellow that adorned her eye-popping cape. The cape tiered down her body in waves, but stopped abruptly midthigh, allowing her red tights to be visible over approximately two miles of leg before her polished riding boots carried on the rest of the sartorial triumph down to her feet. And sure enough, they were flat-soled platform boots.

Nikki's mask, as Visione had decreed, was a feminine dama mask that was pure gold, with wide eyeholes and miniscule additional holes tucked up under the nose and between the full, sensual lips. "Can you even breathe in that thing?" I asked.

"At least I can see."

"Fair point."

It wasn't that my mask had been built with a design flaw, but I wasn't used to any obstruction on my face, least of all a vaguely raptor-like bird mask with a sharp beak that extended out several inches, then swooped down, obscuring my lower face. I could breathe, but the eyes of the bird were shielded by a profusion of blue-black feathers, the same feathers that adorned my full-body cape. The result was a strange disorientation that made me think that objects in front of me were farther away than they were.

Nikki squeezed my arm, and I stopped abruptly, barely avoiding bumping into the woman in front of us as we waited our turn to catch a gondola ride. Despite the late hour, all the canal-side stands were open for business, with tourists queuing up. A wave of murmurs started as we stood waiting, and Nikki started fluffing her hair beside me—an immediate tell that we were being watched.

"Anybody interesting?"

"Everybody's interesting tonight, dollface, most especially us." She laughed with delight as a masculine voice called out the word "Bellissima." Apparently, that was our cue to board. We cut across two other lines to a waiting gondola, and Nikki handed me aboard, then swept into the boat herself. The man started singing a love song before he'd even pushed off.

"I love Venice," Nikki sighed.

When we reached the middle of the canal, an unexpected obstacle bobbed into view—a wine barrel. Our gondolier broke off his song to cluck in dismay. "Be careful, bellissime," he directed. "The barge masters, they do not always make sure their cargo is lashed down properly, you see? It can make for an interesting tour, but someone is out quite a bit of wine, I'm afraid."

Several more barrels bobbed along, and a few were caught against the far edge of the canal, ramming into the pier with the rhythmic push of the current. Still others dragged against the stone outcropping of a bridge, the sound of scraping wood audible across the lapping water. The gondolier steered expertly through the wreckage, resuming his song. When we were once more in the clear, he leaned a little closer. "You have a destination in mind? Or simply the tour."

Nikki sat forward. "The Riva de Biasio."

The man clucked. "Ah no, bellissima," he said, though he dutifully stuck his pole back into the water and the boat glided forward. "That is a place far away from the bright lights and beautiful people, yes? You should not be going there this night, when not even the beauty of Carnevale can quiet the cries of the children."

"So you know the story?" Nikki said, sounding fully engaged. Behind my mask, I rolled my eyes.

"But, of course, I know the story. And in Venice, there are many different ways to tell the same tale. But I will tell you the story of the butcher Biasio the way it was told to my father, and to my father's father before him, all the way back to the year 1532, when the story happened."

"Excellent." Nikki fluffed her feathers. "I know it's terrible, so don't spend too long on the poor children."

"They were the ones to suffer the most, but not the longest, bellissima." Like the well-trained gondolier he was, the man launched into the tale of the butcher of Venice, but right from the beginning, the story was subtly different. In the gondolier's tale, the butcher was a modest, hardworking man who couldn't seem to get ahead, and he was willing to try anything to make his wares the talk of the city. "One night, as he was closing up shop, a *stregone* came to visit."

"Stregone?" Nikki tilted her head as I looked up.

"A doctor?" I asked, though I knew that wasn't quite right. Nikki touched my arm and pointed as we glided past a four-story canal house with a circular window adorning each of its top three floors. Ca Daria, I realized instantly. Our eventual destination.

"Not exactly," our gondolier said, still deep in his story. "In that time, the doctors didn't know as much as they do now, and they relied on natural medicines and healing spells that were more magic than science. And so it was with the stregone. He proposed a deal to the young butcher that he would bring him great money and fame, as long as he never asked questions or varied from the recipes the stregone gave him, and he used the cuts of meat the stregone supplied. The young butcher did these things, and in no time at all, he was famous, his sausages and stews the talk of the city. But this Cargnio, he knew something was not right. His guests would eat certain stews and complain later of headaches and terrible events, while others would enjoy sausages and return the next morning speaking of extraordinary dreams or sharing breathless tales of windfalls of good fortune. It was all very peculiar, and it seemed to only get worse. One day, Cargnio looked where he should not look and saw what is in among the cuts of meat."

By now, both Nikki and I had stopped looking at the passing houses and were staring at the young man, completely rapt. "And then?"

"The poor butcher, he is distraught. He goes to his priest, and his priest tells him he must turn in the stregone, but he knows he cannot do this. He must protect his family. So he arranges for his family to leave the city without telling them why, and he makes his terrible, self-destructive plan. He slips something he should not into a sausage stew, it is found, and the rest, well, you know."

"So he wasn't the one killing the children."

"He was not, but he could not live with himself, eh? Knowing what had been done under his very nose, the terrible remains he had handled. Knowing what he had been willing to do for money. He truly could not live with himself. *He* is the one who begged the senate to punish him in the manner of a warning, and they did exactly that. It was a message to the stregones and dark sorcerers of every ilk not to use Venice as their testing grounds. And that is why the street is still named for Biasio to this day. He is still remembered, still famous. Simply not at all in the way he wanted to be."

"Anyone know the stregone's name?"

"That remains a mystery," the gondolier sighed. "But they called him the Red King."

The man fell silent then, with nothing but the sound of the pole dipping into the water filling the air around us. Our minds roiling with this new potential piece to the puzzle, Nikki and I stared across the canal as we approached the landing point. The gondolier had been right—there was no one this far away from the activities at Piazza San Marco at this hour and on the first night of Carnevale. The pier was deserted. "Shall I wait for you? The butcher's shop is long gone, of course. No one knows exactly where it is."

"Wait for us, sweet lips, and we'll pay you double on the way back. But if you get called away, no harm, no foul," Nikki said. "We'll only be a minute."

We stepped out of the gondola, listening to the creak of the wood against the water, and stepped up onto the pier. The Riva de Biasio looked like any other location along the Grand Canal, with shopfronts and homes stretching up and away from the murky waters, but it seemed unusually dark despite the cheery lamplight that lined the canal.

Setting off across the pier, I pulled my mask off, welcoming the cool brush of air against my skin. "It was worth it to come all this way just to do that," I moaned.

"I second that emotion," Nikki said, her voice far clearer now that she'd removed her own mask. "You see where we're going?"

I let my third eye flicker open, and once again, as it had in the courtyard of Balestri's palazzo, I could see an overlay of the world as a network of circuits. These electric streams zigged and zagged and rounded on themselves in a rush of light and movement for all that the pier was empty and dark, and they led down the street in a tumbling profusion until…

I stopped short, staring, and Nikki bumped into me.

"Whoa—what?" she asked, her voice instantly guarded. "You see something?"

"No, I don't," I said, my voice slightly awed. "I see…nothing."

I moved forward almost automatically, Nikki by my side, her firm hand on my arm as if she thought I might topple over with my compromised sight. She wasn't wrong. The cheerful blur of electrical circuits I could see showed the flow of natural and manmade electricity as well as the circuits of other sorts of energy, the ones that flowed between all living things and particularly between all Connected organisms.

But they all stopped at the doorstep of a nondescript storefront, a card shop, from what I could tell. The place didn't look deserted. The printing of the signage in the window was neat and stylized, the items on the shelves looked new, the place was clean. But from a magical standpoint it was…

"It's like a blank slate," I said, confused. "Like a hole in space."

"Help me out here, dollface. I don't know what that means."

"It's like someone cut the circuits clean through and never reconnected them."

"Huh." She tilted her head. "Can you join them back together? Or is it better to leave well enough alone?"

"I…" I swallowed, unnerved by the complete absence of magic. Still, I'd healed people, certainly. I'd put buildings back together after they'd been broken by magic, and I'd filled in holes in the world. How hard could it be to reconnect a couple of lines of magic?

The sound of a crash and tinkling glass echoed faintly behind us, a trick of the wind. I could almost hear the far-off sounds of laughter as the Carnevale festivities got underway.

Still, I hesitated. "Who would have done this? And why? The ground wasn't evil, the air, the stones. Why cut the area off from the energy of the world?"

"Are we thinking it was done at the time of the butcher's story? That long ago?"

I looked at the dead space in front of me. "What else could it be? This damage is old," I said. "I don't know how old, but it would almost have to be tied to the butcher shop, wouldn't it?"

Nikki nodded, squinting at the building, though she couldn't see what I did. "Almost as if the magic was completely wiped clean, the earth sewn with salt."

My brows lifted as I felt the truth in her words. "That's exactly what's happened here," I said. "

"Bellissima!" The sound of running feet down the street made us turn, and Nikki straightened as our gondolier came racing around the corner, his eyes wide, and his face scorched. Only then did I let my third eye snap back closed, and I realized that there was substantially more light than there had been at the canal when we'd left it.

"Bellissima, there were men—bombs! They bombed my boat! And they—they're coming!"

He ran into us at full speed, his arms spread wide, catching us with surprising strength as a flare of gunfire zipped overhead. "They've got guns!" he said, a little unnecessarily.

"Ease it up, buttercup," Nikki said harshly as she hustled us across the cobblestoned street and behind a low wall. "What happened exactly?"

The gondolier spoke in a rush of English. "I was at the pier, waiting for you, and they came. They told me to move along, and I said I was waiting for my charges and—no warning at all—they threw glass bottles in my boat! They burned my boat!"

"We'll get you a new boat, sweetie," Nikki said.

Another round of gunfire burst across the open space, and she chanced a look. "You know what I'm thinking?" she asked thoughtfully. "I'm thinking it's a hella long walk to Ca Daria. I'm thinking maybe someone doesn't want us to get there on time."

"They burned my—"

"Gun!" Nikki barked, and as the young man looked back, she cold-cocked him. He slumped in her arms, and she sighed. "I really didn't want to do that, but he was kind of getting on my nerves."

I snorted. "It happens." A third blast of gunfire rang out, but it wasn't advancing. "I'm getting the idea they don't really want to hurt us. Because they certainly could have well before now if they'd wanted to."

"Unless they realize you can command flaming balls of death," she said.

"True. But where does that leave us? We can't sit here trapped all night. We're going to be late as it is if we can't pole our way back to Ca Daria." I pressed my lips together. "It's almost as if someone's trying to make us late."

"Not all that surprising, if we're dealing with a wolf in the magician hen house. Maybe the Red King wants the party for himself tonight." She looked at me and waggled her brows. "Lucky for us, we have options.

You do remember the Grand Canal stop for the house, right?"

I groaned, but she was right. It was the quickest way. "I remember it enough to get out of here," I tugged on my mask before grabbing her by one arm and the gondolier by the other.

"Try not to singe my feathers this time," Nikki said, sliding her own mask back into place.

"And you try to hold on to your admirer. And find out where he lives or whatever so we can get him money for his boat." I closed my eyes and pictured the picturesque pier by the Grand Canal…too late remembering that it would be filled with people.

Whoops.

Chapter Seventeen

After an unfortunate collision with a family of unsuspecting tourists, all of whom thoughtfully assumed responsibility for our poor passed-out gondolier—who would shortly be substantially richer despite the fact that we had no idea how much a gondola cost and he was in no shape to tell us—it took us several minutes to extract ourselves and break away. We made it to Ca Daria with only five minutes to spare.

"How do I look?" Nikki asked, smoothing down her cape.

"You forget, I can't see in this thing. Not well, anyway."

"Seems like kind of an idiotic design. You sure you have it on right?"

"I have it on the way Signora Visione put it on."

"Well, she's a little short. And old. Maybe she got confused. Here." She reached out and fussed with my mask, even as I jerked away.

"Maybe you should mind your own—hey," I said, looking around. I could see much more clearly now. "What'd you do?"

"There's false eye sockets in that mask. I have no idea why. I simply flipped them up like eyelids."

I blinked at her through the suddenly unfiltered holes. "You're kidding me."

She grinned, then tapped her own mask. "Anything you can do about the mask-phyxia I've got going on here?"

"I…" I poked at her mask, marveling at the softness of the sculpted surface. "You can open the mouth from this side."

"You can?"

"Here." I pushed at the soft surface of the mask's mouth, grimacing as its lips parted into a delicate moue. "This feels a little rude."

"Keep it up, it's the most action I've gotten all da—hey, that does make a difference. I can breathe."

"You're welcome," I said, rolling my eyes. "Is it time?"

The question was answered for us as a bell tolled somewhere deep in the heart of Venice, probably at Piazza San Marco.

We moved up to the front step, and the door opened as we approached. No one else was in sight, which once again put my nerves on edge. Who would want us delayed from our appointed time? Only someone who knew when our appointed time *was*. That cut down the crew of likely suspects to right around…

"Um, how many of these magicians are supposed to be here tonight?" I whispered.

"More than enough, I suspect." As we moved deeper into Ca Daria, which looked like nothing so much as an ordinary house, no haunting required, a series of motion sensor lights tripped on as soon as we entered their space. It gave the eerie effect that the house was watching our every movement, and I shot Nikki another look. She snickered. She didn't need to read my mind to be open to belittling the hocus-pocus the magicians of Venice were serving up.

"They're not motion sensored." The voice beside us was so unexpected, I jumped sideways, smashing into Nikki, who, fortunately, was solid enough not to go flying.

Valetti stood beside us, masked and caped, but it was definitely him. No one else in Venice could manage to be so fiercely proud and self-effacing at the same time.

"What?" I managed.

"The lights. You must suspect they flicker on and off electronically, but they don't. We've had the wiring checked more times than we can remember. It's a quirk of the building that it follows guests through their first time. It only happens the first time too. After that, the lights stay dark unless you flip the switch." He shrugged. "And sometimes they stay dark even if you do flip them on."

I tried not to stare at him. "You're joking."

"I'm not. Forgive me for indulging myself in the delight of a new guest. It's been some time since Ca Daria welcomed a stranger into her midst."

Valetti moved past us down the corridor. Sure enough, the lights remained dark as he passed them, illuminating only when we drew close.

"He's gotta have some sort of remote," I muttered to Nikki.

"Well, you're the one with the magic eyeballs. What do you see?"

Belatedly, I allowed my third eye to snap open. It was getting a workout tonight, but when it surveyed the hallway in front of me, there was nothing out of the ordinary. Hallway, lights, electric signature of Valetti, Nikki, myself, and some people in a room at the end of the hall. No bright sideways electrical pulses, no Slimer waiting behind a door. "Nada," I confirmed.

"Huh. I was kind of banking on the remote control idea, myself."

"Yeah, well." We quieted as Valetti turned and gestured us into the room, and my stomach tightened as I stepped inside. This room was brightly lit, and though I was completely prepared for a séance, the men sitting around it—assuming they were all men—appeared relatively normal. Not counting the masks, hats, and giant capes, of course.

"Gentlemen and ladies, Magicians all, we welcome you to Carnevale," said the man at the head of the table—instantly recognizable as the prelate when he spoke—without a trace of irony or self-aggrandizement in his voice. "There's much to discuss."

"There's not much to discuss, at least not yet." A heavy man's voice boomed from the body of a diminutive jester, making me blink. "I received one of Butcher Biasio's book of recipes, and I'm not happy about it. I thought that bastard had been so damaged there wasn't even enough left of him to haunt this city. Why now?"

"Well, the reason for now is obvious. The influx of magic. But why him?" Another man with a plague doctor mask leaned forward. "There were far stronger magicians in the city than he ever could have hoped to be. If he was practicing today, he'd have been relegated to the side alleys like Balestri."

"Balestri who's dead, it should be noted. Why bother?"

I listened, spellbound by the callousness of the voices, and my mind couldn't help but stray to Armaeus. He was a magician, the only real magician I'd known since I'd started working on the Arcana Council.

He was a little on the calculating side, but he still didn't seem quite as cold as these people. Granted, I didn't exactly know what a magician was supposed to do to qualify for the senate in Venice, now that I thought about it.

"Marrow and Greaves planned to visit him, I heard," another voice, equally callous. "They've not been located."

That made me sit up a little straighter. These were the two missing magicians Valetti had mentioned earlier. News apparently traveled fast in the senate.

"Still low-level," Valetti said, his suddenly cold voice jarring me. How could these men turn from such genteel hosts to, well—asshats? And was one of these guys the Red King?

Beside me, Nikki shifted. I wasn't shielding my mind from her. It suddenly occurred to me…should I be shielding it from the rest of the room?

"Only if you wish, Miss Wilde. You're a member of the Arcana Council, which is several steps higher on the evolutionary scale than the magicians' senate. It accords you certain…protections that might not be otherwise available to the average magician."

I'd been working long enough with the Magician that I didn't jump, but it was a near thing. But his presence in my mind gave me the chance to ask—

And…then he was gone.

Of course.

I refocused on the group. They were listing other magicians who'd not yet arrived for Carnevale, apparently waiting to see if anyone else had died. Another subset of the sorcerers were making what sounded like a gentleman's wager on who the most likely next targets were, based on who had already gone. Suffice to say, it wasn't anyone in the room.

After this went on for some time, the prelate delicately cleared his throat. The soft sound had the effect of a sonic boom, and everyone shut up. I found my brows lifting as I watched the clear respect accorded to Alfonse. Though he wasn't a high-level magician, he clearly made the other members of this senate nervous. Why? Maybe the man had more in his library of arcana than I'd given him credit for…and maybe I'd have to return to it to see for myself.

"Magicians all," the prelate boomed. "We have not been idle as this threat has brushed up against our most sacred of celebrations. Through the good graces of a colleague, we welcome a member of the Arcana Council to our midst."

With a flutter of noise and movement, the magicians turned to their fellows, trying to seek out who was who. Enough of them hadn't spoken yet, and so, arguably, they were still in the running.

"You?" a man on the other side of Nikki said, his voice faint. "You're on the Arcana Council?"

"Not in this lifetime, love chop," Nikki said, her loud, wry voice once again striking the group mute. I allowed my third eye to slide open as I spoke.

"We're not going to take up much of your time," I said. "We'd like to see this matter ended as quickly as—"

"Justice!" blurted a man on the opposite side of the room. So far, this really was turning into an all-male revue. "I'd heard there was a new Justice on the Arcana Council. But true magicians are exempt from that role."

My eyebrows shot up, an effect sadly diminished by the fact that I was wearing a mask. *Exempt?* Was there no end to what I hadn't been told about my new job?

"Always have been," harrumphed another man who heretofore had been silent. From the jerk to attention of the costumed figures on either side of him, he was someone of importance. So, what, they didn't think I could make magic? My fingers started itching a little.

"Always will be." My attention shifted to the far end of the table, where a slender figure in a cape of obsidian feathers and a traditional bauta mask inclined her head toward me. Definitely a her. I racked my brain, trying to place a female magician at any time during my six years as an artifact hunter or a purveyor of stolen goods on the arcane black market. But I had nothing.

"I appreciate the Arcana Council giving this matter the focus it deserves," the woman continued haughtily. "We have long been far too isolated in our work within the magicians' senate, and their emissary has been more than lacking these past several decades. Sharing of our resources would be better…at least with *actual* magicians."

"To be fair, this is a very specific situation in which I—we—thought an outsider would see things that perhaps we would miss." Valetti's words sped up toward the end of his sentence, his slip about his specific involvement in my recruitment curious to me. Was it intentional? Did he want people to know he was behind this potentially game-changing addition to their team? Or was he still uncertain how it was all going to play out?"

"So neither of the women can conjure," came another scoffing voice. "We've opened up our ranks, risked our exposure, to people who aren't even magicians."

"Do you think they can't conjure?" A new voice broke through the ranks, and the men turned once again, clearly rethinking the idea of showing up in masks in the midst of so much turmoil. "Are you calling for a demonstration?"

The voice was silky, smooth, and…vaguely familiar, emanating from behind a mask in the shape of a lion's head. The man's hat and cape were also shaded a light, tawny gold. And he seemed hell-bent on causing chaos in an already untenable situation.

I scowled behind my mask. *Kreios?*

There was no response to my mental door knock. For the moment, it appeared the Devil would be a dumb spirit.

In the ensuing silence, I lifted my hands. "I'm not here to impress you with magic tricks. I've been asked to rout out a threat to the, ah, senate. If I can do that, I will."

"How?" It was the woman who spoke now, and as she did, she moved sinuously around the room for all that she wore a blank mask and a shapeless smock of feathers. She passed Valetti, who steadfastly refused to look at her, and stopped by the prelate. My eyes narrowed behind my mask as I observed the room react to this rearrangement of players—because there definitely was a reaction. It seemed everything that was done in this room had a timing and purpose to it, and I grimaced. I hadn't spent much time in high school when I'd been growing up, but it'd felt a hell of a lot like this. And right now, I was looking at the council's self-appointed Homecoming King and Queen.

But the female magician knew that she'd captured the room's attention, and she wasn't about to let it go.

"I have learned a little about you, Justice Wilde," she said, shifting forward slightly. As she did, her back did a weird arching thing that positioned her closer to the prelate without her technically moving. I never knew how women did that. Maybe they taught that move in magician school. "I understand you use Tarot cards to find your marks. No one knows Venice better than we do, however. We can help you."

I opened my mouth, then shut it again, a move made infinitely easier by the fact that I was wearing a mask. Despite how sensually she made the observation, the femme magicale had a point. And I did have my cards on me, under all these feathers.

"I can do a reading now," I said, and I could feel the tremor of anticipation in the room. Rolling my eyes was also much easier from behind a mask.

"You could do that," drawled the caped man I suspected was the Devil. "But what if the perpetrator is someone in this room? Surely that would be…inconvenient."

"I'm afraid you have us at a disadvantage, sir." It was the prelate who spoke, which surprised me. His tone was laced with ice, though, and I amended my opinion of him. "I am eager to ensure that each of our members is accorded the proper respect, but you, sir…I don't remember welcoming you at the front door."

"Nor do I," said Valetti gravely, almost apologetically.

"You didn't welcome me," the man said. He raised a hand, and the lights in the electric sconces flickered—as if they were actual candlelight. "But that doesn't mean I'm not a favored guest here. The Palazzo D'Aria has long been a favorite haunt of mine, for all that I have very little occasion to occupy it when you do."

"What sort of devilry is this?" muttered the diminutive man across the table, costumed as a jester complete with the floppy harlequin hat, despite the admonition that we were all supposed to wear tricorn headgear. Even the female magician tilted her head, her mask doing a credible job of looking perplexed.

The lion's mask turned in a lazy arc as the man I suspected was the Devil focused on the jester. "There are only so many meetings that I can keep up with, and these simply don't rate—except, of course the Magicians' Ball. But as to this bit of, well, cloak and dagger, the charm of it is already wearing thin."

The room of magicians shifted with indignation.

"Look," I said. "I don't need to listen to your watercooler fights. I'll find your butcher or, more likely, whoever is styling himself as your butcher." I couldn't help but remember the words that had tumbled out of Balestri's mouth, taunting me about the Red King. That hadn't been an illusion by an untrained hand. Someone with real strength was behind the butcher's attack, and someone knowledgeable enough to transform garden-variety Black Elixir—deadly enough in its own right—into the instantly lethal Nul Magis toxin. That took a pretty impressive magician. Was it one of the ones assembled here? "And I'm going to start that search now."

They all watched as I reached into the slitted pocket carefully concealed in the seam of my cloak and felt along my body for my cards. Without preamble, still focusing far too much on the tension in the room, I drew three cards. I stepped quickly toward the table as I drew them out and flipped them on the table.

Everyone froze.

Except Nikki. Who snickered.

"Oh, for the love of Christmas," I grumbled.

"What?" the jester half shouted, moving forward. "What is it?"

"The cards pick up your energy, and believe it or not, your energy isn't on the murderer who may or may not be in your midst, it's on the chess match you're all playing to one-up each other." I pointed to the Five of

Wands. "You don't want to work together, that's your problem, so this is the last reading I'm going to be doing anywhere near you people. Second is the Hermit—which is the search for knowledge. It could have been the Moon, but there's no mystery here." I reached down to gather my cards. "I'm wasting my time."

"But the last card," the jester all but moaned. "What does *it* mean?"

The tawny caped figure stepped forward and reached across the table, his elegant fingers picking up the card to study it before I could sweep it away.

"Old man Waite never could take a joke." The Devil of the Arcana Council sighed, surveying the claw-footed, goat-headed, fat-bellied image on the card. "If my predecessor hadn't upset the pompous fool so much, my life would have been *so* much easier."

Kreios's cloak and mask disappeared into curls of smoke, and the senate exploded into a fury of sound and magic.

CHAPTER EIGHTEEN

I snatched the card out of Kreios's hand and then swept up the rest cards, stepping out of the way the rest of the room converged on the Devil—who, if I was understanding his veiled, heh, comments correctly, was the Council's official emissary to this group. Perhaps not surprising, since the Devil was a master of illusion.

Aleksander Kreios had ascended to the Arcana Council in the early 1930s, taking the place of his predecessor in a handoff which had been much more up close and personal than mine and Abigail's passing of the baton.

The female magician appeared beside me. "While they all fawn over the newest stallion in the stable, do you want to get a real reading done? I'm Chiara, if you didn't know. Chiara Marchesi." I looked beyond her to see Valetti walking up quickly behind her, wringing his hands.

"If you don't mind, Justice Wilde, we should at least try a reading in more quiet surrounds," he said. "I do feel responsible for ensuring the safety of the senate…"

"Of course, of course." I let them lead me into another room, Nikki by my side. I'd already pulled three cards and scanned them quickly, then dipped back into my pocket for the full deck.

We stepped into the library. It was a sumptuously appointed room, a chamber that looked like people had actually lived in it. The artwork on the walls was both original and European, of course. And there was a lot of it. The chairs were plushly upholstered, and the coffee table was thick and sturdy, the kind of table you could put your feet up on or argue world politics over with equal aplomb.

I spread the deck in an arc and drew three cards in quick succession. “Hermit again. He’s popular tonight,” I said quickly. “Not surprising for people who seek the truth. Then we’ve got the Six of Wands.”

“Victory?” murmured Chiara, and I gave her an approving smile she couldn’t see.

“Definitely could be that, but when you shift the focus of the cards over to the physical search side of the equation, they can be read more literally. That picture most clearly represents—”

“The parade!” she said, looking up at me. The effect of the movement of her beaked mask was almost comical. “You mean the parade of Carnevale tomorrow. That’s where you’ll find him.”

“That’s where I’ll start looking, yes,” I said. “And the third card is the Four of Swords.”

“Four of Swords…” Chiara considered, now sounding perplexed. Even Valetti leaned forward, though I couldn’t see his expression, of course. I felt a little twinge of remorse at how I was about to mislead him. He’d brought me here on Luca Stone’s recommendation. But he wasn’t the only magician in the room, and I didn’t know this Chiara at all.

So I spun a line of credible bullshit.

"The Four of Swords in a search capacity could mean a number of things, some that might not become clear until I see them in the context of the second card, so in this case, at the parade. But there are some clues to look for. If there are any reclining figures, whether sleeping or dead, that's a possibility. Or, it could be more specific—a hospital or a hotel. A place of recovery."

"That's it?" Chiara's voice conveyed the derision that the placid expression on her mask could not. "That's all you have to go on?"

"I find that once I get close, the rest tends to fall into place."

Valetti patted Chiara on the shoulder. "She did ascend to the Council on the merits of these skills, Chiara."

Once again, I was grateful for the covering of the mask. My ascendance to the Council as Justice was based on a lot of things, but my Tarot card reading skills were likely *not* at the top of the list.

Still, those were the skills I was working now. With Valetti's assistance, and under cover of the senate continued fangirling over Kreios down the hall, Nikki and I exited the front door of Ca Daria a few minutes later. The moment I stepped away from the ancient palazzo, I breathed a sigh of relief.

Nikki followed my gaze back to the gorgeous building. "You think it was Kreios's doing, all those dancing lights?"

"I wouldn't put it past him." Kreios excelled at distractions, the more upsetting, the better.

"True."

We moved farther down the street, twisting around until I was sure we weren't being followed.

"So," Nikki said, drawing out the word. "You want to tell me what that card trick was you pulled back there? Because that was some prime bullshit about the Four of Swords. What I would've given to see your face through all that."

"Keep those cards in mind," I said. "Even if they were my second draw, they could become important."

"And your first draw? Enlighten me on *those* cards."

We were walking down a quiet residential street, God only knew where, but I was coming to understand that the glory of Venice was that there wasn't all that far you could go and remain truly lost. You'd either run into a lagoon or a canal. We pulled off our masks and enjoyed the soft night air on our faces.

"The first card was the Five of Swords, which I hate on general principle in a search reading."

"You win, but you're not happy about it."

"Exactly. Which could mean just about anything. I could discover the identity of the butcher too late, I could discover it as he's or she's about to kill me, or I could never discover who the butcher is at all, but my mere interest in the case stifles his little spree."

"Well, that wouldn't be satisfying."

"No, it wouldn't. Alternatively, the card could literally mean that I should look for the man on the battlefield or cemetery. So, two things to keep in mind. Next up is the Three of Cups, which to me says party."

"I like the way that sounds a lot more."

"Agreed. And we're about to launch into a week of balls that are going to get bigger and grander as time goes on, so something to look for. I think I agree with Valetti to some extent. This isn't a wide strike, despite the fact that Balestri and the other two sorcerers supposedly were scrubs. The butcher is targeting magicians, so those are the parties we should count on."

"I'm going to need a new cape," Nikki said, looking down at her flame-red feathers.

"I have a feeling that won't be a problem. The third card, though, can go anywhere. The Queen of Cups."

"Wife to the Red King," Nikki offered. "Maybe a relative?"

"Could be. Or a mistress, a daughter, a muse."

"Well, that narrows it down."

I sighed. "Court cards. I've never been a fan of them in a search reading. They tend to make the most sense after you've already independently verified your choice."

"It gives us a place to start anyway," Nikki said. "Which is more than we had going into Ca Daria. It doesn't solve who might have wanted us to be kept away, though."

"No, it doesn't. But I've got a feeling once we know who the Butcher is, we won't so much need to worry about the rest." I blew out a sigh. "So, the Five of Swords, Three of Cups, and Queen of Cups." I frowned. "The Queen of Cups… What women do we know so far in the city? Chiara and Signora Visione?"

Nikki scoffed a laugh. "I'm not thinking it's the signora."

"I'm not either. But she *is* surrounded by children."

"Her own children—or grandchildren, anyway." Nikki hesitated. "As far as we know. But though she's a wizard with a needle, she doesn't strike me as the kind of Connected we're looking for, if this reading is about helping us identify the Red King."

"Right. So, Chiara."

"Much more the kind of Queen of Cups we're needing, but we don't know her at all." She pulled out her phone from a pocket in her cape. "Simon will. Might as well use team resources."

I nodded. It was odd to think of the Arcana Council as teammates; they hadn't always felt like that. And I had traditionally not been a great team player. Something else to learn in my new job.

"What do you think of the senate we've met so far?" I looked over at her typing on her phone. "Fill Simon in on the others, and maybe Kreios is doing the same thing. We need names and locations, particularly where they were last night, though..."

She glanced up at me, grimaced. "Though if Balestri went down with a blow dart, that could have been from anywhere. And we still don't know the disposition of Marrow and Greaves, the two missing magicians. I'll ask Simon if he's heard anything about them too."

I nodded, my gaze going out over the Grand Canal. Across the water and deeper into the city, the festivities of the opening ceremony were still going strong. I checked my watch. It was almost midnight, and Venice typically rolled up the sidewalks long before nine p.m. But this was Carnevale, and anything was possible.

Anything.

"So we've got a group of magicians who meet every year for two weeks of parties and catching up."

"And maybe undergo completely whack ceremonies to amp up their mojo," Nikki put in, still typing. "Otherwise, why do it every year? There has to be a draw."

"Agreed. And this year, right before their meet-up, there was an event that potentially already supercharged some or all of their magic. No one knows how much any one magician was affected, if at all, but everyone assumes the others got a disproportionate impact."

"Kind of makes you want to get a job in corporate to get out of the rat race, huh?"

I smiled, resettling my feathers as the cool breeze picked up. "We've got at least one female, but most of the magicians are male, most are legacy, and at least in the group we saw tonight, most are entitled Europeans. Maybe all of them with ties to Venice?"

She waved her phone at me. "Definitely all of them with ties to Venice, or at least to Carnevale. Which takes us to another Venetian magician, the butcher Biasio. Who is either a tragic dupe or a sinister madman, depending on how you learned the story."

"No one in the magicians' senate was airing the second version, though. For all we know, our gondolier made it up to improve tips. Certainly a nicer story than a guy deliberately hacking up kids for malicious profit."

"Fair enough," Nikki said. "We can track down our boy at the canal later, if he's found himself a new gondola. With the scratch I'll be wiring into his account once we verify his identity, he shouldn't have too much trouble."

"Or he could pack up his gondola pole and leave the city."

"Or that…" She finished her text and also looked out over the water. "I don't get the impression that a lot of these people leave, though. At least not for good. Hell, even the ghosts want to stick around."

"Which takes us to the Casino of Spirits and Ca Daria."

"Two of the most haunted locations in Venice and happily under the control of the magicians. And if you noticed—we got no actual hauntings. I feel cheated."

I snorted. "I suspect a lot of that is staged to keep out the riffraff, unless there are kid ghosts from Biasio's reign of terror still floating about."

"That's an interesting idea." She eyed me. "I don't suppose you can talk to the dead?"

"I think I would have noticed that. But…" I frowned. There was teamwork, and there was taking teamwork too far. Still, if I was going to begin working full-time with the Council, they needed to make themselves available to me. And there was one major Arcana card that was represented on the Council in a particularly vibrant and relevant way. "Death could, I'd assume."

Nikki nodded. "I'd think that would be part of the job. Or maybe she was on hand for the butcher the first time through."

"You know, we kind of crab-stepped our way into this job. Going forward, it might make more sense to ask more questions up front. Like questions of people who've lived for hundreds or thousands of years on this planet and might have been around when this crap actually went down."

"It's not too late to do that now," Nikki said reasonably. "You're Justice of the Arcana Council. Who all would you need?"

"I have no idea. I didn't know I'd need any of them at the beginning. We picked up a job, we went out on the job—"

"We got mired down in a bog of crazy on said job. But it seems to me the Arcana Council would appreciate knowing the deets or at least revel in the chance to dish the dirt on this magicians' senate, especially if there's a new player who wants to elevate the profile of the magicians to Arcana level…or, arguably, turn them all into walking zombies, their magic burned out."

"Why in the world would that be an advantage?" I wondered aloud. "They're killing their own people."

"Or they're pruning the bushes in advance of the big flower show. What's better, a dozen magicians with a few hangers-on who are little more than glitter tossers, or a highly motivated set of eight or nine sorcerers with a firmer grasp on their own powers and an up-close-and-personal performance enhancer?"

"Win or die," I muttered.

"Pretty much."

We carried on like that around the gentle curve of the Grand Canal, the lights growing brighter and the houses more palatial as we neared Valetti's residence.

"First order of business, we need to get into the police files, find out what happened to Marrow and Greaves, specifically. I assume they died the same way Balestri did if they were at his house, but we need that nailed down. If it's poison, source the poison. If it's a technoceutical, source the manufacturer. We should be able to get that tracked if we can get a blood sample—assuming we can find the bodies."

"On it," Nikki said. "There may have been trace evidence at the scene if they were able to get skin cells, hair, anything like that. It'll take time, though."

"Except we're the Arcana Council. It shouldn't take time. Should it?"

"Ah…is there a CSI: Supernatural division of the Council I wasn't aware of?"

"Maybe when Justice still walked the earth, but now? I think I would've run into it. From everything I've seen, the Council's never been too big on getting involved with the Connected community.

"Well, maybe it's time for that to change."

"Maybe…" I looked again at the flowing waters of the Grand Canal, then stopped, my heart squeezing tight, as if it could take back its last several heartbeats. But it was too late for that. It was too late for a lot of things.

Oh no.

"And maybe it'll need to change now," I sighed. Nikki turned as well, her curse low and brutal in the evening breeze.

Floating in the canal amidst several curved strips of wood were two bodies, their matching Union Jack capes flowing out around them. Twin coronas of purple light surrounded their heads. Purple, not silver, and the meaning of that illumination was finally clear to me.

These men weren't marked for Justice—they were owed it.

"Hello, Marrow and Greaves," Nikki said.

Chapter Nineteen

After we advised Simon of our discovery of the bodies, we moved down to the canal. Before we got there, someone else had sent up the alarm, saving us the trouble. Two gondoliers had hauled the magicians out of the water. They were draped across the boats, our vantage point allowing us to take several distance photos, which Nikki sent to Simon as well. There wasn't any question in our minds, of course, as to who the magicians were—but if Simon could determine anything about how they died, that would be helpful.

A crowd was already forming, the holdovers from the Carnevale celebration mostly, I suspected. Everyone in masks and feathers and hats and capes. It occurred to me I didn't know whether or not Venice had any increase in crime during the festival. I couldn't imagine the police were huge fans.

After a brief deliberation, Nikki and I decided to take the higher road, literally, moving up to another tier of sidewalks overlooking the canal. From this vantage point, we were well out of the way when the cops showed up, a cluster of bustling techs plus a tall, dark, and brutal-looking man who had to be a detective. That man turned smartly when Valetti arrived, conspicuously without his festival garb.

"I may know these men, I may know them," Valetti shouted in authoritative tones. The combination of his assertiveness, patrician outrage, and ordinary garb got him to the front of the action quickly, and he greeted the detective like they were old friends. Interesting.

Then Valetti leaned over the two bodies for a long moment before he seemed to visibly recoil. He straightened, turning shakily to the detective, his face white and drawn. Whatever conversation they had at that point, it was too low for us to hear.

"I didn't get the impression that Valetti was all that big a fan of Marrow and Greaves," I commented. "But he seems pretty broken up."

"He wasn't a fan of Balestri either," Nikki pointed out. "I think death has a way of creating a cumulative effect. It's tough not to feel one's mortality when everyone around you is dropping like flies."

"Fair enough."

We made it back to the residence well ahead of Valetti, and his butler showed us to the same terrace we'd dined on that morning for breakfast and the previous evening. Notably, its forward view overlooked a section of the Grand Canal that was not set up with crime scene lights. Except for a faint halo of reflected light, you would've never known that anything had happened around the bend in the canal.

Valetti arrived more than an hour later, and he entered the terrace with slow, heavy steps. When he saw us sitting there, however, he rushed forward.

"You know, yes? I assume you know," he said, breathing quickly. "You must know what we've found in the Grand Canal. I have never seen…this is simply horrible. I fear we've lost everything before we have even begun."

I tried to reassure him, but in truth, I didn't know what to say.

"You suspected they were dead," I reminded him.

"I did…" Valetti tried to pull himself together. "I did. But I thought with you and your associate here, perhaps—perhaps whoever was behind their killings would keep them hidden, out of the limelight, that you'd scared them off. You haven't hidden the fact that you are here. Those who know who you are know the power that you represent. When Signore Stone let me know you were coming, I had hoped that would be enough."

I felt a flush of defensiveness rise through me, but the count did have a point. Unbidden, Balestri's own accusation came back to me. *"You were supposed to save me."*

Valetti looked at me with wide, red-rimmed eyes. "If the threat of the Arcana Council is not enough to turn this demon back, what power on this earth can truly stop him?"

"Hang on there, slow down," I said. "This guy isn't a real demon, or I'm pretty sure he isn't, so that's a plus. And as you say, you have the full weight of the Arcana Council now focused on this issue."

Valetti stopped, his bleary eyes struggling to focus and failing. "I do?"

"You do. There are elements to this case that go beyond a simple search and recover mission. You're part of an old and venerable organization, and your senate demands respect and careful handling. The Council will be there for you." I didn't want to lay the accolades on too thickly, but with Kreios showing up for the first senate meeting in a long time, I figured Valetti was primed for stroking. It was no secret that the Arcana Council was both admired and reviled by the magicians of Venice, the ancient rivalry between the senate and the Council made worse because the Council paid no attention to it.

If anything, however, Valetti looked worse. "I have failed in my charge to protect my own. Never in the history of Carnevale have we experienced anything so dire. It's a turning point for our organization, and one which none of us anticipated. We are not ready."

"It may not be as bad as all that," Nikki assured him pragmatically. Nikki kept her drama strictly to her clothes. "We've got two dead guys, that's it."

"Three," I corrected. "And the assassins. And Valetti's water taxi captain."

"Okay, multiple dead guys, all adults, no kids. We've got the supposed butcher of Venice running around, but so far as we know, no children have been sacrificed." She tapped her lip. "Probably because once you get kids into the mix, the whole city would blow up. So it may not be the butcher at all is what I'm saying. It may be someone else."

"You don't understand," Valetti moaned.

I looked at him sharply. He was right, we didn't understand. Suddenly, the story of the gondolier from the Grand Canal came back to me, as well as the gunfire that'd followed it. The butcher of Venice hadn't used guns to get his work done either.

"Is there something about the butcher story we're missing, Valetti?" I asked quietly. "Because with the arrival of the Devil of the Arcana Council, we're going to need to know everything. You're not going to want to hold back. And it might be easier for you to tell us what you know here and now rather than face uncomfortable questions from the Arcana Council."

I wasn't kidding here, though I didn't want to lean on Valetti too much. The Devil had a way of weaseling out the truth from people and using it on them at the worst possible time. If Valetti was at all a private man, he needed to stay away from Kreios.

"Of course, I..." Valetti seemed to visibly shake himself. He touched a button on his phone, and a few moments later, his houseman appeared at the door to the terrace, carrying a tray that held a variety of crystal decanters and small glasses. He delivered the tray to the table, then poured Valetti three fingers of a dark brown spirit—scotch, I assumed. Because life's most difficult moments demanded scotch.

Valetti took a deep drink, then turned back to us. His voice, when it came, was hollow. "What we know is this. The butcher of Venice was working on a specific combination of spells when he turned to the darkest arts. As you may have gleaned from the prelate, he wasn't seeking to augment the Connected powers of himself or anyone else. Rather, he was seeking to destroy them. To leave nothing but a husk behind of a formerly psychic soul."

This was getting uncomfortably close to what I'd seen in Balestri's mind.

"He was using Nul Magis," I said, echoing the prelate's words from earlier in the day, though the jury was still out on whether it was the butcher or some witch doctor behind the concoction. "Why?"

Valetti spread his hands. "The reasons are lost to history, I'm afraid. It could have been to take down his enemies or to ensure his own primacy of place, but there are easier ways to do that. By all accounts, Biasio Cargnio was, first and foremost, a butcher. That he turned to the creation of bespelled recipes was one thing, that it got twisted into something so dire…we cannot even speculate as to why."

"I can speculate," I said. "I specialize in speculation. But there's something I don't understand. Say the butcher fed his clients the special stew to get them to lose their psychic abilities. Did it work?"

"I'm sorry?"

"For there to be a truly sinister twist here beyond the obvious horror of the sacrificed children, something had to *happen* to whoever ate those sausages tainted with the enchanted meat. Did anyone lose their woo?"

"Well, as I said, he—"

"And these recipes from his enchanted cookbook, have any of you tried them?"

Valetti looked at me aghast. "You can't seriously think that respectable magicians would try a concoction that required a human sacrifice."

"Oh, come on, not the whole human," I pushed, watching him closely. "A hand. A kidney. With today's technology, even the smallest slice of tissue from a Connected would be enough to work into a tincture, wouldn't you say?"

I tried to ignore the horrified expression on Valetti's face. There was something here, I was sure of it.

"So let's say that a dozen of these books went out, and ten out of the twelve magicians were too delicate to do anything about it," I continued. "But two tried out the recipe. Where would that leave us?"

"I cannot see—"

"It'd leave us with two potential perps," Nikki said. "Both of them willing to try their concoction out on anyone, to see what happened."

"But if that's the case, and the blend was truly dangerous, then we'd have more dead psychics in the canal or, at a minimum, some very unhappy newly minted Muggles. But from everything I'm seeing, that hasn't been the case." I fixed my attention on Valetti. "Have there been any other disappearances within the psychic community? Whether adult or children?"

"I wouldn't have any idea about children," he said stiffly. "And I can assure you that the entire magician community is present and accounted for, less Signore Balestri and now Marrow and Greaves, of course."

"Of course," I murmured. But something still wasn't adding up. "There had to be a testing period of some sort, though. There simply had to be."

Though I wasn't keen on Valetti knowing this specifically, I'd witnessed what'd happened to Balestri's brain under the influence of the drug that had indirectly taken his life. By the time I'd gotten to him, his mind had been a hollow shell, all the areas that should've been lit up like a Christmas tree for a man of his psychic ability totally dormant. Particularly if he'd recently gotten an upgrade courtesy of the recent resurgence of magic on the planet, that was the exact opposite of what I should've seen.

Which meant that had been some seriously potent stew someone had plunged into his bloodstream.

But Valetti was shaking his head. "If you're suggesting that we keep track of all members of the Connected community in Venice, you are sadly mistaken," he said. "The senate, yes, of course. But as to the rest of them, psychic or not, we leave them to do what they will."

It was all I could do not to make a face. Back in Las Vegas, with far fewer years of history to back us up, the Connected community of the Strip had done a better job of looking after itself.

Venice had a Strip too—anything that was directly on the lagoon or that abutted the Grand Canal. Did they have their own psychic community? They had to, surely. Signora Visione was a member, and even, potentially, the gondolier. Certainly the two tailors the prelate and Valetti had recommended to us.

Something to check into, potentially, but I didn't think Valetti would be of any use to us there.

His next words confirmed my suspicions.

"If someone was preying on the members of the Connected community, there would be no way of telling," he sniffed. "This is Venice, a city with all the crimes, vices, and sad stories any other city has. Half the time, you'll find that the Connected are most likely preying on each other."

"Fair enough." I decided to take a different tack. "Have you noticed any changes within the magician community, then? You mentioned that some of your number had been affected by the recent energy spike. Has that caused any rifts within the group, any confusion?"

"Not at all," Valetti said firmly. "We are, at heart, an organization of academics. The events that led to the change in magical ability for many of the magicians, not merely in Venice, but worldwide, has been a subject of intense conversation and intellectual debate. But it wasn't as if we stood around trying to see who could make the largest fireball."

"Would any of you consider yourself competitive? With each other?" Based on my reading in the Casino of Spirits last night, the answer to that was a resounding yes.

Valetti merely shrugged. "I suppose if we ever attempted to conduct magic in a group setting, that would be an issue, but that's simply not how we work. The art of magic is predominantly an isolated experience."

I thought of Armaeus in his fortress back in Vegas and had to concede the point. Valetti wasn't wrong. All my questions kept spinning around, but instead of finding answers, they merely found more questions, a Möbius strip of insanity. "And there aren't—weren't—any disagreements within the group? You said yourself that you weren't exactly friendly with Balestri. Did he have any outright enemies?"

"Signore Balestri was not powerful enough to have enemies," Valetti began, but then he checked himself as if considering it for the first time. "Although I dare say, he certainly must've attracted some ill will for him and two of his associates to have met with foul play in his own home. Perhaps he'd run afoul of the dark practitioners. He *was* dabbling in the drug trade."

It was all I could do not to let Valetti know what I'd found or hadn't found in Balestri's brain, let alone share the fact that someone had tried to forcibly keep Nikki and me from attending the meet-up at Ca Daria tonight. But I didn't want to scare the man any more than he was. He was already on his second hit of scotch. I detoured down a different conversational side street.

"Well, whoever is doing this isn't too confident in themselves or in the results of their little experiment."

"What do you mean?" Valetti sat back, looking confused.

Nikki picked up the tale. "Think about it. We've got someone going around hitting people with drugs—and killing them on top of it. That's not what the butcher's recipe was supposed to do."

"Signore Balestri's death was ruled a suicide," Valetti said quickly. "And we have no way of knowing what the effects of the technoceutical in his system was, or if there even was any sort of toxin present. He could simply have killed himself."

"Excellent point." I sat up. "What was the finding in the canal with Marrow and Greaves?"

"It's far too early to tell. The police were adamant that no firm determination could be given, however, as to cause of death."

"You saw them with your own eyes, Valetti. What did you see?"

He held my gaze, the picture of misery, and didn't speak for a long minute. When he did, his words were raw and agonized. "I saw nothing on them, no mark at all. But regardless what had been done to them *before* they died, they definitely weren't intended to be found. At least not if the shattered wine barrels in which they'd been stowed were any indication."

He reached again for his glass with a shaking hand.

CHAPTER TWENTY

"This doesn't make any sense," I grumbled, pushing through the crowd.

"I can't tell if you're frowning. Are you frowning? Because if so, knock it off. People are starting to stare."

Despite my foul mood, I managed a chuckle. Nikki and I were at Piazza San Marco, part of the roiling throng waiting for the opening parade of Carnevale to begin. We were dressed relatively circumspectly today, she in a long white cinched robe with a gold mask beneath a white feathered hat, and I in a black robe and silver plague doctor mask. We'd already seen Chiara and two other members of the magicians' senate roaming around, looking suspiciously casual. Oddly, they wore the same garb they had the night before. It seemed to defeat the purpose of a mask, if you didn't change your attire once you'd been identified. Then again, maybe they wanted to be known, at least to each other.

"So we've got someone who's riffing on the butcher of Venice but instead of hitting kids—as far as we know—he's restrained himself to dropping off cookbooks of doom," I said. "We've also got a theory that the original butcher was working on a recipe to nullify the magic of his opponents, but absolutely no verification that the recipe was successful. We know the butcher died under brutal circumstances and that he'd had some very bad things happen under his roof, but that's about it."

"Bringing us up to now, where we've got three dead magicians, one of whom we know was poisoned, the other two…were probably poisoned, since they were also at the main dead guy's house. But even if Greaves and Marrow were poisoned, they definitely didn't hop into a couple of wine barrels or dump their own bodies into the water. Which, frankly, is a sticking point." Nikki tapped her finger on the chin of her mask. "If you're trying to make a big point about how magically intense you are, why leave the bodies hanging around, even stashed in wine barrels? Why not simply make them disappear?"

"Because you need the bodies for some other reason. Has to be." I scanned the crowd. There were several hundred people filling Piazza San Marco that I could see, and I suspected the actual count was well into the thousands. Nearly everyone was in costumes and masks, the adult-sized revelers decidedly more decked out than the children, but even the children were sporting colorful capes and face paint. How many kids actually lived in Venice? I suddenly wondered. Were there schools? Gondola bus stops?

Oblivious to my thoughts, the knot of children that'd caught my eye raced through the crowd, laughing and shouting, and my gaze lifted briefly to the adults through whom they were weaving. Most of them paid no attention as the kids brushed by, of course, their eyes fixed on the parade route. I glanced back to the children. Quick, darting hands, fast-moving feet.

Were the little scamps pickpockets? Not the easiest gambit when your marks were all wearing costumes, but—

"Yo, dollface. Is that the Devil talking to Chiara?"

Nikki's intrigued question brought my attention back to the opposite side of the parade route. "Yup, that's definitely Kreios."

Chiara stood with her head tilted back, her tricorn hat covered with a profusion of feathers and flowers, her attention fixed solely on the man in front of her. Kreios, for his part, had changed his costume slightly in that he no longer wore a lion's mask. Instead, he wore a plain white bauta mask, and his hooded cape was knocked back to reveal his long, tawny locks.

"Well, they're looking a little chummy." Nikki's observation wasn't at all jealous, merely astute. And I agreed with her. "I'd had it in my head that Kreios was at the powwow last night to keep an eye on us, but he *is* the official emissary to these guys, whatever that means. Do you suppose there's business they're conducting? Business we should know about, since we're ass-deep in the senate's problems right now?"

"I..." I let the word trail off. My boasts to Valetti about the Arcana Council's full support notwithstanding, I had no real idea what the political machinations of the Council were, and up to now, I hadn't needed to know. "So far as I've ever been able to tell, the only time the Arcana Council has reached out to other people is when they're looking to add to the ranks."

"Fair," Nikki allowed, her gaze still pinned on Chiara. "And supposedly, these are the most powerful mortal magicians in all the world. Which means Venice right after a rift in the magical universe probably wouldn't suck as a recruitment trip. When's your next check-in with Armaeus?"

"I don't have one scheduled. Kreios said he was keeping a low profile on this job, which, if they're looking to recruit new sorcerers to open seats on the Arcana Council, is an interesting approach."

Nikki nodded. "Let them get sucked in by the Devil and have them agree to terms before they meet the Magician and realize exactly how powerful he is. Seems sort of shifty, but that tracks with Armaeus. Don't think I haven't noticed how your job as Justice gets weirder with every new thing we learn about it. I also had Simon run down anything he could find on Mrs. French, as well as whatever information he could dig up on Abigail Strand before she ascended to Justice."

"You know his loyalty is first and foremost to Armaeus." Even as I said the words, I winced. I knew I needed to trust Armaeus more, and I did. Mostly.

"Yup. But the beauty with Simon is that when it comes to matters of the heart, he's—pardon the pun—pretty simple. You and I may understand that the Magician keeps his cards close to the vest, but in Simon's eyes, Armaeus loves you more than life itself. To him, there is no secret that two lovers of your caliber wouldn't share."

I snorted. "I don't think I was ever that young."

"Roger that, but it helps our cause until the Magician figures it out. Simon may tell Armaeus we've been snooping, but at least he isn't shutting us out. And the intel he's found is useful. Turns out, Mrs. French is a Revenant—not immortal, not a superhero, not even super Connected, just really long-lived."

"I wondered about that." Currently spread all over the world in tiny communes and protected villages, Revenants were Connecteds with varying levels of psychic abilities, but their biggest claim to fame was their exceptionally long life spans. More than a few vampire tales had sprouted up over the reclusive race, which they leveraged when they needed but avoided as much as they could. "She's legit old, then."

"Probably only about a hundred more years left in her, maybe less." Nikki nodded. "Simon found nothing on the Lost Boys, but I think we can take Frenchie at her word on them. They healed quicker than they should've from the attack in the library and are now up and around, no worse for wear. All those boys were probably low-level Connecteds before the evil shrink got a hold of them. That kind of augmentation would go for a lot of dough on the arcane black market, if someone could figure out how it was done."

"Abigail knew."

"Maybe, maybe not." Nikki shrugged. "What Simon was able to dig up on your predecessor is a little murky at best. She stayed in her position about three years before she iced herself, or was iced. During that time, she closed approximately fifty legitimate cases and an untold number of ad hoc inquiries."

"Fifty," I repeated. "And her mind was well past fried by the end."

"No one knows for sure how far she was gone, but yeah, it doesn't look good."

I recalled once again the horrified cry of the young librarian, begging me not to open Mak'rep's box. "I don't see how I can effectively do my job if my mind is going to crack with every new case I open. I definitely didn't feel well after the first one, which doesn't bode well for future job performance."

"You pulled out of that, though, pretty quickly." It wasn't a question. Again, Nikki couldn't read my mind, but she could read my memories. And my memories were chock-full of obsessing over my bobbleheaded reaction to Mak'rep's magic box.

"I did. By the time we landed in Venice, I wasn't even thinking about it anymore. Not much. But it certainly doesn't make me want to jump on the next case that comes through 'official channels.' So, we're going to have to fix that."

"Or take it as an occupational hazard, one that you're far better equipped to handle than Abigail was. Simon was able to discover that while she hadn't expressed any magical abilities of note prior to her work with the psychiatrist, her uncle had been fairly notorious during Regency England for his connection to itinerant tinkers, presumably members of the Romany caste. Uncle Strand apparently had a thriving trade system with them for tinctures, tonics, and cures."

"Old-time technoceuticals," I said, turning to stare at her. "He was a dark practitioner?"

"It would appear. From everything Simon was able to find, Abigail herself didn't practice. Then again, she apparently was the victim of sleepwalking even before her employer started experimenting on her. And who's to say how Connected she was prior to those experiments, or how twisted? We've already begun to see how the nutcase gene seems to travel quite happily down the family line, if the case files in the library are any indication. If the Strand family had a history of mental instability, that's something we can check. It's possible that Abigail was dramatically more impacted by the mental slog of the casework than you will be."

"I hope you're right," I said. "But I'd like it better if there was a way we could know that for sure besides trial and terror."

She snorted. "Agreed. I'll keep Simon on the job and see what he can find out about her earliest cases. Maybe something she encountered helped the crazy along."

I lifted my brows behind the mask. I hadn't thought of that, but it made a lot of sense. Every time you opened a box in the library, or a pneumatic tube or a scroll case, you had no idea what lay inside. It was completely reasonable that those cases had been bespelled by Justices long since passed. I had no idea why anyone would want to do that, but that didn't mean it hadn't happened.

"Speaking of, crazy at your six," Nikki muttered, and I barely turned around in time to fend off the rushing attack of a short man in a jester's costume, his pointy harlequin's hat bobbing in alarm. The same jester from the senate's meeting last night, I was almost certain. He hadn't struck me as unusual last night, but now I could feel the energy rolling off him in waves.

"What have you heard, what do you know?" he panted, and Nikki grabbed one of the jester's flailing hands, dropping it as quickly as the man practically ripped his arm away.

"Stop it, stop it, stop it!" he blurted. "Please, I beg you, don't *touch* me."

"Okay, okay," Nikki said, both of her hands going high, and though her face was a blank mask, I could hear the surprise in her voice.

I flicked my third eye open and trained it on the jester, then forced myself not to flinch back as well. Dude was *jacked*. His electrical circuits were vibrating off the charts, and his biological processes were struggling to catch up—stomach churning, heart thudding, blood pulsing. But he still had us at a disadvantage, because I didn't know who the hell he was.

Nikki, fortunately, had gotten what she needed. "Signore Samuele Budin, Venice resident, midlevel magician—but not midlevel so much anymore."

"Not so loud!" Budin made an urgent gesture with his hand, and I looked around, surprised. The noise of the parade route had been abruptly and effectively muffled, as if someone had thrown a blanket over the crowd. Over the crowd—or over us.

"Whoa," Nikki said, though she resisted the urge to poke the cone of silence around us. "That's pretty cool."

"Of course it is," Budin said, finally relaxing a notch as he straightened to his full height of five foot five. "I have very recently become one of the strongest magicians in Venice, but does your precious Arcana Council realize it? No. Kreios spends his time sniffing around Chiara as if she can conjure more than regrets the next morning."

I stifled a snort, but instantly knew what must have happened to the magician. "You were affected by the recent shift in magic?"

"I was *transformed* by it." Budin revealed this with such candor, I was taken aback. "I was on holiday in the Diego Ramírez Islands." When I didn't react, he clarified. "Nothing much there but birds, but I *like* birds. And the islands are situated at the very bottom tip of Argentina." He eyed me meaningfully.

"Argentina," I said weakly. "Oh."

The South Pole had been ground zero for the influx of magic that the war on magic had unleashed on the earth. If Budin had been getting his bird on below Argentina when the burst happened, that put him directly in the path of all that magic. I was surprised he wasn't actually glowing at this point.

"Yes. *Oh.* Whatever you and your people were fighting there, I was struck to the ground with it. When

I woke up hours later, I was so sick, I could barely move. But by the next morning…" He waggled his fingers, and tiny sparks swirled around them, looking remarkably similar to my own blue spectral fire. "I came back to Venice immediately and have been working to control my abilities ever since. Control them and *hide* them, which is why you haven't noticed me before."

I pressed my lips together. The only reason I noticed him now was because he was as annoying as a gnat, but he did raise a good point. What if other magicians in the senate were hiding from me? How would I know?

Budin leaned toward me now, fairly bouncing. "You haven't noticed me, right? Of course you haven't. I haven't done anything to merit the censure of Justice. But the Devil should have, last night. I mean, yes, I was taking care not to show my cards, but he's the Devil. He should know that I at least *have* the cards."

"I thought you guys were a bunch of academics," Nikki objected. "I totally missed any steaming cauldron at your little committee meeting last night."

"Ordinarily, yes. But all that is changing now. Magicians are stepping out of the shadows, ready to do real work. And with the butcher and his recipe booklets returned? All these whispers of Nul Magis and what it can do to the truly gifted? I *know* I'm the next target. And I'm not going to let him get to me, you hear?"

"Okay, okay," I said, lifting my hands to ward off another round of Budin hand flailing. "We're looking for the guy now, and I appreciate the information that you've been augmented. It helps. Has anyone else, that you know of?"

"Not Chiara," Budin sniffed.

"Besides her. The prelate? Valetti?" I frowned. "I honestly don't know who else was in the room yesterday."

"Most of them are posers, but has that stopped Kreios from talking to them—them, not me? No. No, it has not."

"Well, by your own admission, you were kind of working not to be noticed."

"But he is the Devil of the Arcana Council," Budin said again, more petulantly this time. "He should know."

I was beginning to suspect that the Devil knew more than he was letting on, no doubt for his own nefarious reasons. "Well, you're not wrong. But who else is amped up?"

"I have no idea," Budin said with a huff. "At first I thought Valetti was brighter, stronger than usual, but he downplays himself so well, I have lost the ability to see what is real and what is an act. The prelate hasn't offered a display of his abilities since he rose to his position, so he's worthless. Marrow and Greaves had amped up, but they're dead now. *Dead*."

"Amped up how? How do you know?"

"They told me. And before you ask, I was with my family yesterday before the meeting at Ca Daria. I didn't kill them. Why would I kill them? They were only in the city for Carnevale. It was their bad luck that they went to visit Balestri and not me."

"Any reason why they would do that? Was Balestri amped at all?"

"He wasn't—but he was pure-blooded, and he felt his time was finally coming to step into the full light of the senate. He knew—*knew* that he'd been targeted, but given his relative paucity of skills, he had no idea why. He was planning to leave the city."

"You know this how?" Nikki asked levelly. "Are you taking Black Elixir too?"

"Don't think I haven't considered it," Budin spat. "It's no good for general premonitions, though, only personal ones. And I've been careful. Everyone thinks I'm a fool." He reached up and meaningfully batted one of the floppy ends of his harlequin hat. "It's time for that to change."

"In your opinion, where should we look, then?"

"Everywhere but at me," he said. "And in a hurry. The senate of magicians isn't like most organizations. Our biggest events aren't at the end of Carnevale, it's over the next three days. First there's tomorrow's Spectacle, then there's the Magicians' Ball two nights later."

Nikki tilted her head. "You mean everyone comes into town and it's over in a few short days? Who planned that party?"

"It's not over, but it can't begin until the alliances are struck. The rest of Carnevale is spent executing against everything decided on by the alliances, which happen at the beginning. Otherwise, the big party takes place, everyone leaves and…it all dissipates."

"That…does make sense." As Budin talked, however, I noticed that the kids were back at the fringe of the crowd. And they weren't alone this time. A trio of tall and lanky costumed figures trailed the jumble of elbows and knees, keeping a careful distance. There was something about their attention on the children I didn't like. Kids weren't my total focus anymore, but old habits died hard.

"It also cuts down our timeline pretty significantly," Nikki observed. "And so far, we don't have a lot to go on."

"You have more than you think," Budin said. "Balestri may not have taken Black Elixir, but Marrow and Greaves had, and they knew what was planned for them. They called me from their hotel rooms, left a message for me—but I was with my family."

"So you've mentioned," Nikki said, eyeing him a little more sharply.

Budin poked his finger in the air, hard. "Talk to the police and have them check the two Englishmen's abdomens."

It was my turn to sharpen my gaze on the magician. "Their what?"

"Their abdomens. If what they feared would happen to them was true, they'll be missing several organs, without a single incision mark on them," Budin said, his breathless voice turned horrified. "They were eviscerated by *magic*."

CHAPTER TWENTY-ONE

"Valetti in five," Nikki murmured, glancing up.

"What? No!" With another flurry of finger movements, Budin dropped the cone of silence around us and smoothed down his costume. "He can't know about me."

"You don't trust Valetti?"

"I'm a magician!" he hissed. "I don't trust anyone."

"Signorinas!" Valetti called out boisterously enough, and I didn't miss Budin's flinch as he turned. "And old friend," Valetti continued.

He and Budin embraced in the kind of European air kiss that might originally have been invented to accommodate costumes. "The parade is bigger this year than ever, yes? So many people, so much excitement." The count swept his arms out as he turned, and true enough, the parade had started. I squinted at the crowd around us and frowned. The kids were gone. So were the dark-garbed men trailing them.

Without hesitating, I flicked my third eye open, laying out the crowd in front of me in a sizzling electrical map.

To my utter surprise, Budin's jester had gone back to a totally normal level of movement. The man was still quite obviously Connected, but his abilities were sufficiently banked to the point I wouldn't have looked at him twice if I didn't know what he was hiding. He really was a high-level Connected if he could hide from even me. Beside him, Valetti glowed with a far stronger Connected vibe. Off into the crowd, Chiara glowed with levels similar to Valetti's, though her agitated circuits were due in part to the proximity of the Devil, I had no doubt.

I took the moment to survey the Devil with the advantage of my special sight and noticed something else too—his circuits glowed a different color from Chiara's and Valetti's and even Budin's did. While the magicians maintained the usual whitish blue of Connected energy, Kreios's circuitry had taken on a decidedly golden hue. What in the world…

"Welcome to the Arcana Council, my dear Sara Wilde."

The words popped into my mind with Kreios's pure, seductive drawl, and my brows leapt behind my mask as he chuckled. But he didn't dampen the golden hue of his energy signature.

"Not didn't. Couldn't. There are some benefits to Council membership, no? But for now, I'll bid you a fond addio." The Devil turned, then turned again—and I lost him in the shifting throng.

Interesting. It would be helpful to know there were Arcana members lurking about, no question.

I swept the rest of the crowd for other Connecteds—there were surprisingly few, and those that were tended to stay in small clumps, barely moving at all, as if caught up in deep conversation. A trio of women right next to the parade route, their energy arcing even higher than the plumes of their feathered hats, a pair of beak-faced plague doctors hunched together near the edge of the square, looking like vultures awaiting the first death at the party—

And then I saw them. The energy signature of children was unmistakable, darting through the crowd at waist level, reeling and bouncing along as the children themselves ran and darted in and out of clusters of people. With my regular eyes now focused as well, I could spy the dancing feet, the fluttering hands. These were definitely pickpockets at work. Then the kids moved farther, out of focus of my regular eyesight, though I could still follow their electrical trail with my third eye.

"—Police report," Valetti said, and the words drew my attention back enough to refocus on him. He was looking at me expectantly.

"Sorry—the parade. It's amazing," I said, gesturing lamely at the brightly colored horse-drawn carriage that was lurching forward in front of us. "I got distracted."

Where I expected annoyance, I got only indulgent understanding. "Venice, it is a city like no other." Valetti sighed happily. "I am so glad you are coming to understand. But the police report, I was saying, is due within the next day. I've used what small powers I have to expedite its completion."

I was beginning to suspect that where Valetti was concerned, there was no such thing as small powers, and I wondered how deep his influence went in the city. I decided to take a shot.

"How are the police handling the return of, ah, your troubles?" I asked, catching myself almost too late. Certain words tended to draw the attention of others, no matter how general. "Butcher" was one of them.

Valetti nodded at me appreciatively, then made one of his trademark dismissive hand gestures. "They do not respond because they do not know, you see? As far as we can tell, only the magicians received the book, and only the magicians are at risk."

"But—the children." I glanced back to the far end of the crowd. More people had thronged into the square, but I could still track the boisterous, rampaging energy of the children. "Shouldn't they be warned about possible attacks on children?"

"In the midst of Carnevale? With absolutely no proof that such a warning is needed? I assure you, they would not thank me for that. They have far too much other work on their hands with so many visitors to our fair city."

"Yes, but…" I tried to reassure myself by watching the tumbleweed circuits of the children, clearly Connected, clearly safe, laughing and rushing and shouting through the crowd of those unsuspecting tourists—

And then a rush of darkness overtook their energy.

"Hey!" Without waiting to explain, I pushed between Valetti and Budin and took off at a run, barreling along the parade route for several feet before I was forced to leap back into the crowd. The children had moved away from the edge of the parade, and even now I could see that trail arrowed back toward one of the cobblestoned side streets of the square.

But between me and that tumbling, sparking dance of light was another type of energy, malevolent and smoky, stronger than anything I'd seen from the dark practitioners before. And there was no question that these men, these Connecteds, were dark practitioners, or at least the minions of dark practitioners. I remembered the golems that Mak'rep had sent into my library, but these weren't like that. These were humans.

I pushed against the crowd like a salmon swimming upstream and then kicked it up a notch, making headway as I reached the edge of the square. The energy of the children had changed as well. It was moving at a fast, steady pace, no longer darting and dancing. The energy of beings trying to escape. They cut left into a particularly dank-looking street, and I had no choice but to run after them. I plunged left—

Straight into a virtual brick wall.

The impact of the magic leveled at me was so strong, I felt the separation of each of my bones, down to the tiniest bits in my fingers. I was flung back into something at least reasonably soft, but before I could react, I was bound tight with restraints that momentarily trumped my own magic. With both my third eye and my regular eyes blinded, I struggled to lift my hands, the heat of my spectral fire billowing around me as I jerked and twisted, trying to break free.

"Enough," hissed a voice right up to my ear as my mask was ripped away and replaced with a black sack.

"Let me *go*!"

"You want to know the truth about Abigail Strand, about the legacy you've inherited?" The voice was heavy and dark, speaking in rapid Italian. "Then you will let us take you and tell you. It isn't far. But you must come now."

At the sound of Abigail's name, some of the stuffing went out of me.

"What do you know about Abigail?" I asked mutinously. I couldn't see, and my hands were still lashed to my side, but my legs were still free. The man with his arm around me hustled me along, and I let myself be hustled. Once I got free, I would blow up an entire city block of these asshats, but for the moment, my curiosity was stronger than my pride. "And what did you do with the children?"

"Give me five minutes to get you where we need to be, and you'll know everything." The man's voice had dropped. It was soothing now, placating, and I instantly distrusted it. Still, I could blindly trot with the best of them, and in far less time than the five minutes he promised, we slowed again. The hood came off my head, and I was turned around, blinking with my ordinary sight as I took in the view.

A half-dozen children stood before me, their eyes wide with excitement, the expressions on their faces one of pride and satisfaction. Children who'd just done a very good job, I decided. The same children I'd seen in Piazza San Marco.

I grimaced. If this was any indication, my reputation for saving all the children, everywhere, was going to be a problem. I needed to toughen up in a hurry. And with another glance, it was easy to see *why* this particular group had known what button to push with me. I could tell immediately who and what they were. Dark practitioners—more than half of them scored with the silver mark of Justice at their temples. I'd circulated among them for several years, and though I didn't recognize the particular crew in front of me, I didn't have to know them by name.

"Do you know who I am now?" I asked, and I didn't recognize the sound of my own voice. Low and malevolent, it shimmered in the air around me. Another second later, the bindings on my arms fell away, burning to a crisp in my sudden spurt of righteous fury. Another helpful discovery: I had righteous fury.

To their credit, the men in front of me didn't move. They were Venetian from what I could tell, gaunt and dark haired, their skin tanned deep bronze by the sun reflecting off the lagoon. Their eyes were dark as well, sunk into their weathered faces, and they watched me now with the indifference of men who knew their time would eventually run out.

"We know that you may well come for us, yes," one of them said, clearly their leader, though he looked no different from the others. "But not today. Today we come for you."

My energy jacked up another notch, irritation riding high. "You want to explain what you mean by that?"

"I mean we are not stupid, Justice Wilde. We aren't now, and we weren't back in the time when it was Abigail Strand who was plucked out of obscurity and raised to the highest level our kind had ever reached."

"Your kind. Abigail's uncle was a dark practitioner. She wasn't."

"Are you sure about that?" My third eye focused on the man in front of me, and sure enough, his Connected abilities were off the chart. Higher than Valetti's, even higher than Budin's. In another place, it might well have been him that the Devil would be chatting up for potential work with the Council, not Chiara.

Who was to say those conversations weren't already taking place?

"Who are you?"

"My name is Lorenzo Garcia, and I am at your service. You have come to Venice for the senate of magicians, and in truth, they are a worthy group. But we have our own assembly, yes? And we are here to tell you, you cannot lay the evil that is taking place in this city at our feet. The original butcher—yes. He was a dupe that we used horribly to advance our own causes. We make no apology for that. But the acts of this Nul Magis? No. That is not us."

"Why should I believe you?"

"Because you have very little time to find out who is behind this. The magician who has stolen our history is very strong, and he is very much aware of the impacts of the recent shift in magic. He will not wait to use his potion more widely, to secure his position in the senate and among the magicians of the world. He will negate the magic in any he considers his rival."

"And you won't?"

Lorenzo spread his hands. "I am telling you, we have our own agenda, much as we have since time immemorial. The recipes we created were not intended to kill the magic within the practitioners, only to augment it. That a few of them went terribly wrong—only a few—is the reason no one knew of them. The Connecteds they affected were lost to history, the magicians who were affected, well, they exacted their revenge. But the truth is, all the recipes prepared by Biasio Cargnio should have worked to enhance magic, not destroy it. They didn't. We improved the formulations, found the problem, created new formulations. By then, of course, it was too late for the poor butcher. And his recipe book that contained the spell for Nul Magis was lost to us."

"Who was the witch doctor?" I asked. "If Biasio was an unwitting dupe, who was the man who lured him down the primrose path?"

"The sins of the father…" The dark practitioner in front of me sighed, gesturing to himself. "He was my distant ancestor. I have his strength and his depravity in my blood."

I curled my lip, disgusted. "He was the Red King?"

"The Red King! No, no, not at all. That was a name reserved for far grander magicians than we."

"Really. Like who?" Once again I thought of the books in the library of Justice. There had to be something in them.

Lorenzo tilted his head. "That will take some research. It would be a favor I'd be happy to grant—"

"I don't need your favors, since most of you are marked, whether you know it or not. Just as your forefathers probably were in Abigail's time when she apparently cut you a break. I'm a hell of a lot less inclined than she is, though. But say I help you get this Nul Magis off the market. What does that get me from you?"

"What is it you want?"

"You know what I want. You guys want to prey on magicians your own size, you knock yourself out. But you're preying on the weak and defenseless, and that's gotta stop."

Lorenzo glanced toward the knot of children who were staring at me, transfixed. "The life of a child burns the brightest."

"You have no idea how sick you sound right now."

He tilted his head, clearly understanding my demands. "I cannot speak for everyone."

"Oh, I think you can."

"But no, it is too much. Too much work to ensure compliance. There must be more in return for such a concession. And of course, it is nullified in the event of your death."

"Lucky for everyone concerned, I don't plan on dying for a long time. But I don't mind hearing you out. What else do you want?"

To my surprise, he leapt on the question, leaning forward. "What every dark practitioner has wanted since they first struck out to carve out a place of magic for themselves," he said. "We change one of our most fundamental processes, we work with magic that is fully formed, we build our strength, then we want a voice. A place. A right to coexist even if our methods are not your methods, our code and creed are not your code and creed."

"You are *murderers*," I reminded him.

"And so is your Judgment. And your Emperor. You cannot deny it."

I opened my mouth, then shut it. Lorenzo smiled. "That's right, Justice. You have our terms. We do what you ask and protect the children of our community…we want a guaranteed seat on the Arcana Council."

He couldn't be serious…and yet, I could tell that he was. Worse, I could feel my own deep-seated desire to believe in Lorenzo, to trust and support, to imagine that a lifetime—several lifetimes—of depravity could be washed away with one simple promise. I was a fool to accept him at his word, I knew it in my bones. And yet…

Inspiration struck. There was a reason why I'd ascended to Justice; my judgment wasn't always ironclad. Fortunately, I knew someone's who was.

"Very well…" I said, and it was my turn to smile. "But even to begin that process, you're going to need to be judged worthy. And from where I'm standing, you've got an awful lot to prove."

Lorenzo stiffened. "I don't understand."

"You don't have to. I know someone who will be happy to explain."

I pulled my bands free and set upon the score of dark practitioners, as the alleyway exploded into smoke and fire.

CHAPTER TWENTY-TWO

By the time I dragged myself back to Piazza San Marco, the parade had long since left, but the revelers were still going strong. Nikki didn't ask about the smoke damage to my costume, and I didn't share Gamon's enthusiastic greeting to the tea party of dark practitioners I'd dumped into her parlor. If Lorenzo and his crew were serious about their promise, I'd see them again.

If not…they were dark practitioners. The screens that had flared to life to catalog their misdeeds had made that obvious enough.

Nikki and I spent the rest of the day going over the recipe booklet we still had, avoiding Valetti and hassling Mrs. French to find the books I'd located in the library. So far, she'd not found any mention of the Red King, which irritated me no end. There had to be something there.

The invitation to the Spectacle came to Valetti's palazzo the following morning while we were dining al fresco on the terrace. I could get used to dining al fresco, especially high enough up that you missed out on whatever aromas were hunkering in down at sea level.

A staffer knocked respectfully at the door, and Valetti looked up, all arched-brow surprise. I didn't so much mind his exaggerated responses anymore. After multiple days and multiple masks and costumes, it was a pleasure simply to see someone's face and be able to read their reactions in a glance.

"Excellent." Valetti beamed as he took the invitations from the silver salver. For a moment, I felt like we were in the middle of a Regency romance, minus the hunky guy at the head of the table. And come to think of it, I'd gone way too long without a hunky guy to look at. I knew Armaeus had decided to let me fly my first job solo, but surely Kreios had receiving hours today. I needed to see where he was staying. "There are three invitations, so I'm very happy to extend the warmest wishes of the magicians' senate to both of you to attend *lo Spettacolo* tonight. You will be absolutely enchanted, believe me."

He chuckled at his own joke, then eagerly handed over the invitations, waiting expectantly until we both dutifully opened the envelopes. No sooner had we unsealed the flap than the envelopes burst into feathers in our hands.

We reacted instantly.

"Hey!" Nikki snapped back in her chair, her hands going up as if to ward off a fireball. She turned to me, and her startled expression turned into a grin as she eyed the smoking ruin of my envelope. "Well, that's going to be tough to explain if you're supposed to show up with the card."

"You…" Valetti stared at me as well, his eyes as big as saucers. "There was no flame."

"There was flame. You just didn't see it," I said grumpily. I poked the ashes away, but whatever actual invitation might have come along with the magic trick was definitely down for the count. "Next time, don't give me a bunch of exploding feathers without warning. Don't give me a bunch of exploding anything."

"I thought it was cute," Nikki said, leaning over the silver-tipped white feathers that had collapsed into a neat pile atop her invitation. She slid the card out from beneath the plumage and read aloud. "We're to meet at the Palazzo Mystere tonight."

"The Mystere!" Valetti said, as if this was news to him. He tore open his own envelope, tossing it a little as he did so. The explosive effect was much more impressive that way, a profusion of flying feathers that cascaded in a happy little storm over the card. He picked up the invitation and scrutinized it. "You are quite right. But there hasn't been a Spettacolo there in all the years I have served on the magicians' senate. A true coup indeed for the prelate to have kept this so secret."

Was that a tiny bit of jealousy I heard in Valetti's voice? "The prelate runs the Spectacle every year?"

"He has for the past ten years. He also hosts the Magicians' Ball at the Casino of Spirits, but the Spettacolo is, as they say, a movable feast."

"And this palazzo they've chosen is awesome?" Nikki asked. "It seems like every house I've entered in this town is cooler than the last."

"The Mystere is one of the oldest and most beautiful palazzos in Venice," Valetti said, but his voice was more perplexed than enraptured. He pocketed the card, then placed both hands on the table. "If you will excuse me, I have much to prepare. Please do accept my apologies, Justice Wilde, for startling you with the invitation. I should have warned you."

"I should've warned you that I don't like surprises." I added the slightest bit of emphasis to my words, but if it made an impression on Valetti, he gave no indication.

We watched him leave with bemusement, and Nikki turned to me.

"Was it something we said?"

"Not us," I reached for her invitation. She handed it over, and I read its contents. Though the envelopes had been hand addressed, the card inside looked generic. I could only assume that Valetti's had read the same as Nikki's. And there was nothing there of interest. The name and address of the Palazzo Mystere—which sounded a little ridiculous, frankly—the attire of "standard" and the time. That was it.

"What's standard?" I asked. "Are we wearing the same costumes we wore to Ca Daria?"

"That would be negative. I already got a call from Signora Visione that she's expecting us at three o'clock for a fitting. I think she got a kick out of us."

"Or she wants something." I'd shared my run-in with Lorenzo Garcia already with Nikki, and we were both still coming to terms with it. I had no love for the dark practitioners, but the carrot they were dangling was pretty hefty. And the man was right: I had made my peace with Gamon, whose crimes were numerous, specific, and brutal.

"Or that." Nikki nodded. She gave me a long look over her espresso. "You haven't told Armaeus yet about Lorenzo and his gang."

"There's nothing to tell. I'm Justice of the Arcana Council, and they were marked. I brought them to Gamon's door, and she can hear their case. If Gamon judges them worthy to approach Armaeus with their request, they'll be given that chance."

She made a face. "You know he'd support you if you wanted him to at least listen to the guy."

"That's not the question." And it wasn't. I knew without a doubt that Armaeus would support me, no matter what I did as Justice. Setting aside his personal feelings for me, he wanted the Council to be strong. You couldn't get that if you micromanaged your members, beyond a few hard and fast rules. Only trouble was… "I suspect he supported Abigail Strand as well when she was Justice. Not in the same way, maybe."

Nikki scoffed. "I sure as hell hope not."

"But it sounded like he gave her a pretty long rope. And with that length, she entered into some relationships that maybe she shouldn't have with the dark practitioners. Relationships he let happen."

"Or she was already in those relationships, and she couldn't find an easy way out." Nikki's phone pinged, and she scanned a few screens with evident satisfaction, then stood. "Either way, you're not her, and we've got our own itinerary. You ready to go?"

"You mean go, go, or teleport, go?"

"The latter. The morgue is closed today, and you've got a clear shot at…this. Simon snapped it before he shut down the cameras early this morning." She flipped her phone around and showed me a utilitarian room with a lot of metal drawers lining one wall. It was dark, and empty, and creepy as hell.

"You've got to be joking."

Nikki waved me quiet as Valetti's housekeepers entered to clear away our plates, apparently signaled to do so by Nikki standing. I followed her as she moved to the side of the terrace, and waited until she continued in a low voice.

"No matter what Valetti said, the police aren't releasing the report on Greaves and Marrow anytime soon. In fact, it wouldn't surprise me if he's squashed it. But Simon did some digging around and found out where Greaves is stowed."

"Of course he did."

"Simon also told me that Greaves's brother is flying in tomorrow to identify the body as next of kin and sign the papers for release. We all suspect those signatures will be meaningless if someone wants the disposition of the remains to remain, well, indisposed, but they've kept the body close at hand for viewing, which means you can also see it. You know…really see it." She tapped her forehead with a long, manicured fingernail. "With your magic eyeball."

I grimaced. "What's it going to be stuffed with, sawdust?"

"Don't know. But if they aren't doing an autopsy, or if they're quashing the results of that autopsy, no one will ever know if they've got beanbags for kidneys or not. In real life, Greaves and Marrow were unmarried and lived together. Possibly partners, possibly just roommates. Either way, a hell of a way to go for them. They deserve better."

I thought about the purple corona that had surrounded both men. They did deserve better, I thought. They deserved Justice.

In the end, teleporting into a morgue was a lot more exciting than it should have been. While Simon's image was solid on the broad strokes of the room, apparently the morgue wasn't quite as closed as he'd believed. I poofed into existence close enough to a dead body to check its back molars.

"What in the—" I wheeled back and crashed to the ground, barely scrambling behind a rolling metal chest of drawers before a tech blew through the door. For the next twenty minutes, I died a thousand deaths as the tech helped prepare a guy who'd endured just one. Finally, he deposited the corpse in a drawer and exited, and I peeked up from behind the chest of drawers.

I scuttled over to the wall of shelves, found the drawer for Greaves, and pulled it out.

My third eye did the rest. I gazed at Greaves's bloated, mottled face, then swept my gaze swiftly down his body. He'd been a magician of some power, I could see even now, despite his light having been so forcefully stamped out. There'd been no Nul Magis administered to him either. He'd been killed by some other drug.

But that wasn't the piece that was important. I didn't have to fake my gasp as I staggered back from the gurney.

The magician Greaves had been hollowed out, then expertly rehealed...with a jumble of what looked like extra parts shoved inside him. I couldn't even tell if the extra parts were human.

"Sweet Christmas, I'm sorry, Greaves," I murmured. The purple corona around his head was fainter now, but still present, convicting me.

The thick voice behind me made me jump. "Explain to me, if you will, why I should not arrest you right now and turn you over to Interpol, Ms. Wilde."

I jerked around so fast my head spun, and came smack up against Detective Tall, Dark, and Dour from the night before last. "I'm sorry, I think there's been some mistake," I offered lamely, never mind that I was standing in the middle of a Venetian morgue without any right to be there. "I mean, I happened to be walking by, took a wrong turn, I don't know how I ended up in—"

"Ms. Wilde." At the detective's stern tone, I looked at him—really looked at him. And beneath the badass dark eyes and short, cropped hair and lantern jaw, he was definitely Connected. Which meant...

My eyes went wide. All three of them. "You know Greaves and Marrow are magicians," I accused.

The detective's expression didn't change. "I got the request from Count Valetti to expedite cremation today. Count Valetti is a longtime patron of the Venice police, and we are grateful for his support. There have also been rumors that Valetti has…esoteric interests, but at first I thought nothing of that. These men, this Greaves and Marrow, they were not Venetian citizens, however. It is not so easy as that. But there was definitely something that did not feel right about these bodies, you see? And there was also something odd about their energy, even in death. So I thought I would wait, and I would watch. I confess, I was curious to see who came for them."

"Maybe I was curious too."

"Perhaps so, but I also paid attention these past few months when a particularly striking brunette was designated first with a Blue Notice, and then with a Red Notice, and then with no notice at all, from Interpol. I rather liked the looks of her, so I took notice. I did not expect to meet you here, however."

"That makes two of us." I directed his attention back to Greaves. "How much do you know?"

"You understand, we see many, many drowned bodies here in Venice. This one bothered me, and I am not without resources of my own. While I did not have the advantage of second sight, I do have access to a hospital with ultrasound scanners. It took very little convincing to find someone to help me."

"I'm sure," I murmured. Even for an Italian, he was unreasonably attractive. I suspected a lot of people were happy to help him.

"In their scans, I saw what I suspect you saw as well. Only, unlike me, *you* were expecting there to be…animal parts where human parts should be. I would like to know why."

I rocked back on my heels, wondering how to play this. I was on this case in my role of Justice, with the task of protecting the Connected community from itself. The police were not supposed to be part of the equation. Nearly everywhere on earth had police, however, and most of the time, I'd be dealing with criminals. How had the previous Justice handled this?

Then again, Abigail had been certifiable, so her methods were probably less than ideal.

The detective seemed content to wait and watch me as I worked through the finer points of the problem, but I had a fitting to get to.

"You want the truth?" I asked abruptly. "I'm inclined to give it to you."

"I would find that very…unexpected," the detective said.

I plunged ahead. "Greaves and Marrow were magicians, part of an order that meets in your fair city every year at this time. They were targeted for their organs because human organs go very well with the production of magic-based drugs. With me so far?"

The detective's face had shut down, but not for the reason I immediately suspected. "Technoceuticals," he said.

Okay, so maybe the guy was more than a pretty face. "Yes. Someone wanted these magicians' parts for a new strain of drug, and they got them. But, being the tidy sort, they cleaned up after they got what they needed. I'm not really sure how they did that, honestly, but there's a lot of rogue magic running around that we haven't quite accounted for."

The detective let the rogue magic reference pass without comment. Good man. "And you're here…"

"To get who did it."

"And then?"

"And then suggest that they turn themselves in to the local authorities," I said, offering him a winning smile. "I can't say for sure they'll be willing to do that, but that's the plan."

"You think I'll believe you?"

"I do." I nodded. "I think you'll believe me for exactly four more minutes while you walk me outside and let me go. And then I think you'll remember that the word of a woman who was on Interpol's most wanted lists not all that long ago is probably not worth anywhere near as much as the proof you have on your medical scanners. Except sharing what's on your medical scanners will cause you a lot of headaches, because someone will eventually have to acknowledge that organs were taken out of a human being without any visible incisions. So you'll think, what the heck, maybe I'll give Sara Wilde the time she needs. And then you'll quietly put Greaves and Marrow back on ice, and you'll wait for another, oh, say, seventy-two hours. If within that time period I provide you what you'll need to get the people who killed these British nationals, without the trouble of explaining everything that happened, specifically, then I'd say we have the makings of a beautiful friendship."

The good detective stared at me a long, quiet minute, working out the details. Then he smiled and gave me an exceptionally dismissive Venetian hand wave.

"I can do that," he said simply.

Chapter Twenty-Three

The Spettacolo was already in full swing by the time Nikki and I showed up at the front door of the Palazzo Mystere. The palazzo occupied an unusually large section of real estate down a winding side canal off the Grand Canal, not appreciably far from the Casino of Spirits. We could see the elegant white stone building rising behind the walls, illuminated with what looked like industrial-strength lights, and we could hear the music from half a block away.

It sounded like we'd arrived at the circus. The doorman greeting people in front of the imposing iron gates was wearing a suitably staid top hat and tails, but his cravat was bright pink and his waistcoat a garish green. Inside the courtyard, fireworks burst above the walls, and there were cheers and laughter audible over the brightly playing calliope music. By the time we'd reached the front door, there was only one couple in front of us, both of them in identical costumes of dead white, including white tricorn hats and short capes over long body-fitting shifts. They were approximately the same build. They would be impossible to tell apart unless they were standing right next to each other.

No one would have that difficulty with Nikki and me. She stood in a new pair of platform riding boots, these in crimson red, a color that contrasted dramatically with her deep black robe and black-and-gold mask. Her red hair flowed magnificently beneath her tricorn hat and long crimson satin gloves. I'd traded up as well to a feathered cape of white and silver, my silver hat and white mask making me look like a walking incarnation of the ill-fated invitation that had summoned me here. I'd asked Signora Visione if there was any significance to that, and she'd stared at me like I was a lunatic. Helpful.

The guardian at the gate didn't bother asking us who we were, merely checked something off in his ledger book and stood to the side. I wondered at that, and as we walked by, eyed him with my third eye. And blinked.

His own third eye winked right back at me.

"C'mon, c'mon, you're ruining our entrance," Nikki complained, reaching back to hustle me along. Once through the imposing door, there really wasn't anywhere else to go but down a long red-carpeted walkway, flanked by tall, skinny vases of sputtering sparklers. The circus theme continued into the surprisingly large courtyard, with colorful tents set up every few feet, the smell of popcorn and cotton candy in the air, and even a straight-up menagerie of animals ringing the space. That part had to be an illusion, but it was a very effective illusion.

We reached the end of the walkway, and a harlequin dressed in all the colors of the rainbow hustled up, carrying a tray of champagne flutes. "Welcome! Welcome, Benvenuto!" she sang out as we took our glasses, then she twirled off. I noticed several other similarly dressed women and men moving through the crowd, clearly the waitstaff of a supremely indulgent catering group.

"Justice Wilde, Miss Dawes."

I'd seen the prelate enough times to recognize him when he strolled up to us, even though he'd changed his austere attire of the night before last to a midnight-blue cloak and hat that offset his stark white plague doctor mask. I glanced around to see if anyone had paid attention to him calling us out by name. Once again, it sort of defeated the purpose of costumes if people knew who you were. But that didn't stop anybody from wearing costumes, clearly. Even the illusionary menagerie animals wore masks.

"You honor us with your presence."

"I get the impression it's the most sought-after invitation in town," I said.

"We like to think so. I understand you also paid a visit to our local police today, as well. Did you find what you were searching for?"

I didn't need to hide my surprise, given the advantage of the mask, but I worked to keep my voice steady. "The magicians don't have a mark on them," I said. "I assume you already knew that?"

"That and, I have come to be informed, they are missing enough of their internal organs to produce an unreasonable supply of Nul Magis." The prelate nodded. His mask's mouth was tilted up in a benign smile, belying the darkness of his words. "Valetti informed me of this a short while ago, having recently gotten word himself. He's…understandably distraught."

"Why's that?" Nikki asked, while I gritted my teeth behind my own mask. Exactly how many Connecteds were working in the morgue today? "From what I could tell, the count didn't have much use for Greaves and

Marrow. And he already knew that they'd been stuffed into wine barrels."

"Killing is one thing. Any fool can kill another human. But that these two supposedly low-level magicians were targeted by the butcher raises three issues. The first, the butcher is not only targeting children—perhaps isn't targeting them at all. The second, Greaves and Marrow were clearly far more advanced than we thought they were for the butcher to make them his target. And three, the butcher is taunting us with his invincibility." As he spoke, the prelate tilted his head, his dark eyes gazing at me through the mask. "I understand that you were brought here to solve this problem, Justice Wilde. It would seem we need your assistance more than ever. And soon."

"With respect, we'd barely gotten off the plane when these magicians were murdered—" Nikki pointed out tartly, not missing the censure in the prelate's words.

"Of course, of course. Not a criticism, merely an observation. But we are now up to three murdered magicians, as well as the assassins and Count Valetti's man. The two most popular events of Carnevale are over the next few days. It would seem time is short for us to stop more bloodshed."

The calliope music changed, and the prelate glanced up, murmuring his apologies as he moved off to rain on someone else's parade. I scanned the crowd in his wake, seeing the profusion of blue-white Connected magic, and…I frowned. Golden circuitry too? Were there more Council members here than Kreios?

"Well, he's a barrel of laughs," Nikki muttered. We were on the move as well, naturally shifting to the edge of the crowd, closer to the illusionary menagerie of animals. There were already far too many people crammed together outside the Palazzo Mystere, thronging the streets of Venice for Carnevale. This courtyard, with all its sparkling lights, raucous music, and riotous colors, seemed far too oppressive on top of that, the Spectacle its own affront against us.

"He's not wrong," I shrugged. "We haven't done our jobs yet."

"Dollface, we've been here three days. You've barely had time to get over jet lag, let alone solve a crime that's befuddling what're supposedly the greatest magicians on the planet. There's more we have to learn about all this."

"Yeah, maybe—"

"Justice Wilde!"

The voice was so small, so pathetic, that I instinctively looked down, expecting there to be a child at my feet. There was a diminutive figure, all right, but it wasn't a kid. "Budin?"

"What in the—" Nikki began, but the man crouching behind the potted plant hissed at us.

"Don't look at me!" he cried. He was no longer wearing his jester costume, but instead was in a nondescript black tricorn hat, bauta mask, and black cloak. The very simplicity of his outfit conspired to make him stand out. That and the fact he was crouching in the foliage. "They're all around me. They *know*. I'm in danger, and you have to save me!"

His words were too close to Balestri's, and I stiffened. "You're going to have to stand up, Budin, or this isn't going to work. You're safe now."

I added that last bit almost as an afterthought, but it seemed to have a galvanizing effect. "Oh, thank God." Budin stood and threw his arms around me, hugging me tight.

"Whoa, whoa, now, you're okay, you're okay." As I looked down at him, my third eye engaged, and I noticed the complete change in his circuitry. "Well, not completely okay. What are you on, Budin? Have you been drugged?"

"I took it," he said, pulling back, his eyes flaring wide behind his mask. "I had to know—I couldn't let them creep up on me unaware! And it happened exactly how the Black Elixir said it would."

I snapped my gaze to Nikki, and she looked hard all around us. "There's an empty tent down to the left. I'll get food or whatever. You got him?"

"I got him."

Budin whimpered and clung to me as we turned.

"Dude, pull it together and walk like an adult," I ordered as Nikki strode away toward the buffet. "We're going to sit down away from all the people, and you're going to tell me what you saw."

"No." Budin straightened suddenly as if he'd been shocked. His head swiveled on his neck, his gaze darted everywhere. "If they see me with you, they'll know. They'll know! I have to hide. But you must know what I have learned."

"I have to know," I agreed, wishing that Nikki hadn't disappeared so convincingly into the crowd. "Tell me right here, then. You're safe."

"Safe..." He nodded three, then four times, drawing in a ragged breath. "The drug said that my palazzo wouldn't be safe, but this isn't the first time I've been threatened. I have cameras, guards, dogs. Only the first proved helpful. But not their fault, not their fault...not when what came..."

"Focus, Budin," I said as his words trailed off. "I need you to tell me what you saw." I glanced around again, taking in the riot of colors. The circuits of energy dashing around the courtyard of the Palazzo Mystere were all rushing at full tilt, it seemed, exactly what you'd expect at a party full of magicians.

Budin gave a wet cough. "I went into my safe room and took up watch. I could see everything, every room, every window, every door. No one knows that I have built such a modern room in my ancient home. And sure enough, they came."

He swiped for me again and missed, so he contented himself with clasping and unclasping his black-clad hands, giving the effect of someone deeply under the influence—but of what? Black Elixir still? I refocused my attention on him, but I couldn't tell anything in the chaos of his neural circuits.

"Who came?"

"*Ghosts,*" he said, the word almost a keening wail. "They flooded into my home, past my guards, past my dogs, wraiths of shadow and death."

"Actual wraiths." The work of an illusionist? I thought of Balestri again, and the illusion of the Red King speaking through him. Someone was showing off, flexing his magical muscles.

"Were they carrying anything? Knives? Guns? Anything like that?"

"No." He shook his head forcefully. "I should have waited, but I panicked. Sounded the alarm. The men rushed to my aid, dogs baying, but the wraiths disappeared. Of course, there is no longer any sight of them on the camera feeds, but I saw them. I did!"

"I believe you—"

Budin reached into his cape and pulled out a small cap in a plastic bag. "And then I found this in the kitchen. I hadn't even been watching that room but, but..."

"You were distracted." I took the bag and studied it. "What's this from?"

"It's a cap from an apothecary's vial. It'd rolled behind a stoppered bottle of wine. I—I had already poured myself a glass from that wine, and it was sitting on the counter." He turned at me with enormous eyes. "They poisoned my *wine*."

I was able to hide my grimace of disbelief. "Signore Budin, you can't know that for sure."

"I *can*," he said, shaking his head. "And to confirm it, I gave the wine to il Diavolo. He will tell you. He now most certainly knows I am a far greater magician than Signora Chiari."

"You gave it to Kreios? To test?"

"They're coming," Budin batted me at the arms, and I turned, finally seeing Nikki heading our way. "You must save me, you must—"

I heard the strange sound a moment before the flash of silvery light shattered across my vision, and I didn't breathe, didn't even think, I merely reacted. With my hands already moving to fend off Budin's panicked assault, I jerked my wrist upward and felt the sting of the dart as it buried itself in the back of my hand. I flinched, feeling the injection push through fabric and skin and into my bloodstream as Budin froze in front of me.

"You will save me," he gasped, his eyes so wide, I thought they'd roll back in his head.

Though he hadn't been struck, Budin collapsed to the ground in front of me with a bleat of terror even as my own sight swam, my body feeling…strangely slack. Loose. Not right at all. A flower of unyielding darkness blossomed deep inside me, and I felt myself tipping backward—

Then I was caught in a pair of warm, strong, strangely familiar arms.

"Now, now, my dear Sara Wilde," purred the Devil in my ear. "You die on my watch, and there will be hell to pay."

CHAPTER TWENTY-FOUR

When I came to again, I wasn't in the circus setting of the Palazzo Mystere, I was sitting on a very well-appointed terrace that was quite noticeably not Count Valetti's. Calliope music still played far too close, and I was by no means alone.

"Whoa," I said, sitting back. "Please tell me you didn't call out the cavalry on my account."

Sitting, standing, and lounging around the elegant teak furniture of the palazzo rooftop were more of the Arcana Council than I'd seen assembled since the world had caught on fire. The Devil sat nearest to me, all Mediterranean chic with his flowing sun-kissed hair, deeply tanned skin, and an open-necked white shirt over his trademark ragged-hemmed khakis and beach sandals—never mind that it was February. His casual pose was ruined, however, by the tension in his clenched hands. Opposite him but all the way across the terrace was the Magician, dressed impeccably in a four-thousand-dollar ebony suit and what were probably eight-thousand-dollar loafers. Two females rounded out the Council. Death perched on the short terrace wall in a muscle shirt, jeans, and combat boots, her stark white-blonde hair shaved close to her skull on one side, and spiked high on the other. The High Priestess lounged in a nearby chair, regally nonchalant in her toga-styled gown, accessorized by a whole lot of amethyst jewelry. I hadn't seen her in amethyst before, I realized, my brain tugging hard at the sight of it. What was important about amethyst?

Then I noticed the other person on the terrace, sitting stock-still in a cushioned teak chair, his back straight, his eyes wide, his hands white-knuckling his mask. Signore Samuele Budin, looking like he was about to pass out. Again.

"Where's Nikki?" I asked.

"Still downstairs at the party," Armaeus said, his voice clipped. "We were able to get you out without anyone noticing, but she was too far away to not be a distraction. She's stripped off her gloves and is doing what she can to see who might have blown the dart that struck you."

Everything came crashing back in my memory, and it was my turn to stiffen—and by stiffen, I meant propel myself backward and almost over the couch cushions, my headlong reaction stopped only by Kreios's sudden grip on my shoulders.

"You're safe, you're here," he snapped. "You're healed."

"Healed?" The thundering of my heart refused to abate, the blood in my arteries jackhammered against my cells. I dragged in a heavy breath as adrenaline jacked and whirled through me, racing around like a crowd of first graders on the last day of school with no way to get out of the building. "What happened?"

Armaeus moved then, so quickly I couldn't fully process it. He caught both of my hands and brought them down, pulling the right one slightly forward. I glanced down at it.

"My hand," I said dully.

"You caught a dart intended for Budin," Armaeus confirmed. "The dart was laced with Nul Magis. It hit your system and…" He gave me a soft but undeniably fascinated smile. "You summoned us. All of us."

"I *what*?"

"Believe me, no one was more surprised than I was," the High Priestess said, her tone laced with condescension. "I was dead asleep."

I scowled in her direction. "That's what you wear when you're sleeping?"

"Be glad of it," she said, lifting up one arm bedecked with amethyst bracelets. "You drew upon the healing strength of these stones before I fully appeared on this terrace. You pulled everyone to you, except Kreios, who was helpfully on scene when you were struck."

"He g-grabbed me, pulled me with you, brought me here," stammered Budin, a breath before his mouth slammed shut and his eyes widened, as if he was shocked he'd said anything aloud. He swiveled his head around, taking in the luminaries that surrounded him. "I didn't mean to hurt her."

"You didn't hurt her. Don't take on karma you didn't earn." Death slid off the terrace wall and stood, walking over to Budin, who seemed to shrink into himself at her approach. I didn't blame him. Death had that effect on people. Though she'd served on the Council since ascending around the start of the Common Era, she'd made it a point to blend in with whatever the current version of badassery was. Right now, when she wasn't doing her part to shepherd souls into the next life or keeping demons from hurrying that process along for mortals, she was known as Blue, a famed tattoo artist and airbrush virtuoso who was a regular feature on the international auto circuit. Her torn clothing and sleeve of tattoos took nothing away from the harsh, otherworldly beauty of her sharply cut features and pale eyes, but as she got down in Budin's face, I could practically see the man's hair turning gray.

"What you have done, however, is a little on the stupid side. You're not a cat, Samuele Budin, with nine lives to waste. Regardless of what happens to you on the other side of this one, you need to live this existence to the fullest. That's not going to be possible if you keep hitting Black Elixir."

"I was frightened," he whispered, staring Death in the eye. We all sat riveted, watching this play out. I didn't know much about Death, but I realized that I'd rarely seen her interact with a human for more than a passing comment. Now she held Budin's full attention, his eyes almost glassy with shock. "They were coming for me."

"I know," Death said. "But we've figured out that Black Elixir's so strong because it is made with the blood of demons. That's why the premonitions worked so well, and that's why people die so quickly."

I stiffened in horror at this revelation, but Budin seemed focused on something entirely different.

"But I won't take the fifth hit," he said, shaking his head to emphasize his sincerity. "I know better. I just needed to see—to *see*. To *protect* myself."

"Your senate of magicians is supposed to protect you," Death said. "They didn't, and I'm sorry about that. But you can't keep that demon blood inside you. Not as a magician of your strength."

Budin blinked at her. "My strength?"

He looked so forlornly hopeful, my heart lurched sideways. Thank God, Gamon wasn't here, or I wouldn't hear the end of it.

"Yup." Keeping her gaze hard on him, Death reached behind her, and only then did I see the long, wicked-looking tattoo needle sticking out of the back of her jeans, the tip shiny and cruel in the moonlight. "Your strength. You told Sara you were the strongest of the senate of magicians, and you're not far off. We need strong magicians. We *don't* need demon hybrid magicians."

She moved so quickly that I jerked in Armaeus's hands, only vaguely realizing that it took both the Devil and the Magician to keep me on the cushions. Before Budin could react, Death whipped the tattoo needle around and plunged it into the side of his neck. His scream ended quickly on a garble as Death lifted her other hand, seeming to catch something that shimmered in the night air above Budin's head.

Meanwhile, a spout of black goop arced out from Budin's neck where Death had punctured him, splattering to the floor. I flinched back, and I wasn't alone. No wonder everyone was standing so far away from the poor guy.

As the geyser lost strength, Blue tossed the tattoo needle down and caught Budin's sagging shoulders with her right arm. Laying him down on the couch with a gentleness I wouldn't have expected, she cupped her left hand back over his eyes, and whispered words I couldn't hear.

Budin convulsed, let out a horrified gasp, then slumped on the couch once more…the steady rasp of his breath the only indication of life. But he *was* definitely alive.

Blue straightened. "Humans," she muttered, and she flicked something at the goop on the floor. It must've been a match, because the whole mess of it caught fire and burned with white-hot heat for the space of a heartbeat before evaporating into a thick dark smoke.

"If that stench remains in this toga, I'm stiffing you with the cleaning bill," Eshe, the High Priestess, flapped the hem of her toga and wrinkled her nose.

Death snorted. "What're you going to do? Fieldwork is messy."

"Are you serious with the world's slowest—*dollface*." Nikki Dawes came out onto the terrace, the wave of her focused attention hitting me full force even at twenty paces. She'd lost the mask and hat, but her unadorned face was stark with concern. "You're fine? You're…" She blinked, her thoughts clearly catching up with my memories, memories I hadn't fully been able to process yet. "You're fine," she said, more firmly this time. "What was in that dart?"

Kreios lifted a lazy hand and drew a small barb out of his jacket. "Nul Magis," he said. "Shot from a high-powered gun, it appears, with a sniper's level of proficiency. Nobody at the party could have shot the device, because the trajectory didn't work. In order for it to reach its target, it had to be coming from a position above the courtyard walls.

I frowned, looking out. "One of the other palazzos?"

"Given the specific direction, undoubtedly the palazzo directly opposite ours, which is owned by the head of police. This, unfortunately, does not narrow anything down. After the briefest of searches, well before any of this unpleasantness, Simon ascertained that three-fifths of the magicians' senate here in Venice is in one way or another in collusion with the local constabulary."

"But why would anyone want to hurt Budin?"

"There are several reasons," Armaeus said. He released my hands with the slightest squeeze, then stood again, strolling over toward the terrace wall. Below him, the party continued apace. "First, Budin had made his anger with the magicians' senate quite plain over these past several weeks. He wanted to be given due credit for his improved abilities, and no one wanted to give him the forum he needed to perform."

"He does seem like kind of a needy dude," Nikki said.

"Secondly, Budin knew more than anyone suspected about Greaves and Marrow," I put in. "He shared that information with an outsider. Me. That might not have gone over so well, though I don't think it'd be worth killing a man."

"It might not have been, but then he got caught up with the Black Elixir." Death made a face. "Stupid of me not to have figured this out before that sample you gathered from the drug dealer, but I'd only seen the effects on the dead, not the living. And I hadn't seen it at all in its pure form."

I turned to her. "Is that really possible, that it's demon blood?"

"Whoa, whoa, whoa," Nikki waved her hands in front of her, and locked eyes with me. Two heartbeats later, she grimaced. "Gotcha. So Black Elixir is black because of demon blood. That's just gross. And how exactly do you get a demon to donate its blood?"

"That's an entirely different problem," Death said, her lips twisting. "But, at least we know this technoceutical is definitely not the result of someone preying on children. I wouldn't even mind the hit the demons are taking, except for how badly it jacks up humans, who will simply never leave well enough alone."

I raised my own mental barriers carefully to keep my thoughts to myself, at least for the moment. I still had Lorenzo the dark practitioner's offer to process, and I didn't quite know how to present that yet. And there was also the problem of what the High Priestess had intimated.

"How many of you were in Venice already?" I asked. "I didn't summon you from across the globe."

"You didn't," Armaeus said. "Though I do believe you could have. We were staying...locally enough."

"Locally." Suddenly, I remembered the golden circuits I'd seen among the guests. "You were here. Like, here, here. In costume."

"I was not in costume," Eshe advised frostily. "I was *asleep*."

"It is customary for a quorum of the Arcana Council to attend the Magicians' Ball that marks the announcement of the magicians' alliance." Armaeus tugged his cuffs. "Normally we come in exclusively for that event, but given the unusual circumstances surrounding this year's event...we came early."

I stared at him, suddenly remembering the menagerie. Specifically, the skill with which the illusion had been rendered. "This palazzo is yours?"

"It's one of several properties the Council holds here," Armaeus said. "Rarely used, but it comes in handy when we need it."

"No wonder the prelate hasn't had access to it for so many years," I mused. "And that explains why he was able to get it at a moment's notice this year."

"He thought it best if no one knew the precise method of his acquisition of such a prime location. I thought it expedient to cater to his pride."

I swung my gaze back to the High Priestess, unable to let her comments go. "So let me get this straight. You were asleep when the, um, summons came. My summons."

"I was."

"Wearing amethysts."

The flash in her eyes betrayed her. "Not all of us require demon's blood to read the future," she said, her chin high, and suddenly, the dots connected for me. Before her ascension to the role of High Priestess, Eshe had been a Greek oracle of high renown, quite possibly the actual Oracle of Delphi, though she'd never a hundred percent come clean on that. And she'd apparently read the future…and seen me.

"You knew I was going to be injured?"

"I knew you were going to rashly put yourself in danger to save a human who was beneath your dignity," Eshe sniffed. "I decided I should probably be prepared. I was. When you arrived on the terrace, Kreios was able to lay you down on a bed of amethysts to draw the poison out of your system. Armaeus was able to hold the darkness of the Nul Magis toxin at bay until you could accept healing."

"And Death?"

Eshe sniffed. "She was here specifically for the human. She hates parties."

"I'm going to need to go back down there," I said.

"You are," Armaeus said. "Budin, for his sake, would be better served spending the rest of the night out of sight, and ideally the next two days. He believes most sincerely that a specter has moved into his home, and I am inclined to believe him. We are dealing with a magician of great strength, and unfortunately, a magician that we currently have no way to identify. There are simply too many people who have been exposed to the influx of magic to know how it affected any one person."

"Uh-huh." I sighed, sitting back in my chair. And how are we going to figure that out in time for the Magicians' Ball? That's only two days away."

"We aren't, my dear Miss Wilde." Armaeus arched a winged brow. "You are. As Justice of the Arcana Council, you are our righteous hand. We may support you, but we cannot replace you. Both for the sake of the position and the sake of your personal safety, it has to be you."

I stared at him, then cut my glance around the terrace. Four sets of serious eyes stared back at me, while Nikki's eyes were filled with pride and more than a little worry.

I stared at my hand, the one that'd taken a blow dart full of souped-up demon's blood. "I'm so asking for a raise."

CHAPTER TWENTY-FIVE

"I find myself somewhat at a loss for why we're here." Armaeus's dry comment carried over the breeze as we approached the Casino of Spirits from the water, and unlike the rest of the pleasure boats and water taxis surrounding us, we angled toward the private dock with a sense of purpose. Two days had passed since the Spectacle, and the grand Magician's Ball was supposed to occur in this very place, later tonight.

But I wasn't here to party, quite yet. Armaeus stood beside me on the water taxi in what I supposed he considered casual wear—a cotton shirt fine enough to have been spun by the hands of angels and a pair of trousers that draped so effortlessly, they no doubt cost as much as the taxi we were on. Still, he'd gone along with me without any hint of objection until now.

"Aw, c'mon. Afraid to spend some alone time with me?" I fluttered my lashes. I wasn't very good at it, but I deserved an A for effort.

"Simon has already downloaded and cross-referenced the contents of the library, comparing it against the older, rarer texts we have at our disposal," Armaeus continued, ignoring my baiting. "He found no significant discrepancy in the translations, nothing redacted beyond normal loss of data to be expected with books that have no doubt been damaged and retranscribed countless times. There's nothing here that we don't already have."

"Good." I'd thought as much, in the wee small hours of the morning as I chased the last vestiges of the Nul Magis around my system. The faintest shadow of the magical concoction lingered, more to taunt me than to cause any danger, and I was almost glad of it. If I'd been easily rid of its taint, I would have discounted the drug altogether. The fact that it remained in my system nearly two days later, stubborn and cloying, had been enough for me to pay careful attention to everything I'd seen and heard since I'd set foot on Venice's shores. "How long has it been since you've been inside the Casino's library?"

"It can't even be called a proper library," Armaeus sniffed. "The collection they have on display is only a fifth of their total inventory."

"That's what Alfonse said." I glanced at Armaeus. "He totally has a magician crush on you. You know that, right?"

"The prelate is not the most powerful of the magicians in the senate, but he's undoubtedly the smartest. And, it would appear, the most discerning."

"Well, there he is. Try not to make him faint."

We pulled up to the dock of the Casino of Spirits, and as he had a few days earlier when Nikki and I had accompanied Count Valetti, Alfonse was waiting for us at the top of the ancient stone steps. But unlike that time, he didn't merely have one acolyte at his side. No, this time, fully a half-dozen men in long tunics and trousers stood watching as we reached the pier, their excitement a palpable wall of energy pulsing toward us.

"Hmmm," Armaeus said, surveying the crew. "These are men of some ability but no training."

"I suspect they're going to want your autograph. Try to keep them busy for, what, at least a half hour?"

"What?" Armaeus slanted a sharp glance down at me, then his mouth twitched. "You brought me along as a distraction?"

"You have proven to be an excellent distraction so far. And I need to get into the library alone to poke around."

"I assure you, you'll be vastly disappointed by what you find in there. The books are nothing more nor less than what they appear to be."

I shrugged. "Maybe. But I still need to look. And I need you to keep Alfonse panting after you while I'm doing that. On the other end of the property, ideally."

"Hmmm," Armaeus said again, this time more noncommittally. But I could tell his mind was turning over the possibilities as he returned his gaze to the eager young initiates. The Magician might be a solo practitioner, more comfortable locked up in his glass-and-steel fortress than he was interacting with the great unwashed, but he wasn't immune to adulation. Very few demigods were.

"Welcome, welcome," the prelate practically gushed as we stepped off the boat. He gave me the briefest of salutes, then turned his full attention to Armaeus. "I'm so glad you were able to visit today, Signore Bertrand. It was all I could do to keep the attendants to this select group of our most promising new practitioners in Venice. They, of course have heard about you, and—"

"And I have been deeply remiss in my absence from your fair city for so long," Armaeus acknowledged, his rich, rolling tones striking the prelate temporarily mute. The men surrounding him looked equally poleaxed, and I struggled not to roll my eyes. "I would very much like to see the preparations for tonight's Magicians' Ball, but I brought Justice Wilde along for some quiet study in the library. To assist with her recovery."

"Oh!" The prelate turned back to me even as I schooled my expression into one of wan Post-traumatic Magic Disorder. I'd been feeling pretty chipper, but of course, Alfonse wouldn't know that. He'd known only that I'd taken a barb intended for Budin—who was still out for the count, though for far different reasons. I didn't know if Budin was having such a hard time detoxing from the demon blood or getting over his up-close-and-personal brush with Death. "Forgive me, Justice Wilde, I didn't even ask. You are so very strong."

"It's okay, I'm much better, really," I demurred, flicking my third eye open to survey Alfonse's circuits as he dithered over me. From everything I could tell, he remained Johnny Straight and Narrow. He was concerned about my illness, embarrassed more than a little, but otherwise, his emotions read as completely guileless. I recognized that a not insignificant part of me *wanted* him to be guileless, however, and that made me uneasy.

I managed a slight tremor in my hand as I gestured to the building behind me. "The Magician was so interested in seeing the changes here, and I thought I might spend some quiet time in rest and meditation—perhaps in the library? While you show him all around?"

"The library! Of course." The prelate's eyes flew wide at the prospect of having the Magician to himself. He turned eagerly to one of his acolytes. "Please show Justice Wilde to the library and ensure she is comfortable, then return to us immediately. We will start in the Grand Hall, and I know you will not want to miss any of that conversation."

"Of course, Your Grace," murmured the unfortunate man who was designated my tagalong. He politely gestured me toward the beckoning entryway as the prelate made an attempt at small talk about the weather with Armaeus, but as soon as we'd crossed the threshold into the Casino of Spirits, I turned to the initiate and smiled, reaching out to touch his arm. I didn't miss his jolt as my deliberate pulse of energy shot through him. His eyes widened, and I knew immediately that the prelate had not shared with any of his people who I was or how powerful I was. It was possible Alfonse didn't know that last part, sure. It was more likely that he couldn't wrap his head around the concept of anybody being more powerful than the Magician.

Either way, his single-minded focus on Armaeus was all to the good as far as I was concerned.

"I've been here before," I said, infusing the words with ultimate confidence. "I know my way around. It'd probably be best if you returned to the prelate."

He blinked at me. "If you're sure? The library is all the way down this hallway, a door to your left flanked with—"

"One black column and one white column, yes," I said, giving him another winning smile. "I appreciate your reminder, but I can find it from here, truly."

I didn't even need to push him mentally. My words were enough, combined with his very obvious interest in returning to the prelate and the Magician. I watched him disappear down the corridor and back into the light with a soft smile that I couldn't help. How long had it been since I had been that eager to learn something new? To head off on an adventure into the unknown, uncertain of anything but my own ability to see my way through whatever reached out to hit me?

Well, okay. That was pretty much every day for me too.

I reached into my jacket pocket and pulled out my Tarot deck.

As I made my way down the corridor toward the library, I shuffled the cards. The same way it had the first time I'd been here, the casino's spirit struck me first and foremost with its age. This was a little odd to me, because it wasn't really that old a building. I'd been in crypts that dated back to the dawn of civilization. By comparison, this building from the sixteenth century might as well have been a Wendy's.

And yet, there was something indelibly sad about the souls that haunted the Casino of Spirits, for all its history as a house of ill repute back in the glory days of Venice. Perhaps that was the problem. Before, it'd been a place to go and drink and laugh and party, while now it was the province of shuffling priests and murmuring acolytes. I could almost understand its yearning for a return to another time, another era, when life was so much simpler.

I paused as a rush of cold air shivered through me. There was something in that realization, I thought, something important. The pull of the past was figuring very strong on the present terror of the Red King.

Up ahead, I could see the flanking columns at the end of the long hallway, and I flipped the topmost card almost haphazardly, knowing what I'd draw. This time, I was right: the High Priestess. Seeing her last night had jogged something in my memory, and not only because she was rocking some serious stones of healing. Eshe considered herself the bastion of esoteric learning within the Arcana Council. While the Magician cared about the magic that moved the world around us, Eshe's province was more the magic that moved the world within. The mysteries of the future, the realm of possibility, the hidden lore of secrets and unspoken desires.

Which was all too close to how the prelate and Valetti had described this collection of library books. Seeing the High Priestess now in the deck reassured me that I was on the right track. The answers I needed would be in the library. But I didn't think I'd find them by scrolling through the card catalog.

The door to the library was unlocked, and I slipped inside as quietly as possible, shutting it behind me. It closed with an audible click. I debated finding some way to block it, to ensure that I'd have as much time as possible to myself. In the end, I opted against anything obvious. There was no point in causing any alarm or, more importantly, tipping my hand.

I moved across the room, bypassing the long table and heading directly for the shelves that lined the far wall. There were several doors cut into the wall, each of them locked tight. I turned and surveyed the rest of the room, noting the sunlight as it played over the dust motes in the air. The room was brighter than I remembered it, almost cheerful in the morning light, and I noticed this time around that the windows were topped with stained glass transoms, which threw colorful patterns into the far corners of the room. I stepped up to the monks' table, settling in a chair as I spread the deck in an arc in front of me. When I was on a job, I rarely took the time to do a focused read. Most of the time, I was forced to check the cards as I was running for my life or about to do something relatively stupid. But now I took a deep breath and expelled it, drawing my fingers across the deck with a movement almost of reverence.

Around me, the room seemed to press inward, though not oppressively. Almost as if the very stones yearned to feel the touch of magic unlocked by the presence of these cards. The cards and someone willing to ask them a question.

"That's right," I murmured, "What've you got for me? What am I missing that I need to understand about the magicians working at dark purposes within Venice's ancient senate?"

Without pausing again, I reached out and selected three cards, flipping them in front of me on the table one at a time. Then I drew in a soft, startled breath and looked around.

The first card was more one of reassurance, I thought: Death.

While not too many people in the world would consider that a card of being on the right track, I'd seen Death not twelve hours earlier, and she'd been instrumental in my efforts so far, helping Budin get back on track. In a more general sense, the Death card meant transformation, but I didn't think that signified in this case. No, the most interesting elements to this card were the image of a skeleton riding upon a white horse, carrying the standard of a single white rose. I glanced back to the doors lining the room, each of them surmounted with a carved flower, symbolizing one of the sacred flowers of Italy.

The middle door featured a rose.

I stood and crossed to that door, unsurprised to find it locked. Fortunately, cards weren't the only thing I never left home without. Drawing a small set of picklocks from the interior pocket of my jacket, I made short work of the lock and stepped inside the room.

As Armaeus had warned, this room was night and day from the larger library room, and I pulled out my phone to use as a flashlight, preferring to wait to use my spectral fire if a more pressing need emerged. Then I fell into the tried and true search methods I'd used more times than I could count.

The third card in the reading was no surprise. The Red King, the King of Cups. Another indication that I was on the right track, most definitely. But the second card I'd drawn was the one I found the most interesting. The Five of Cups. Picturing a young man mourning the loss of three cups of spilled wine, the card was notable for several reasons. First, there were still two cups that were full of promise waiting beside him. Secondly, there was a house on the far shore, over a cheerful bridge, that if the young man could only see, he would know that his future was assured. Looking around this room now, I was at a momentary loss for how to find the next link to that happy state of future bliss. I scanned the room for anything related to wine, but of course, there was nothing here. The room itself looked like it hadn't been explored in years.

I walked forward, my eyes cast down like the despondent man pictured on the card. In this room, the books were shelved from floor to ceiling, several more stacked in boxes on small tables scattered throughout. But the books on the first level were all hoary with dust, clearly tomes read long ago and forgotten. Was my answer in one of those arcane volumes? I felt almost unnaturally compelled to plant myself on the floor and lose myself in their mysteries.

But no—that wouldn't help me. Stopping, I stared at the mysterious books for a long second, then, without moving my feet, straightened my body and leveled my eyes up, exactly where I would have been looking if I were the young man in the card glancing up to see the castle on the far shore.

One book stood out, a slim volume, its spine etched in gold, with a familiar, friendly name: La Casa di Valetti. Without thinking, I pulled the book from the shelf and tucked it into my jacket. As I turned, I felt the entire library sigh with long-held relief.

I stepped out of the room, noting that the sun had crept out of the shadow of clouds, and was now fully shining down on the library reading room, brightening the entire space.

A sound from the corridor made me jump. Someone coming to check on me, undoubtedly. Securing the book in my jacket, I hurried forward to sweep up the cards—and noticed something else as well.

With a trick of the newest rays of light through the stained-glass window, both the King and Five of Cups were now stained the color of blood.

Chapter Twenty-Six

Nikki met me at Signora Visione's, where we had what I dearly hoped was our last fitting of Carnevale. If I never wore another cape again, it'd be too soon.

"Since when do you check out library books without a card?" Nikki asked me, raising an eyebrow as I handed over the volume. "And where's the Magic Man?"

"Presumably, still with the prelate." I peered up at Signora Visione's sign. Her shop looked closed up tight, but as I watched the windows, a tiny twitch in one of them gave me the information I needed. She'd seen us, and she'd be down shortly. "One of Alfonse's flunkies was sent to make sure I wasn't going into withdrawal without access to so many magicians at once, and when I told him I'd see myself home, he almost collapsed with relief. I got the feeling they wanted Armaeus all to themselves."

"They wouldn't be the first ones," Nikki paged through the slender leather volume. "I don't read Italian, and there's no pictures. What am I missing?"

"Not much, except that the House of Valetti is one of the oldest and most favored in all of Venice, probably all of Italy, at least when it comes to magic. The family tree has gotten a little less impressive of late, but back in the day, these guys were the real deal. They were full-on conjurers, illusionists, healers, and mediums at various points throughout history. It's kind of impressive."

"Makes more sense why Valetti gives off the whole benign condescension vibe," Nikki said. Now she was staring at the windows as well. "Dude was one step shy of extolling the value of eugenics, you ask me. He must be thrilled at the influx of real magic in the world, for all that it was an unintended side effect. Oh—that reminds me." Nikki continued to scan the signora's shop front. "Mrs. French finally found the cases you were talking about—the dark practitioners from the sixteenth century. Sad to say, there were no Red Kings among them. He either wasn't a bad enough dude, or—"

"Or he never got caught. Him or anyone in his family." I shuffled a few steps away from the building, unease spidering across my nape as I looked at the design surmounting the shop's heavy door, but I focused on the design above it—a cup overflowing with abundance. A cup to mark the signora's shop. A cup…

"Pretty much." Nikki scowled at the locked door. "Are we ever gonna be let in?"

Cups. Suddenly, the reading at Ca Daria flashed in front of my eyes, including the one card that hadn't made sense to me, the Queen of Cups. Had it not been about Chiara, but instead about Signora Visione? A clue not about the Red King, but about someone I needed to protect from him?

Oh, *crap.*

The high-pitched sound of a child's scream, muffled under several layers of dress shop, rang out from the shop.

We bolted forward. Not bothering to waste time with the picklocks, I jerked my hands up, a ball of spectral fire playing over my fingers before pouring into the locking mechanism of the door. Metal melted, circuits fried, and a second later, the door sprang open—still largely intact, so we could close it behind us, but nowhere near the barrier it'd been. The inside of Signora Visione's shop was the same as it had been the last time, which was to say, dark. I lifted my hands, and the fire burst into four separate directions, hovering in the air like miniature disco balls. Now that we were inside, we could hear better—and what we heard was desperate crying. We darted through another set of sound-damping doors and entered Visione's dressing room, where the old woman lay on the ground surrounded by sobbing children, some of them clutching bolts of fabric to their small bodies.

"What happened?" Nikki barked as I lurched forward. Signora Visione's body was little more than skin hung over bones. My third eye flicked open as I reached her—and then I wheeled back.

"Poison," I hissed, noticing the telltale breakdown of circuitry. "Just happened. What'd she touch? What'd she drink?"

"Nothing—she drank nothing! She was coming to open the door, and she fell!" The children flung themselves at Nikki, clamoring in Italian, which she didn't know, but I didn't have time to play translator. There was no denying what Visione had been struck with, and I was more than ready for the job. I hadn't been able to heal myself under the influence of Nul Magis, true—but I was no longer under its influence.

I reached out with my mind, cradling the frail body of the woman in front of me with a web of energy that picked up the still weakly firing circuits of her neural system. I didn't focus on her physical reactions to the drug—it wasn't the physical part of the old woman I was worried about. It was her mind, her soul, the very heart of her magic. Reaching deep within her, I found myself sucked into the very earliest memories of her history, when she first became a magician. Signora Visione was seriously old. But those kernels of her magic were the root of the power of Nul Magis, I realized suddenly, and probably why children had been the preferred organic suppliers in the butcher's era. It was the newness of their magic that was important, that provided the leverage for the fell concoction to do its work—which had to be why Greaves and Marrow had been targeted now. They'd been Connected, certainly, and magicians of some renown…but their true birth into the arcane had taken place only a few weeks earlier, when they'd been exposed to the influx of magic as the world had nearly been broken.

My mind flashed to Budin as I held Signora Visione's core magic in the palm of my own power, breathing it back to life. The poor man had every right to be petrified, I thought. He'd also been reborn recently, and to far greater effect than Greaves and Marrow. He would be the prime candidate to provide source material for the nouveau butcher's dark concoction.

Signora Visione convulsed beneath me, which sent the children into a new paroxysm of squeals and bleats, Nikki's strident voice ordering them to chill out having a surprisingly galvanizing effect. I glanced up to see her drawing the kids over to the side of the room, half of them still hugging her and the others kneeling at her feet, huddled around her like a human crinoline, their fists to their chins as they watched me labor over the old woman.

I redoubled my efforts. The signora was now responding, the magic at her core opening up again from a tight, withered husk to a new-forming bud as I breathed fresh energy into her, sending it along her circuits like sand scattered across the floor. She shivered, and another layer of power built around the first, then a second, then a third, her body finally beginning to warm as she regained strength and began to slowly fight toward consciousness.

When she surged upward, however, her arms flailing, I barely avoided getting cracked in the face.

"Vattene!" she howled, and, failing to connect with my face, she took another swipe, only this time, her bony fist jammed into my solar plexus. With a grunt, I fell back from her, taking another crack upside the head as she changed directions yet again before I could grab hold of her wrists. "Vattene, vattene!" she railed some more, even as the children started once more to cry.

"Dollface," Nikki protested, clearly not impressed with my fighting skills.

"She's an old lady!"

I ducked a solid kick from said old lady and managed to fling my body onto her, holding her to the ground as the final round of her magical circuits fired and rejoined themselves. Signora Visione still kept screaming at the top of her lungs, but she was old, her screams were faint, and eventually, her lungs gave out. When she drew in a deep breath, I flattened myself on her until I was relatively sure she was close to passing out, then risked letting go of her hands.

"You're very strong. And very heavy," she said, her voice thick with the irritation I remembered so well from the first time we met. "Get off me before you kill me all over again."

I slid back from her, resting my weight on my heels. The kids surrounding Nikki seemed desperate to lunge toward the old woman, but Nikki held them tight in a thrall of magic that had nothing to do with her Connected abilities and everything to do with the fact that she had children of her own, once upon a time.

"You know what happened to you?" I asked as Signora Visione lay on the floor staring at me.

"Do you know what happened to your hair? I don't think so. *That* we will need to fix." She waved at me weakly as I leaned forward, scanning her body for any other issues now that the Nul Magis had been neutralized. There were none. For being on the cusp of death, the old woman held up pretty well.

"There was nothing," she said, shifting her gaze from me to the ceiling. "I go to the marketplace, I pick up the day's needs, I stop at the cloth makers, I come here. No one follows me, no one looks at me. They know better."

She sat up then, cackling a raspy breath when she saw Nikki stationed with her charges. "My hearts," she said, and as if they were a released rubber band, the kids burst forth and rushed her, somehow managing to stop in time so that they didn't break any bones. They lifted her off the floor and stabilized her, engulfing her in a group hug, though she was barely taller than they were. She sighed as she rested her hands on each of their heads, one after the other. This time, there was no fierceness to her expression, only enduring love. "We have work to do, yes?" she murmured.

The kids didn't move.

I tried again. "What was it like when you got to the shop? Anything different here?"

"No. There were the day's costumes to be picked up, and I met with a carrier, and then—"

"No, Nonna." A thin, muffled voice spoke at the edge of the scrum, and a child's curly headed mop popped up. She gazed at the old woman with large, dark eyes. "No one came to pick up costumes. They're all still here."

"What are you saying? Of course they are not." The pile moved with startling speed back through the dressing room and into the front of the shop, and sure enough, several large bags hung on the hooks lining the walls. Signora Visione scowled. "That cannot be. The men, they came! They all came!"

"Who did?" I asked, exchanging a glance with Nikki. "Were these costumes for the Magicians' Ball tomorrow night? Like for Valetti or Alfonse or Budin—"

"Them? No!" Signora Visione scoffed, throwing up her hands. "Those fools do not know from good design. Signora Chiara, yes, she works with me, but she is the only one."

"Signora Chiara," I said flatly. "You've worked with her a long time?"

"Her and her family before. She's the first female Marchesi on the magician's senate, but her father and her father's father was before, and on down the line, since the very first Carnevale. She will have to have children of her own, yes? Or perhaps her nieces or nephews, if she wants the line to continue. But she is very strong. And her costume is there." Signora Visione pointed to a bag that took up a good four square feet. Nikki hissed with interest, and even I fought the urge to peek under the cover. "She will come for it today at three, not before. She sleeps during the day before the Magicians' Ball, as should you." She said these words to Nikki quite sternly. Then she slid her glance to me. "You, eh. There is not so much need."

I snorted. "I appreciate the vote of confidence. But what are we looking at here? You saw someone enter, and no one did? And when you came to open the door for us, you blacked out?"

"Or someone entered, and I assumed it was for a costume. And it wasn't." She frowned. "But entering, it is not so easy. I would not have let anyone in."

"And you don't know who – ?"

"I don't remember. My hearts?"

The children merely stared at her, and she shook her head. "They do not see the customers usually. You are an exception." She looked at Nikki. "You make them smile."

Nikki nodded. "It's what I do."

"I'm going to need the names of whoever these costumes are going to," I said. "Whoever entered did so because you were expecting them. One of those has to be the lead we're looking for."

With grumbling agreement, Signora Visione promised she would give us the list, then hustled us back into the dressing room for another round of fitting. When she was done, she stood back, her scowl once more in place. "You are ready," she announced.

"You got that right, sister," Nikki said, sounding awestruck. She stood in front of a mirror, a vision in a shimmering coat of teal green, a profusion of peacock feathers swirling around her head. Her deep blue boots caught the light. "I don't think I've ever seen anything more beautiful." She glanced back to the old woman. "Do you do special orders?"

But Signora Visione was looking at me.

"And you! You are a masterpiece."

I smoothed down my golden cape, shot through with bolts of white. It was pretty, without question, though it was nowhere near the showstopper that

Nikki's costume was. The tiniest kernel of envy lay in my most hidden heart over that, but I was the one who needed to be circumspect, I reminded myself. I was the one who needed to blend.

"You are wrong, Justice Wilde, you will see," Signora Visione said, and when I glanced back at her, I could see in her eyes that she knew what I was thinking. I supposed you didn't work as a costumer for decades without being able to read your clients. "In this costume, in the Casino degli Spiriti, you will be truly seen by those who love and fear you most. Pay careful attention and know their reaction is both pure and right."

Chapter Twenty-Seven

The grand ballroom of the Casino of Spirits wasn't even in the casino proper but in an adjacent building across a wide, formally landscaped lawn. By the time we arrived, night had fallen, and the place was lit with torchieres and at least a million tiny white Christmas lights decorating every tree and shrub. From the water, it looked like a fairy wonderland, and I was absolutely certain that at least half the motivation behind these decorations had been for what distant passersby might think rather than actual attendees.

Which was not to say the attendees weren't arriving in suitable numbers to pay their respects.

I'd had a vague sense of the crowd two nights earlier at the Spectacle, but I'd been pretty quickly distracted, first with Budin and then with the little dart of joy that'd been intended for him. Even now, strolling beside Nikki with our requisite glasses of champagne, I felt the touch of the Nul Magis within me. Not harming me, not anymore, but not entirely leaving me either. If this was the magical version of an STD, I wasn't a fan.

The crowd tonight had a totally different feel to it too. Where the evening before last, they'd come to be entertained, to chatter and mingle and reconnect with friends old and new, tonight they came for more serious matters. Count Valetti, who'd spent most of the afternoon asleep in preparation for the event, was now totally in his element, blissfully mumbling about alliances and connections, referencing a decidedly analog little black book. Upside, said book was virtually hackproof; downside, the search function was decidedly labor intensive.

"He's still at it," Nikki said, angling her headdress of blue feathers to the right. I looked and caught Valetti looking back. He nodded rapidly as I raised a hand to him, then returned to his notations.

He wasn't alone either. Fully two dozen of the men and women milling through the manicured grounds were carrying some version of the small book, some gilded in silver or gold, some leather-bound, a few consigned to tablets—but only a few. All the magicians wielding these little compendiums of the arcane would glance around the nearest knot of people, check a few pages in their book, perhaps write a note or two, then move on. I didn't know if I was at a party or a show dog competition.

"What notes are they keeping in there?"

"It's for the alliances." The voice was all the more unexpected because it came at my elbow, and I stepped back sharply to once again avoid bumping into a man at knee level. The hat and thick cape rendered the masked figure a particularly shapeless lump, especially sitting on the low garden bench. The voice, however, was pure Budin. Once again emulating a potted plant. He really needed a new gig.

"What are you doing here? I thought you were going to sit this out." My tone was severe, but only because the last time I'd seen Budin, he'd been surrounded with security personnel at each of the cardinal points surrounding him, a virtual compass of protection as he'd dined on a late lunch at Palazzo Mystere.

Budin waved around him. "And miss this? My moment of triumph?"

"You're having a moment of triumph?"

He leaned forward, as bulky as a pup tent. "I was targeted by the butcher of Venice and *survived,*" he said, his voice decidedly more gleeful than it had been in the palazzo. Getting out and about had been good for him. "I was taken in by the Arcana Council overnight—overnight! And nobody knew the nature of the conversations we had, nobody knew the plans we were making, the arrangements."

"Ah…we weren't making any arrangements."

"I know!" He chortled. "But nobody else knows that. Even Alfonse is treating me better than he has in a decade, and I didn't have to do anything but nearly die to get his attention. It's wonderful."

He said this with a distinct lack of irony, and Nikki and I stared at him. "With respect, signore," she finally said. "You could die all over again tonight. I don't think that's the kind of attention you really want."

"No, no, I've learned my lesson," Budin said. "I'm wearing a high-necked cape for a reason, a skull cap, and a mask beneath this hat. Below my cape is full body armor."

"No wonder you're sitting," Nikki put in, but Budin waved off her sarcasm.

"I don't plan on making myself known, and I've been installed here since before the first guests arrived. Most don't even look twice. Plus, as I said, I don't need to keep the book this year. It's more enjoyable than you can possibly imagine to know that I don't need to keep track of the many alliances being struck tonight, because

I've already been ushered into the grandest one of all. Armaeus Bertrand has agreed to meet with me after the close of Carnevale to further my studies!"

I barely kept from spitting out my champagne as Nikki carefully held her own glass away from me. "He has?"

"You can ask him yourself." Budin waved excitedly toward the building at the far end of the gardens, and sure enough, a figure stood there, silhouetted against the bright lights of the entryway. Tall and regal, with a flowing black cape that seemed to shimmer in black and gold, it could only be Armaeus.

"You go inside," Budin ordered. "I'll be along once it's quiet again."

"No, *we'll* be along," Nikki said. "You've got a tendency to get into trouble."

"The bodyguard of the Council," Budin breathed, his voice sounding enraptured. "Assigned to me!"

"Right." I shook my head, but couldn't help but smile. "But hey, one more question," I asked. "What does my costume look like to you?"

"Gold and white, as it should," Budin said, beaming. "You look like the Arcana Council member you are."

Which sounded good but wasn't exactly a showstopper reaction. Then again, I was pretty sure Budin neither loved nor feared me, so maybe his take on my party outfit didn't matter so much.

I managed to down the rest of my champagne and grab another flute from the tray of a passing server, assuming that Armaeus would already be inside by the time I reached the ballroom building. I was wrong. The Magician waited for me patiently at the top of the steps as if we'd had a scheduled assignation.

He watched me climb the stairs, his face hidden behind a mask patterned in black-and-gold diamonds.

It suited him. "My compliments to Signora Visione," he said, his voice rich with approval.

"She isn't half-bad," I said. I glanced down at my own costume, still seeing what I'd seen when I'd first donned it—a shimmery gold-and-white cape, mask, and hat, almost austere in its simplicity. What I didn't realize until later, after Nikki had picked up on my petty dismay over my attire compared to her flamboyant silhouette, was that in my case, beauty truly was in the eye of the beholder, at least if that beholder loved me. She'd marched me over to a mirror, and when I stood in front of it, with her looking at me—I could see what she saw.

And what she saw was astounding. Gone was the simple golden outfit, replaced with a profusion of ebony and white feathers that coated my hat and cape and piled up at my shoulders. My mask was a falcon's beak studded with sequins, and my shoes were blinged up as well.

From there, I'd made it a point to be seen by at least a half-dozen others while I was standing near mirrors or windows—I'd even let my picture be taken in a selfie by an awestruck tourist. Every time, it was different, though other than with Nikki, it wasn't all that impressive. Once again, however, as the signora had told me: I wasn't dressed to impress everyone…

"So what is it you see?" I asked Armaeus as he held out his arm to me. He turned, and we walked into the building, crossing a relatively shallow hallway faced with a wall of open French doors that led into the ballroom beyond. That room, a gorgeous space lit with chandeliers, was already filled with a crowd of elegantly dressed figures of every description—as long as that description included a hat, boots, a mask, and a cape.

"I see Justice of the Arcana Council, looking as beautiful as when I first met her as Sara Wilde the artifact hunter," Armaeus said, his voice pitched low enough that I should have been the only one hearing him, though several masks around us turned our way. "I see you walking in a cape and hat of golden white, but you are not masked to me. I see your eyes, I see your smile, I see your fire. The same fire that builds me, destroys me, and recreates me again every time you walk into a room."

I stopped in my tracks, blinking rapidly behind my mask, trying to make sense of his words. "Are you…" I managed, narrowing my eyes at him, no matter how heavily my heart thumped its ungainly staccato. "Really?"

"You are Justice, you are Vigilance, and you are—" Armaeus paused, cocking his head, though I couldn't hear anything. "I believe they're playing our song, Miss Wilde."

At that moment, the music swelled in the far corner of the room, and Armaeus pulled me forward, gathering me into his arms as if I knew the absolute first thing about dancing.

"Act naturally," he murmured. "Think of it as a very slow fight."

"What are you *doing*?"

"Taking advantage of my moment with the most powerful woman in the room." He turned me again, his mask gazing serenely at the other couples on the dance floor, some pairings of what appeared to be two men, some two women, and others the mix that had been most common when the music wafting over the dance floor had first been played in European salons.

And then, I saw something else—the barest glimpse between light and shadow, two dancers so ephemeral they might have been my imagination, but for their vivid, transcendent emotion. There, among all the masked magicians, a man and a woman danced together in that grand hall—one, in the simple tunic and breeches of a sixteenth-century painter, the other in a gorgeous gown, her hair piled high on her head. The woman—who seemed by far the more sophisticated of the pair—gazed at the older man with gentle, almost bemused affection. The painter stared back at her with unabashed adoration in his eyes, his soul-deep devotion palpable all the way across the room.

My breath caught in my throat. It appeared that Luzzo the painter had finally won over the heart of his fair Cecilia, all these centuries later.

Armaeus tightened his hold on my arms, in silent acknowledgment of what I was seeing. Then he turned me around again.

"The Red King has arrived," he murmured. "His magic is cloaked, even to me, but the signature of the Nul Magis he carries in his weapon responded to the echo of the drug still within you. That much was made clear the moment you arrived, though we cannot pinpoint where his kernel of Nul Magis is. You can rest assured that he knows the danger you represent, however. Fear is building with each passing moment. He's looking for you now."

"He?" That made me straighten a little. "I was beginning to lay odds on Chiara being the one with her hands in the stew."

"Chiara Marchesi. It's not a bad guess, but her family gained its favor well before the 1500s. The Marchesis didn't need the boost of the butcher's concoction to gain their position on the senate—they created the senate."

"Well, you could say that about any of these guys."

"Not Alfonse," the Magician said. "His family is old and storied, but most of those stories, you'll find, are tied to the Church, not the cauldron. He has enjoyed great renown these past several years, but what is different now…"

"Is the influx of magic," I said. "But you can't seriously think Alfonse has anything to do with this. He doesn't seem…"

"Connected enough?" Armaeus tilted his mask down to me. "It is but one calculation of hundreds, but based on the reception I've had from him these past few days, it has merit."

"The reception—Armaeus, he thinks you're a *god*. And given his background, I don't use those words lightly. He's been waiting on you hand and foot and treating you like you're the OG of magic, if that's not redundant to even say."

Armaeus considered that. "I am the OG of magic," he countered.

"Exactly. And Alfonse has a particular passion for history and for everybody being in his proper place. Would the butcher have introduced you to a dozen aspiring magicians, people who reasonably might one day be stronger than you—certainly stronger than him?"

"I doubt quite seriously that he thought any of those acolytes would surpass my abilities."

"But his own?" When Armaeus didn't answer, I wanted to poke him. That was unfortunately difficult to do when both my hands were trapped in a dance I was only barely surviving. "Exactly. He wouldn't have. And I can't see him getting his hands messy with blow darts and poison, either—or hiring someone to do that for him. Neither can I see him killing, what are we up to—four people? Five, no *six*, if you count the attacks on

Budin and Signora Visione. That's an impressive body count for a cleric."

"Clerics have done far worse in the name of their popes, kings, and gods."

"Maybe. But not this cleric. Look."

Armaeus turned, and we both watched Alfonse approach a short, stocky man in a cape, recognizable only by his escort in her profusion of teal feathers. Nikki held herself like a cop, despite the over-the-top glamour of her ensemble, but there was nothing in her stance that made me think she was about to lay out Alfonse. If anything, the man's genuine reaction to the blocky Budin, complete with an attempt at a European air kiss, made his intentions about the man eminently clear to me. Budin had been right. Alfonse had taken his vote of confidence from the Council to heart and was willing to elevate him to higher status in the senate of magicians, and doubtless was about to announce that very decision this evening, in the clustered heart of the core believers.

Apparently, I wasn't the only person who thought so.

As Armaeus turned me around again in another graceful arc, my third eye flickered open almost of its own accord, and I swept the room, my heart beating more heavily as I saw the thriving, jumping, jittering bursts of Connected activity. The magical circuits of energy in the room were weaving together in a frenetic dance that had nothing to do with the swells of music from the musicians, the swirls and arcs of the dancers serving only to blend and weave the streams of power more tightly together. Everyone was caught up in the moment, the magic, the excitement, the splendor. Everyone except—

Except one figure at the far end of the ballroom, his electrical current bursting as well, but not with excitement or joy. It shot up in elegant calligraphied lines—a short slash, then a longer one—short, then longer. I focused on that oddly familiar pattern, unable to penetrate it. The sorcerer was a fiercely powerful illusionist, and his fury seemed to snap in the air like a sheet caught in the wind as he lifted a silver wand in time to the music. Was that an illusion too? Was he really holding up a wand with a spark at its end that beat with a familiar dull black throb of energy?

The same throb of energy that echoed within me, all the way down to the seat of my soul?

"No," I whispered as Armaeus turned me around again. In that moment, I knew I was truly seeing the Red King—perhaps for the first time since I'd come to Venice. Across the ballroom floor, I met the flat-eyed, fully insane glare of the once and future most powerful magician of the Venetian senate. He recognized me too, I realized with a start. He saw me as I truly was.

But this was not the first night he'd seen me.

Not at all.

The energy flares burst up again, one short, one long, graceful calligraphied slashes of power…just like an insignia I'd seen first on a sign, and then in a recipe book of spells, and finally here, in the heart of the magician's senate.

Count Vittore Valetti. The Red King.

With my third eye, I saw the wand quickly change trajectory, flattening out, pointing across the room—

No!

Chapter Twenty-Eight

As if propelled into motion by my thoughts, Armaeus burst into vapor and tore away from me, a profusion of smoke swirling in his wake. Time slowed to a standstill, but the dart containing the fell toxin shot across the room and straight into the smoke—then through it, its unerring trajectory still the two men at the far end of the chamber. I had some vague sense of Armaeus being not where he should be—which was stopping the dart—but all the way over where the perpetrator was even now turning away, but that was no good, no good, not when the—

Budin made a noise I didn't think was even possible coming out of such a small man, a shouted command so powerful that the very walls of the room shook. It wasn't enough to change the trajectory of a magic dart, but he also moved with a speed I'd never seen in a human who wasn't also an Arcana member and thrust Alfonse out of the way. The Nul Magis-laced dart struck the small magician square in the chest, instantly burrowing deep—but Budin didn't stop there. With another thunderclap of an order, the barb froze into a block of ice, then shattered, the shards bursting back out of his chest plate and hitting the floor with a clatter.

A clatter that everyone could hear, since the room had gone dead silent.

"No more!" Budin growled, the girth afforded him by his body armor making him seem like a fierce little tank. "Tonight is for joy, not death!"

I pulled the hat free of my hair and slid off the cape and mask, drawing in a rich lungful of oxygen. "Well, let's not get ahead of ourselves."

Turning away from Budin, I made my way over to where Armaeus held the upper arm of Count Valetti. Whether it was the sight of someone unmasked or merely the drama of the moment, no one spoke as I strode across the hall. Even the count merely glared at me, his back straight, his hands clenched.

"You have no jurisdiction here," he said tightly as I approached. "The senate of magicians supersedes the Arcana Council. It has since the Middle Ages."

I drew in a long breath. Up until I'd seen Valetti's exploding magical signature, with energy that shot out in the same distinctive flares as his calligraphic style, Valetti had been third or fourth on my list of possible bad guys. But he *had* been on it. There'd been the faintest of echoes of his calligraphy in the recipe booklets too. This was a man who wanted to be caught, who wanted to be known for his diabolical crimes. Lucky for him, he'd now get his chance. "Your family has long been a well-respected part of that senate, Valetti. That didn't have to change simply because the balance of magic did. Sorcery is a learned art."

"It *should* be a learned art," Valetti practically spat. "It should be, but it wasn't. Not after you and your precious Council waded in and flailed around, trying to set a world to rights that you didn't even understand. You have no appreciation for history, no appreciation for the worth of spending generations honing the position of your family, the respect, the honor. No. Instead you step in and change it all in the flash of a moment, taking away everything that mattered."

Beyond Valetti, another man removed his hat, then slid his mask up and away from his face. Luca Stone, I realized, his expression unreadable as he stared at his colleague, the man for whom he'd entangled the Arcana Council in the affairs of magicians. The *prelate,* I realized. He was staring at the prelate, not Count Valetti.

Stone's gaze shifted, and his eyes met mine. He smiled and nodded with appreciation.

I returned my attention to Valetti, whose glare hadn't diminished. "You had no right to murder Balestri—" I began.

"Balestri!" The count threw up his hands, a man truly at the end of his rope. "That was my mistake. I know it was. But he was so *annoying*. His constant parties, his dirty little drug trade, his insufferable moaning about how his family used to be the most famous in all the land. He was nothing—he had no power, none! He could barely conjure candlelight, but to hear him talk, you would've thought he was the most powerful magician in the cosmos. And everybody put up with him. Why? Because of his *family*. When mine was so much more obviously the finer stock, and had been for hundreds of years."

"You knew I saw him die," I accused. "You created his final message about the Red King to—what? Taunt me? Why in the world would you do that?"

"Because I *am* the Red King," Valetti said coldly. "I am the monarch who floats upon the open sea, benevolent and good, guiding all that know to follow me. As all the generations before me, the House of

Valetti is the rightful ruler of the magicians of this city—and it always has been."

"Not always, no." I didn't have the Valetti family slim leather volume on me, but I didn't need it in my hands to recall its words, which I now saw in a different light. "You were one of the quietest families of the magicians' senate from the moment it was formed until the late 1500s. Then another wave of plague struck, what everyone thought was plague, anyway, and only the Valettis and a few other families stayed strong. That was when your real power started to build. You became one of the most respected families of the senate, and your magic grew, and gradually, in time, you reached the position of respect you felt your family should be accorded."

"I was happy to work within the construct of the senate of magicians," Valetti said, his voice low and malevolent through his mask. "It was an honor to be a part of that senate, and my family believes in honor more than anything. Honor and the rightful place of those who have done all they could for this city, this senate, these people."

"And then it all fell apart," I said. "You weren't augmented in the rush of magic that swept over the planet."

"I was," he countered. "But not enough. Not to the same degree as Greaves and Marrow, of all people." He curled his lip. "Or even ridiculous Budin."

The disdain with which he said the magician's name was as chilling as it was loud, but the diminutive man didn't step forward to defend himself. I glanced his way, startled to see he'd stepped out of his mask and hat, that he'd even stripped away his body armor. He stood next to Nikki wearing the ordinary clothes of an ordinary man, but still shimmering with power. And he stared at Valetti with an expression I wouldn't have expected.

Pity.

Valetti, fortunately, couldn't see him. "None of them had done the work to move their family into the proper position in the senate. I had! I and all those who had come before me."

"You discovered the butcher's secret," I said. "Your family did, anyway. You knew he'd created the Nul Magis toxin by mistake."

"He wanted to be one of us," Valetti mocked, drawing himself up to his full height. "A simple butcher, with blood on his hands and gore on his feet. We did not kill him. His ambition killed him."

"He didn't know what he was doing."

"He didn't," Valetti said, disgusted. "Until we helped him along with that, whispering the truth that we had discovered, planting the severed fingers, then we destroyed him and his filthy shop. Because we had learned something else too, something the dark practitioners would not use…but we *would*. We would and we did."

"The plague years." A new voice spoke now, gray with horror. The prelate Alfonse stood, still masked and cloaked, staring at Valetti with his expressionless face. "All those magicians who died. How many of them were helped along by the Valetti family?"

"You wouldn't even *be* here if it wasn't for the Valetti family," the count retorted. "Your family should have been burned for heresy for even having the sorcerer's gene, let alone acting on it. It's only through the efforts of families like my own that you were spared."

The prelate dipped his head, acknowledging the truth.

I made a face. "I'd ease back on the self-congratulation, Valetti."

"You don't have the strength within you to know what I know—do what I've done," he seethed. "Back in the 1500s, it was the roughest beginning. The very first iteration of Nul Magis...and of Black Elixir, five hundred years before we would be graced with enough of a supply of demon blood to change the world."

"You killed three people—more if you were behind the deaths of the assassins. I assume your man Alessandro wasn't harmed after all." Valetti made no response to that, and I pushed on. "You attacked us at the site of the butcher's shop, and could have killed our gondolier instead of merely destroying his livelihood. Then there was Signora Visione and your attempts on Budin. Who else?"

"I do not answer to you." With a jerk, Valetti wrenched himself away from Armaeus, who let him go. I caught the look in Armaeus's eye as he did so—it was pure fascination. The Magician was going to be the death of me.

Valetti threw his hands in the air, and I could feel the pulse of magic in the room, my right hand stinging with the recognition of the demon blood coursing through the count's system. "I command you—" he began in stentorian tones

"You command nothing," I countered in my mildest tone.

Or what I thought was my mildest tone.

The walls around me seemed to bow out and snap back again, but I held Valetti's gaze. "You are marked for Justice," I said, and I saw it now—the flash of silver at his temple he'd managed to hide from me for days. "I couldn't see it. Didn't want to see it. But that makes it no less true. Speak your crimes."

"You have no—"

I lifted my hands slightly, and Valetti convulsed, his eyes flashing wide as he spoke the truth I compelled.

"It had taken years," he cried, glaring at me. "Nul Magis wasn't possible, but Black Elixir—that I could create, cobbled together from the most depraved souls who made their way to Venice. Years. Decades. And then…then you and your Council paved the path for me, when I thought it would take yet more time. I could strike! And I would strike. There would be no mercy. I had only to ensure that there was a quorum in the senate to see my triumph."

"The Arcana Council in Venice would assure that no magicians would stay away," Armaeus said, almost thoughtfully. "You could take your pick of targets, ensuring your place. We've stayed away from Venice too long."

At these words, Valetti's fury seemed to renew itself. "Your Council is on the verge of being overtaken by the real magicians of this world," he seethed. "You have no jurisdiction over—"

Another wave of my hand and Valetti got back on track.

"The recipe books?" I pressed.

"To stoke fear. Fear is necessary, right, true. Only fear made the senate work together, you see?" He whirled, but a sea of faceless masks stared back at him. "You *see*. You must see."

"They see," I said. "And they're not the only ones who do."

I stepped forward and grabbed Valetti by the hand as another man broke free of the crowd, lifting off his mask with one hand as he clipped a restraint on Valetti's wrists with the other.

Detective Tall, Dark, and Doin' His Job. Good man.

However, Valetti was one of the most powerful magicians in Venice, if not all of Europe. So for good measure, I slid my own cuff around one of Valetti's wrists too. It'd keep him under control while the local police dealt with him, and then would be there when he was ready for his date with Judgment.

Valetti jerked as he felt the touch of magic, whipping around to growl at me. I lifted a casual hand, and the cuff delivered a jolt of electricity all the way to his toes, leaving him gasping.

The detective eyed Valetti, then me. "I trust you'll be leaving Venice soon?" he asked me. "I don't know how long we'll be able to hold him."

"I wouldn't worry so much about that," I assured him. "He's got a date with Judgment, no matter what."

The detective nodded, but it was Valetti's reaction I was looking for. The count stared at me, bug-eyed with understanding.

I felt good about that.

As the two of them left the ballroom, a new surge of music swelled and eddied through the suddenly electrified space. Around me, another dance began, this one with steps so ancient, I had no hope of trying to mimic it—nor did I want to try. It was over, finally. The moment passed, the case closed. It was over.

And, I realized…that felt—really good.

"Miss Wilde."

I glanced up to find Armaeus Bertrand standing over me, his mask and cape gone, his riveting black-gold eyes now entirely focused on me. He took my hands and lifted them to his heart. "You've won, it would seem," he murmured.

I grimaced. "I wouldn't go that far. Valetti was a grenade waiting to explode. All I did was pull the pin."

"That's not what I meant." He shook his head. "You have succeeded where Justice Abigail, and the distant Justices before her could not. What do you see around you?"

I looked where he gestured. There were the magicians talking and laughing, several of them in knots around the High Priestess and the Devil, who were masked and caped but easily recognizable by their golden circuitry. Some of the magicians were now gathered around Budin, still others around Alfonse.

"I…see a lot of really uncomfortable clothes?"

"You see the Arcana Council interacting with the Connecteds," Armaeus corrected me. "Arguably with the most relevant group of Connecteds on this earth, albeit one which we have barely acknowledged for generations. Yet you simply reached out and took on your first case…and here we are. Communicating. Teaching. Listening."

His voice seemed to wobble a bit, and its unnatural tenor was doing odd things to my heart.

"Well, you knew I was in trouble," I said. "Of course you would come."

"To help you, of course. But there is more happening here than simple help. What is begun this night will not end this night, but will continue, a pathway for magic to grow and thrive. The Connecteds of this world and the Council, working together, in a way that no one has been able to accomplish in longer than any of us can remember…" He smiled ruefully. "Especially me. And thus you are Justice, and Vigilance, and even more than that. You are the Grace that balances the scales. The Supreme Triad in one."

"Supreme Triad," I repeated, remembering Signora Visione's slip of the tongue. Nikki was going to be stoked to have the mystery of my new moniker solved, but… "That seems like kind of a mouthful."

"I concur." Armaeus tilted his head, his golden-black gaze once more threatening to swallow me whole. "For me, it's more than enough that you are Justice. And, now and ever more…my Justice."

I stared back at him, lost in the inexorable pull of his magic, unable to fully process the emotions rolling through me, but desperately wanting whatever was happening to last for a very long time.

Armaeus, of course, could easily read my thoughts. Something sharp and intense flashed in his eyes, and he lifted my hands to his lips and brushed a kiss over my fingertips.

"Then I suggest we start with eternity, Sara," he murmured, as a new whisper of power swirled around us, "and see where life takes us from there."

Chapter Twenty-Nine

I stood in front of the door to my office in Las Vegas a few mornings later, catching myself as I lifted my hand to knock. I didn't need to knock, this was my space. My very own proper place in the world.

The door opened in front of me anyway.

"Come in, ma'am!" One of the young librarians stood there beaming, his bright eyes dancing. "I'm Tobey, and we saw you coming all the way down the hall!"

"You did?" I glanced at the door, which looked no different than it had the last time I'd seen it, but as I entered the room, I saw a new station set up to the side of the entrance lobby. Two additional boys manned that desk, peering at a screen about half the size they were. They seemed so engrossed in their work, I felt a twinge of nerves at my first task of the day.

"Is Mrs. French in?" I asked, watching Tobey scamper back to the desk as well, whispering and nudging his fellows to change the view. Another boy came out of the library, snatching off his cap when he saw me.

"Right here!" came the brisk British voice from the office, and a second later, two other boys trotted into the lobby from that doorway, touching their caps before they headed for the library.

"Wait," I shouted, and that stopped them short. "Is this all of you? Can you tell me your names again?"

There were six boys in the room, and they looked at each other, then back at me, grinning. I lifted my hands slightly to my sides, not enough to alarm them, but to balance the moment, preserve it in my mind. My right hand throbbed with the extra effort, but not quite enough to hurt.

"'Tis all of us accounted for, Justice Wilde. I'm Bobby, Bobby Haymoor," began the first. Then each of the boys chattered off their names, the sound of their young voices pinging around the room. When they were done, I dropped my hands, and they pushed and shoved and went on their way—four of them disappearing into the library, two still manning the desk like impish guard dogs.

I shook my head, stifling a laugh, for all that my heart was inexplicably heavy. By the time I reached the entry to my inner office, Mrs. French was halfway across the room toward me. She saw my face and stopped.

"What is it?" she asked. "What's wrong?"

"Nothing's wrong," I said quickly, but I tossed my bag on the couch and stood there, immediately unsure. This was exactly why I'd never had employees before. I had no capacity for crucial conversations. "Well, that's not true. Something's wrong. A lot of somethings. Starting with them."

I gestured toward the main lobby, and Mrs. French stiffened. She nodded once, sharply, then moved forward toward the door, closing it quietly before turning around. "Would you like some tea? Scotch?"

"No." I shoved my hands into my jeans pockets, wishing I was anywhere but here—then catching myself as I felt my cells start to destabilize. Poofing out of existence wasn't going to solve this issue, as tempting as it was.

I launched in. "I want some answers, Mrs. French. Why are those boys still here? Surely someone could have set them free a long time ago. They should be free, and they should be living a normal life."

She blinked at me. Whatever she'd expected me to say, that wasn't it. "The boys," she repeated.

"For starters, yeah. In nearly two hundred years, you mean to tell me you never once asked Armaeus or even Death to look into reversing whatever spell Abigail's boss laid on them? Because I don't believe they wouldn't have helped."

"What makes you think the boys wanted such help?" Mrs. French asked staunchly.

"Nothing. But it doesn't matter what they want. They're ten-year-old boys—perpetual ten-year-old boys. You knew better than to keep them in the library. What happens when you die? That will happen, eventually, right? You're not immortal."

"I'm not." For just a moment, Mrs. French looked like she was going to stiffen to the point of her spine splintering, staring at me across the room. Then something shifted in her eyes, a look of inexpressible sadness, and I knew I had her.

I didn't feel good about it, but I had her.

"You know what I am," she said, her voice resigned.

"A Revenant. A very long-lived one. Gamon's the only Revenant I know all that well, but she's only been around about eighty years."

"She is a scary one, I'll grant you that," Mrs. French said, but the stuffing had gone out of her. "But barely a child. And now that she's on the Council, she won't have to worry about aging at all."

I nodded, watching her closely. "But you do."

"I do," she said, her voice wan. She moved over to a straight-back chair and sat on the very edge of it, all that she could reasonably manage with her bustle. She folded her hands in her lap. "You have me dead to rights, Justice," she said. "I could have—should have—taken the boys straightaway to the Magician for his help. I had no right to keep them with me all these years when they didn't know anything of the world beyond this library, whereas I knew all too well what it held."

"You wanted to protect them."

"Oh, of course, but that's not the whole of it, as you well know. I wanted their company. It was no good for me on the outside, not once I saw what..." She swallowed. "Well, there's no matter the why of it. It was wrong, plain as day."

"Once you saw what?" I asked. "What happened to Abigail, Mrs. French? What is it that happened that made you stay locked up in the library with the boys for almost two centuries?"

"Abigail..." Mrs. French's smile was inexpressibly sad. "It wasn't like what you think. She did nothing to harm me or the boys. But she suffered for her job, Justice Wilde. She suffered mightily every time she encountered the dangerous men and women she needed to bring to Judgment. And, worse, Judgment wasn't as absolute back then."

I frowned, surprised. "In what way?"

"In the way that resulted in some of the marked being released back into the population. Poor Abigail would go out not knowing if she'd be faced with an angry Connected who was more prepared than she was for their second altercation. She was strong, she had her scales and the weight of most of the Council behind her, but she couldn't be prepared for everything."

"Judgment didn't have her back?" I could hardly believe it.

"Not always," Mrs. French said. "Not enough. And he said—he said that if she pushed too hard, he'd let all her secrets out. He knew, of course. Knew everything about her. You can't stand in front of Judgment without him knowing your every sin."

"Really." I thought about what Gamon would be able to judge me for, but I didn't think that particular issue was going to be a problem between us. "And she cared about that?"

"She cared about *us*. The boys. Me. She cared about our safety and the safety of her family, black sheep though they were. She knew where she came from and she knew what she'd done, and it ate at her day and night. The cases were added pressure, but nothing compared to the pressure she put on herself."

I lifted a hand and rubbed my brow, trying to keep everything Mrs. French was saying straight. "Abigail ascended to the Council even though she was a dark practitioner."

"Her family was. Not her."

"Right, her family. But she was broken from that, from that and from what her employer had done to her. Her employer, whom she murdered."

"While rescuing someone else!"

"Another young woman."

Mrs. French bit her lip. "Yes. When the Magician interrupted Abigail, she was truly distraught and truly powerful. He told me once that he knew he needed to elevate her or kill her, there was really no other option. And he was in desperate need of Council members in that time period. Your Devil hadn't ascended yet, nor the Emperor, or the Hanged Man, or—"

"I get the picture. But Abigail was deeply and irretrievably broken. Surely he knew that too."

She shook her head. "At first, he knew only what she allowed him to know. Which was only what she allowed herself to know when she was with him. Her employer thought her a sleepwalker, but that…that wasn't truly her affliction."

I stared at Mrs. French. "And you know what it was?"

"I surely do. I saw it right away. It helped that I had seen it before." She gave me another rueful smile. "My family may have been Revenants, but that didn't mean they were the nicest people. They disapproved of my choices. When I became pregnant by a young man who wasn't of my kind, they took the baby and—" She cleared her throat. "Incarcerated me at a public institution. It was only supposed to be for a short while, but a short while in a Revenant's life is a far different thing, you see. I saw…a great many things in that place. It had been built for the pauper insane."

I felt like ice was running through my veins. How had I not known this? How hadn't I guessed? "You were harmed?"

"Not irredeemably, no. I had the advantage over most of the inmates and a fair number of the keepers in that I was in full possession of my faculties. I made sure I was a favorite of the superintendent. He was a kind man, and there were far too few of those. Eventually, however, I was treated by a visiting psychiatrist, and, well…" She lifted her chin. "He was *not* a kind man. And he knew there was something…different about me, as Connecteds often do."

All the dots didn't merely connect, they lit up like the Strip. "It was Abigail's employer. You were the girl she saved."

"When Abigail visited that night, it wasn't merely that she was in a trance. She was in a different mind altogether. One of thirteen alternates who would surface as time needed, some less manageable than others."

"But if you knew this, surely the Magician knew it as well." I thought back to what he had said, that Abigail wasn't damaged *because* of her job, that he'd thought she'd be uniquely suited for it. "She had dissociative identity disorder, and he thought she was perfect for the role of Justice?"

"Before Abigail, the role had gone vacant for seven hundred years," Mrs. French said simply. "You can do the math."

I blinked at her. "Armaeus didn't know anything about what the job took."

"He didn't know. And when he did finally learn the truth about Abigail's condition, she appeared to be thriving. Anything one alter experienced, the others covered over, and of course, there were so many other jobs to manage, ad hoc cases that weren't as dangerous in the main. But one day, she simply couldn't face it anymore. And when she went…" Mrs. French shrugged. "By then, I had a purpose and a place. I had the boys to care for and so much shelving to do. The Council fed and clothed us and gave us anything we wanted. It wasn't a bad life." She glanced up at me. "But you can take me to Judgment now, Justice Wilde. I do understand."

"Judgment!" I blinked, but there was no slash of silver at Mrs. French's temple. All her misery and self-recrimination was internally driven, and always had been, I suspected. "No. That's not what this is about. I just think the boys need a chance to grow up, is all. Children aren't meant to stay children."

"But..." Mrs. French's eyes filled, and her words, when they came, were barely audible. "They'll leave."

I nodded, more gently this time. "They'll leave, hopefully. Once they get a little older. They'll leave, and they'll find friends and maybe eventually make families of their own. Being a gifted Connected doesn't mean you have to stay alone your whole life, after all. Not everyone out in the world is an asshat."

She gave me a watery smile. "Most of them are. I've had a long time to study this."

"Most of them are," I agreed.

"Very well, then," she said heavily. "You tell me what I need to tell them, what I need to do, and I'll do it, Justice. And if you don't want me to stay, I understand. Of course I understand. I couldn't possibly not understand—"

"You'll be staying as long as you'd like, Mrs. French. And there's nothing at all you need to do. At least not about the boys."

I turned away from her startled face, and moved to the desk. Fully thirteen canisters, unopened, lined the sleek black surface. "Is this everything that's shown up since I've been gone?" I asked, and she gave a rueful chuckle, quickly wiping her tears away.

"Not at all. That's everything that's shown up since we cleared away the overnight deliveries. Since you left for Venice, we've received one hundred and seventeen cases."

I jerked my gaze to her, staring. "You're kidding."

"I'm afraid not. Granted, a full fifty-three of those were grudges and family disputes, and another twelve were poppycock, bits of stuff and nothing created to draw you out on false pretenses, but the remaining fifty-two appear to be quite legitimate. They've been categorized and prioritized, and except for a few that you might consider addressing immediately, they've all been shelved."

"Fifty…two. And it's only the legitimate cases that were the problem."

"For Abigail, yes," Mrs. French said. "But there's nothing that says they will affect you the same way. You are two very different people."

I grimaced. Armaeus had said much the same thing. "How much do you know of the cases she worked on? And is there a list? Maybe if I went back through them, see where maybe she got tripped up…"

Mrs. French straightened. "There most certainly is a list!" she said brightly. "I hadn't even thought of that. Maybe it's not a question of any cases being the issues, but the cases she happened to choose."

"Maybe…" I still remembered the sloshing-brains reaction I'd had to opening Mak'rep's box. I wasn't too sure how much I believed my own theory. "Worth a try."

"Absolutely." Mrs. French bounded up. "I'll go ask. I mean…" She paused, looking uncertainly at the closed door. "The boys," she said. "What shall I say to the boys?"

"It's already handled," I assured her.

"But—how?"

"By these," I said, wiggling my fingers in the air. Mrs. French's eyes widened.

"You *are* a very different person from Justice Abigail," she allowed.

"Well, they'll simply start growing older now, bit by bit. When they come to you with questions, you can tell them it's because there's a new Justice, and that they can stay as long as they like."

She clenched her hands together in front of her, managing another shaky breath. "I…I don't know what to say."

I smiled, shrugged. "Then it's a good thing you don't have to say anything."

Mrs. French left, and I stared at the desk, unseeing for a long moment. Gradually, with only the slightest wince, I pulled my hands back together. There, in the palm of my right hand, remained the tiny core of power I had most unexpectedly kept from my experience in Venice. The Nul Magis. Not enough to kill a bona fide sorcerer, not enough to destroy their magic. At least I didn't think so.

But enough to break a spell that had lasted for nearly two hundred years?

That, it seemed, I could do.

And if I could do that…

Drawing in a deep, steadying breath, I reached for the nearest glass canister to me and opened my next case.

~~~
~~~

THE LOST QUEEN

Not all who wander are lost.

As Justice of the Arcana Council and an experienced artifact hunter, Tarot-reading Sara Wilde prefers to track down the missing on her own. With her latest case, sadly, everyone's dying to help her out.

Determined to locate the Lost Queen, a witch destined to fulfill a dark and twisted prophecy, Sara finds herself corpse-blocked at every turn. Not even the electric, provocative, and deeply powerful Magician of the Arcana Council--whose newest arcane pursuits test Sara's emotional and sensual boundaries--can help her find her mark.

Worse, Sara isn't the only hunter on the case. From the shadowy labyrinths of Budapest to the ancient churches of Moscow to the glittering lights of Los Angeles, the world's most powerful male witches are gunning for the Lost Queen, demanding her as their rightful consort. Right before they end up dead, each more gruesomely than the last. There's definitely a pattern here...and one Sara needs to break, before her own mercurial Magician becomes the prophecy's next target.

Better hope you don't find what you're looking for when you hunt *The Lost Queen.*

~Now Available!~

A Note From Jenn

Sara's adventures in The Red King brought her face to face with the King of Cups, who definitely wouldn't thank me for making him a villain in this tale! In truth, drawing the King of Cups is almost always a very positive experience. Turn the page for an interpretation for the King of Cups!

ALSO: Interested in learning more about the Tarot, upcoming book releases, and other bits of arcana and mayhem? Get Connected (heh) and sign up for my mailing list at www.jennstark.com/newsletter!

The King of Cups

Court cards are generally about people—the ones you know, the ones you'll meet, or possibly even yourself—and the King of Cups is someone you definitely want to associate with. Emotionally balanced and truly caring, he sits atop his throne surrounded by the flow of energy, in tune with the world around him. When this card represents a person, look for someone who is jovial, caring, sincere, artistic and creative...with potentially intense feelings, authentic sensitivity and powerful emotions (no matter how balanced he is, this King's emotions run deep!). When this card does not represent a person, you are most likely involved with a spiritual, creative, or artistic project, something that speaks to your deepest emotions. It's considered a card of abundance, flow and good luck! In fact, in some readings it's called the god card, signifying that a higher being is blessing your endeavors. So, when you see the Red King, celebrate! Unless he's a dark practitioner. In that case, you should probably run away.

Acknowledgments

Wow—THE RED KING launches a whole new series of books for Sara Wilde, with a slightly different spin. Thank you to all my readers who have stayed with me on my journey so far, and to those who are joining me for the first time! I hope you enjoy the ride. As always, my deep and abiding thanks to Elizabeth Bemis for her beautiful work on my books and my site—especially my fantastic cover. My editorial team of Linda Ingmanson and Toni Lee went above and beyond the call of duty with THE RED KING, as I introduced a mystery into the story that kept us all on our toes. Any mistakes in the manuscript are most definitely my own. I am deeply grateful to Edeena Cross and Sabra Harp for their brilliant beta reads, and to Kristine Krantz, whose careful eye (and skeptical side-eye) kept me on the right track, as always. And, of course, sincere thanks go to Geoffrey, who helped bring this series to life. It's been a *Wilde* ride.

ABOUT JENN STARK

Jenn Stark is an award-winning author of paranormal romance and urban fantasy. She lives and writes in Ohio. . . and she definitely loves to write. In addition to her Immortal Vegas and Wilde Justice urban fantasy series and Demon Enforcers paranormal romance series, she is also author Jennifer McGowan, whose Maids of Honor series of Young Adult Elizabethan spy romances are published by Simon & Schuster, and author Jennifer Chance, whose Rule Breakers series of New Adult contemporary romances are published by Random House/LoveSwept and whose modern royals series, Gowns & Crowns, is now available.

You can find her online at jennstark.com, follow her on Twitter @jennstark, and visit her on Facebook at facebook.com/authorjennstark.

Made in the USA
Middletown, DE
10 June 2019